"I thought you understood me . . . agreed with me," she said. "We are like a keg of gunpowder and a careless spark, Lucas. No matter how cautious we are, something terrible always happens when we are together. You said as much yourself: There is no way for us to have a comfortable meeting of the minds."

"To hell with our minds, then," he growled, and hauled her out of her seat and back into his lap, where she belonged.

Any chance to protest was lost immediately. Deirdre's hands were helpless between her chest and his. And the moment she opened her mouth, his descended to cover it with a searing power that took her breath away. Then she thought she might never breathe again. . . .

By Emma Jensen
Published by The Ballantine Publishing Group:

CHOICE DECEPTIONS
VIVID NOTIONS
COUP DE GRACE
WHAT CHLOE WANTS
ENTWINED
HIS GRACE ENDURES

Books published by The Ballantine Publishing Group
are available at quantity discounts on bulk purchases
for premium, educational, fund-raising, and special
sales use. For details, please call 1-800-733-3000.

HIS GRACE ENDURES

Emma Jensen

FAWCETT CREST • NEW YORK

A Fawcett Crest Book
Published by The Ballantine Publishing Group
Copyright © 1998 by Emma Jensen

All rights reserved under International and Pan-American Copyright Conventions. Published in the United States by The Ballantine Publishing Group, a division of Random House, Inc., New York, and simultaneously in Canada by Random House of Canada Limited, Toronto.

www.randomhouse.com

Library of Congress Catalog Card Number: 97-95346

ISBN 0-449-00233-0

Manufactured in the United States of America

First Edition: June 1998

10 9 8 7 6 5 4 3 2 1

For Margaret Evans Porter and Susan Lantz.
Boundless thanks, *mo bhanchàirdean,*
for the countless cups of kindness. *Slàinte.*

We twa hae paidl'd in the burn
    Frae morning sun till dine,
But seas between us braid hae roar'd
    Sin' auld lang syne.

For auld lang syne, my dear,
    For auld lang syne,
We'll tak a cup o' kindness yet
    For auld lang syne!

—ROBERT BURNS

1

IN THE SMALL village of Tarbet, on the shores of Loch Lomond, she was known as Deirdre of the Sorrows. Had anyone bothered to ask, Deirdre Macvail would have said she felt her life to have been quite blessed. But no one asked, and she accepted the label with philosophical grace.

At the moment she was feeling somewhat frayed around the edges, though not in the least sorrowful. Her days since arriving in Edinburgh had been a series of Scenes. A peaceful evening would have been lovely, but too much to hope for. This time a shoemaker's poor eyesight was apparently responsible for the chaos. Deirdre was not a believer in either fate or ill omens, but in retrospect she would have to consider that the situation had been a portent for the night to come.

"I cannot possibly wear these!" Miss Olivia Macvail, prostrate on her bed, could not stomp her blindingly pink-clad toes, but substituted quite effectively by kicking them against the footboard. "I will be laughed from the ball!"

Deirdre sighed and reassuringly stroked her sister-in-law's black curls. "We are not due to leave for another half hour, dearest. I am certain we can come up with a solution before then."

"But I want to wear the pink dress! I *must* wear the pink dress!"

It would not help matters to point out that the pink dress was somewhat the worse for wear due to its participation in the tantrum. Nor would it serve any purpose to suggest that Olivia might have checked the shoes when they had been delivered the day before. Instead Deirdre gently coaxed the younger girl's face from the counterpane. Despite her faint annoyance at the hysterics, she had to concede that Livvy was one of the few women

1

who could still look stunningly beautiful with red eyes and a dripping nose. Her plump cheeks bore the pink prettily; the green of her eyes was made all the more vivid.

Jonas had been impossibly handsome, too, even at the worst possible moments. It came with being a Macvail, apparently. But now was not the time for Deirdre to be thinking of her late husband. She had to see to his sister. At almost twenty-six and with nearly three years of being the girl's sole guardian, Deirdre had become quite adept at weathering far worse dramatics than this one. She did not, however, know what she was going to do about the shoes.

They were due at Lady Leverham's Charlotte Square house promptly at ten. Deirdre was still in her wrapper, and Lady Leverham did not handle disruptions in her social planning well. Late arrivals tended to send her into a distressed flutter. Deirdre, with their hostess's nerves in mind, had expected to have her charge gowned, coiffed, shod, and ready in plenty of time for Deirdre herself to dress. Her own preparations were always a speedy effort. She simply had not allocated time for a shoe disaster.

First things first, and she had to coax her sister-in-law off the bed. "Livvy, dearest, let us go look at your wardrobe. That new blue tissue—"

"Blue? I cannot wear the blue! I must be a vision in pink!" Olivia kicked at the footboard again, causing the entire applewood frame to creak and nearly jostle Deirdre off the high mattress. Then, with an especially heartrending wail, she buried her face in the pillows and commenced to sob anew.

Deirdre waited. Livvy sobbed. The mantel clock chimed. It was time for a new tack. "Well, a vision in pink you'll be, certainly. Pink nose, pink eyes, pink dress complete with a veritable atlas of pink wrinkles. What do you think, love? Can we arrive at Lady Leverham's and tell the assembly that you decided to ride under the carriage rather than in it? That way you could go in your stockings, and no one would question how you managed to lose your shoes."

As expected, there was a faint, watery giggle from the bed.

2

Now Deirdre could only hope the girl's natural humor would win out over tragedy. It tended to be touch-and-go in such matters.

Livvy giggled again, then actually sat up to survey the damage. "I had not thought of the wrinkles." She hiccuped and groped about the disarranged counterpane as if expecting a handkerchief to magically appear.

Ever ready, Deirdre supplied one from her wrapper's sleeve. It was always wise to have a handkerchief about in Miss Macvail's presence.

Olivia snuffled and swung her legs over the edge of the mattress. She stretched them out and stared banefully at the brilliantly pink slippers. With her tumbled curls and lip-thrust pout, she looked like a small child forced to endure a much-needed lecture on deportment.

"I suppose I could wear the blue," she conceded glumly at last.

"Or we could simply remain at home."

As a pièce de résistance, it worked. The concept of missing Lady Leverham's soiree catapulted the girl off the bed and into the dressing room. Deirdre shook her head in fond resignation as she followed. For her own part, she would have been more than content to spend a quiet evening at home. But Lady Leverham was putting herself out for Olivia and would be sponsoring the girl for the London Season. Despite the fact that she would rather spend the evening playing piquet with the devil himself, Deirdre was not about to scorn such kindness or deprive her sister-in-law of her opportunity to dazzle the ton.

Livvy was more than willing to dazzle. In fact, she had already predicted her social success right down to the title of the man she would marry. Nothing less than an earl, she had announced some weeks past. And, despite the fact that she was merely the daughter of a minor baron, with only the smallest portion to her name, she might very well find herself a countess by summer.

Olivia Macvail was a beauty, and a determined one. Lady Leverham was a fixture in society, and a tenacious one. If Miss Macvail wanted an earl, an earl she would have. Deirdre was along for the ride—and for a promise she had made.

As her late mother had wished, Olivia would have her Season, with her first bow here in Edinburgh. Within the fortnight they would be installed in Lady Leverham's Mayfair town house. And if matters progressed well, Deirdre could have her charge happily married off to some unsuspecting earl and herself back in Scotland by June.

If all went as expected, she would be forced to relive the unhappiest moments of her life in the process.

Once she saw Olivia safely disappearing into the folds of the blue dress and in the competent hands of her maid, she hurried to her own chamber. Perhaps the dove gray silk, with its modest bodice and quiet trim, was not quite up to the occasion, but it was appropriate for her role. Seven years earlier she had made her own Town debut in shimmering, embroidered white gauze. But that was before. Now she was a widow with an eighteen-year-old charge. Livvy would dazzle; Deirdre would blend into the draperies with quiet propriety. Then she would disappear.

"I could leave some curls to fall just here," her maid said hopefully when Deirdre was at last settled at her dressing table. "Just over one shoulder—"

"No, Judith." She tempered the terse words with a rare, blithe smile. "And I trust you will use extra pins tonight, or I'll have the curls over my shoulders regardless."

The maid grumbled something about lights and bushels, but obediently scooped the heavy, dark gold mass high into its customary tight knot. Deirdre didn't bother to survey the effect, but did keep a stern eye on the number of pins. It took very little to send her hair into disarray. She did not plan to be dancing that evening, but one was guaranteed to be jostled at even the smallest of Lady Leverham's parties.

She declined, too, the string of pearls Judith proffered, choosing instead the filigree locket on its silver chain. It rested just above her bodice, warming with familiar speed against her skin. She gently touched it once with her fingertips before rising from the dressing table.

"Why, you haven't even looked at yourself, ma'am!"

"No need." Deirdre collected her gray kashmir shawl from the neat, narrow bed. "I know precisely how I look."

"So you say," Judith muttered under her breath.

Deirdre smiled again. "You will tell me should I sprout an extra nose, won't you? Now, don't wait up. I expect we'll be late."

Olivia, looking as much the glorious vision in blue as she would have in pink, was pouting again, this time into the mirror, when Deirdre returned to her chamber. "This parure is wrong," she announced, gesturing impatiently to the delicate cameo pendant and earrings she wore. "It was meant for the pink."

"Your brother thought it would go beautifully with any color," Deirdre said calmly. "That is why he chose it."

"He did not choose it. Mama did. Nasey had appalling taste in ladies' gifts. Mama always said . . ." Olivia's eyes centered on Deirdre's reflection and the silver locket. "Oh, I am sorry! I did not mean . . ."

"I know, dearest. And you are correct. Jonas did not have your eye for elegance." Deirdre glanced over the girl's meager selection of jewels. Of course there was little there. "Would you like to wear my mother's pearls? As you can see, I will not be needing them."

"Oh, could I?" Olivia sprang to her feet, eyes bright and utterly tear-free. "That's ever so kind of you, DeeDee!"

More expedient than kind, really, Deirdre thought. It was simple enough to hand over the strand, easy even to see them around another woman's throat. She had barely known her mother as a child, not at all as an adult. Her marriage to Nasey had ended what little communication had existed. The pearls had arrived in a plain brown wrapper three years earlier, along with a terse note from Deirdre's father, informing her of her mother's death. It was the first and last she had heard from Richard Fallam since she had run out of the Conovar chapel and into Jonas Macvail's waiting curricle.

More than once she had thought to give Olivia the necklace. She certainly did not wear it often. But some faint and piquant impulse had her keeping it, had her taking it from its case every several weeks to rub life back into the pearls with her palms. Now that they would be worn regularly, she would really have no need to touch them at all.

Once the strand was in place and Olivia had slipped into her pale blue shoes, Deirdre gave her a critical once-over. "Well . . ."

"Well?" Livvy gave a nervous pirouette. She looked very young. And very lovely.

Deirdre told her so. "I challenge any ball in Britain to produce so beautiful a debutante!"

"Oh, DeeDee!" With affection every bit as strong a part of her character as the vain tantrums, Olivia threw herself into her sister-in-law's arms. "I do so want you to be proud of me."

"I am," Deirdre said softly against Livvy's ebony curls. "You are all I have, dearest."

"We shall always have each other!"

She smiled at the girl's fervent promise. Oh, yes, they would always have their affection for each other, but Deirdre knew what distance could do. Giving up Livvy would be a terrible wound atop old ones, but the girl's place was among the Haute Monde. Deirdre's was at little Red Branch Cottage along the shores of Loch Lomond, the only place she had ever truly felt at home.

She gently disengaged herself and stepped back. "Shall we go, then? It would not do at all to keep Lady Leverham waiting, nor to delay your presence on the dance floor."

The words were again well and carefully chosen. Olivia was giddy in her eagerness to dance her first waltz. As unwilling to delay as Deirdre was to go, the girl all but leapt down the stairs and into the carriage.

It was a short drive from their tiny house in Rose Street to Lady Leverham's elegant abode in Charlotte Square. Edinburgh had changed so, Deirdre thought, even in the few years since she had first seen it. The New Town was clean, bright, bustling beneath the ancient stone walls of Edinburgh Castle. Charlotte Square, with its rows of houses as imposing and English-looking as its denizens, was nearly complete on all four sides. And Princes Street, with its homes and shops, was a mile long now, as long as the walk between the castle and Holyrood Palace, where the ill-fated Queen Mary had resided—and a good deal more cheerful.

Deirdre loved Edinburgh, every damp old stone and twisting alleyway. She could barely remember the Waterford of her child-hood, and the years in England held nothing but sorry memories. Yes, she had taken to Scotland, as Nasey had said she would.

6

They had planned to spend their lives together there, at Red Branch in the winter and Edinburgh during the Season.

She would have her life in Scotland still, only alone.

Lady Leverham's house was decked out for the occasion, flowers and paper lanterns on every surface not moving. Already a stream of guests ran from street to door. Deirdre thought she saw Henry Raeburn's shiny pate among the throng and looked forward to speaking with him. The well-known portrait painter was a fixture among New Town society and possessed all the Scottish charm most of his hosts did not. Deirdre knew she could count on him to liven up her quiet corner for a few minutes. Perhaps Walter Scott would be there, too, if he were home from his frequent travels. Lady Leverham knew how to assemble a guest list.

By her side Olivia was bouncing on the leather seat in excitement. Only Deirdre's quick hand to her wrist kept her from leaping from the carriage while it was still rolling. "Gently, dearest. We would not want you twisting your ankle before the first dance."

Livvy calmed enough to release the door handle. She did not stop fidgeting. "Do you think there will be any young noblemen here? Agnes MacDonald told me Lord Aubert was at his hunting box last week. She says he's ever so handsome and perfectly charming as well."

Deirdre doubted Olivia's friend had ever been within shouting distance of Lord Aubert, or that the young marquess would be bothered to attend an Edinburgh soiree. But she had to agree with the assessment. She had known Dunstan Somersham, heir to the Earith dukedom, during her own Season, and had liked him very well. No, he would not be at tonight's fete, but perhaps Olivia would meet him in London . . .

"Oh, look, DeeDee! There is Miss MacDonald! She must have at least one of her brothers with her. The eldest will be a baronet someday. Not my earl, certainly, but a girl must practice, mustn't she?"

This time Deirdre prevented her sister-in-law from going head-first out the window in her enthusiasm at seeing Agnes Mac-Donald. "Careful, Livvy. You will tear your sleeve if you go on

7

waving like that. You may greet Miss MacDonald and her brothers to your heart's content once we are inside."

By the time they had descended and reached the marble foyer, Olivia had gone into ecstasies over the appearance of several more school friends, two more baronets, and one mere mister who was, to Deirdre's practiced eye, exceptionally handsome and undoubtedly a fortune hunter. She steered Livvy expertly up the stairs toward the ballroom and away from the appraising gaze of Mister Wants-Pounds. The glorious Miss Macvail would not serve his purposes, and Miss Macvail's dedicated guardian was not about to let him close enough to learn the fact for himself.

Lady Leverham was holding court at the edge of the dance floor. She was a round dumpling of a woman with improbably dark hair peeking from beneath a towering purple turban, and a pasha's ransom in jewels glittering from every available appendage. "Olivia, darling! Deirdre, love!" She threw her arms wide, nearly coshing her diminutive husband between the eyes with one of the boulders on her right hand. "I was all but preparing to send a search party for you."

Deirdre accepted the enthusiastic embrace, exchanging a warm smile with the lady's husband over her ample shoulder. "I am sorry, madam. We had a bit of a pink disaster, but as you can see, still arrived on time."

"Pink?" The lady released her and crossed her purple-draped arms. "I see no pink."

"No, unfortunately you do not. We made do with blue."

"Hmph." Lady Leverham gave Olivia a quick glance. "The girl looks stunning, of course. But you, my dear"—she turned a stern eye on Deirdre's simple dress—"are a disgrace."

"Oh, my lady . . ." Deirdre raised her hands in protest.

"A peacock masquerading as a pigeon! Really, Deirdre, what *are* we to do with you?"

"I am forever asking her the very same thing, Lady Leverham." Olivia had recovered sufficiently from her awe at the glittering spectacle to add her twopence. "For all the time we spend making certain I am fit for company, she insists on being . . . being so . . . *dull!*"

"And you, my sweet, insist on being pert. Best watch that tendency, or you shall be forced to settle for the second son of a baronet instead of an earl. Now"—Lady Leverham gave Deirdre's dress one last sorrowful look before scanning the crowd—"where is that MacDonald boy? He will partner Miss Olivia in the first dance."

Livvy scooted forward to aid in the search. "The elder Mr. MacDonald?"

"Of course the elder. I would not have you wasting your first ball on a younger son."

"Well, I suppose Mr. MacDonald will do. Is Lord Aubert here by any chance?"

Their hostess waggled a plump finger in front of Olivia's nose. "None of that, miss! I will not have you setting your cap at a marquess until we have fully tested the waters. Besides, Aubert has apparently taken himself back to Derbyshire. Most discourteous, I say. MacDonald, however ... You were speaking with him, Leverham. What *did* you say to make him vanish?"

"Well, I—" her husband began.

"Probably some rot about politics. You know the MacDonalds are Tories, my love, yet you insist on baiting them. You did, didn't you?"

"Actually, my dear—" he tried again.

"No matter. We shall find him. Come along, Olivia. It will hardly seem bold of you to walk about if I am in your company. You, too, Deirdre. I suppose one of the other MacDonalds will do well enough as a partner for you." She got a bejeweled grip on each of her guests. "And you, Leverham, will not bait any more Tories tonight. Do you hear me?"

"I would not ..." Lord Leverham was ultimately forced to content himself with declaring his innocence to the glowering portrait of a past baron.

Deirdre allowed herself to be herded along. It was for Livvy's sake, after all, and she really should not permit her spirits to be so deflated by the mere thought of several months of such entertainment. Several months. She felt her shoulders slump. If one Edinburgh ball, surrounded by amicable acquaintances, made her so unhappy, there was no telling what London would bring.

Seven years was a long time, but the ton had a very long memory.

She darted a glance at Olivia around Lady Leverham's impressive bust. The girl was busily trying to smooth her hair and skirts while not missing a single person, portrait, or potted plant they passed. Deirdre reminded herself that it was her sister-in-law's first ball. A bit of gawking was perfectly understandable.

And Livvy was in good company. Gawking was obviously the chosen behavior of the hour. Heads turned as they passed; male eyes widened. Despite herself, Deirdre smiled. Miss Olivia Macvail had arrived, and she was, without dancing a step or opening her mouth, fast on her way to becoming a success.

"Ah, there he is, the scoundrel!" Their hostess bore down on her quarry with the determination of an army general. "Oh, Mr. MacDon—"

Deirdre had never in their many years of acquaintance heard Lady Leverham fail to complete a word. But the lady was, at the moment, staring at the top of the stairs, mouth agape. A good dozen of her guests, including the incompletely addressed Mr. MacDonald, stared at her, their own mouths open as if to help her. When Lady Leverham spoke, people listened, and kept listening until she had quite finished. It was the only way to get back to whatever conversation had been going.

Her silence did not last long. "Oh. Oh, dear. I had heard that he was in Edinburgh, but did not think . . . Oh, heavens. You are not going to faint, Deirdre, are you? But of course you are, and I haven't a vinaigrette about. Oh, mercy!"

No, Deirdre was not going to faint, though she believed her hostess might benefit from a swift whiff of smelling salts. How very odd, she thought as she studied the figure who had materialized not three feet away, that she should be so very calm. It was, after all, a scene from a nightmare.

In all the times she had imagined the meeting, in all the frightening scenarios, she would never have predicted it happening in Scotland. Nor could she have prophesied the dilemma in which she would find herself. For she could not quite decide which was worse: facing the man whom she had jilted quite literally at the altar seven years earlier, or facing the man who had killed her husband. Not that it mattered, really. Both were standing in front of her, in the single, impeccable form of the Duke of Conovar.

2

S HE LOOKED AWFUL. A veritable scarecrow.

Lucas Gower, the Duke of Conovar, stood facing the one woman he had ever hated and waited to feel some satisfaction. After nearly seven years, he was meeting Deirdre Fallam—no, he corrected bitterly, Deirdre Macvail—again, and she looked like hell. He should have been delighted. Instead he was furious.

Stick-thin, pale, and garbed in an atrocious gray dress, she was still the most beautiful woman he had ever seen.

As he watched, one delicate hand reached up to cover the lush mouth. Her eyes, that smoky, unforgettable blue, were as wide as they had been on that long-ago day when he had reached an agreement with her smug father—and bore the same expression. A lesser man, in his position, would have been cut off at the knees by the horror there. A lesser woman, in hers, would have been in a swooning heap on the floor.

But Deirdre Fallam had never been a fainter. She had been a shouter.

Lucas waited, helplessly curious as to what would issue from those wide, velvet-rose lips. If he remembered correctly—and he remembered nearly everything the girl had said during their brief acquaintance—her first speech to him had been, "I will make you absolutely miserable, my lord." The last had been a simple, shaky, "No," and hadn't really been addressed to him at all, but to the slack-jawed vicar.

So he waited, along with everyone in the immediate vicinity, for her to speak now. Deirdre's eyes closed briefly; her hand dropped from her mouth. In that moment it occurred to Lucas that he really ought to spin on his heel, present her with his back, and walk away, perhaps all the way back to London.

He never had the chance. There was a trenchant wail, a soft gasp, and suddenly the young lady at Deirdre's side was leaning toward him—at a swift rate.

Acting more by instinct than design, Lucas reached out and caught the girl before she fell. He grunted and almost went to his knees, but managed to hold on. The room erupted then. Lady Leverham squealed and rushed forward, everyone began chattering at once, and Deirdre vanished in a throng of scuttling guests.

"Oh, heavens! Oh, my darling!" The baroness reached up and actually grasped a handful of Lucas's cravat. "The poor lamb! Quickly, bring her through here, Your Grace. A vinaigrette, someone, please!"

Lucas had no choice but to follow. The woman was throttling him. Stooped, struggling to keep from dropping his somewhat less-than-featherweight burden onto his own toes, he allowed himself to be led into a small salon. Revelers scattered, and Lady Leverham shooed a slow-moving pair from a plush settee. Then she relinquished her grip on Lucas's throat.

As gently as he could manage, he set the girl on the cushions. Contrary to his belief, she was not unconscious, but weeping. The moment her head hit the padded arm, she began wailing as well. The sound pierced his eardrums and had the fine hairs on his nape rising. For all that she resembled a Rubens madonna, the creature had the lungs of a banshee.

Then, suddenly, Deirdre was there, pushing past him to kneel beside the settee. Her cheeks were flushed now, and a heavy skein had come loose from the severe topknot to fall over her shoulder. Struck by memories of wild, burnished-gold curls tempting his fingers, Lucas stepped hurriedly back.

Then she spoke, and he felt his toes curling in his shoes. "Hush, dearest," she crooned, that faintest of Gaelic lilts still threading the husky voice. "Livvy, sweetheart, you must calm yourself."

Livvy? Lucas blinked. This exquisite, caterwauling creature was Jonas Macvail's sister? He remembered black plaits, twig-like limbs, and a habit of leaving sticky handprints on his coattails.

Apparently his old friend's sister had grown into this lush, lovely young lady. And a hysteric.

Deirdre's soothing ministrations were not doing any good. Nor was Lady Leverham, squeezed into the melee and waving some ill-smelling silver box in the general direction of the girl's face, helping to silence the infernal noise. No, Olivia Macvail was deep in the throes of an epic fit, and showing no inclination to stop.

When a well-meaning matron rushed forward with a glass of lemonade, spilling the better part of its contents over Lucas's arm, he decided enough was enough.

"For God's sake, Brat, be *quiet*!"

Whether it was the deep, booming voice that reached the girl or the long-ago sobriquet, it seemed to do the trick. Olivia gave a last, damp squeak and fell silent. So did everyone else.

"Good." Lucas pinned the girl with a steely gaze. "Do you have a handkerchief, perchance?"

"N-no. But DeeDee always . . ."

Deirdre was already pulling a square of lace-trimmed linen from her reticule. Lucas plucked it from her fingers as she offered it to her sister-in-law and dabbed ineffectually at his soaked sleeve. His arm was already feeling decidedly sticky. Then, ignoring her, he addressed Olivia again. "What on earth possessed you, Brat?"

She snuffled. Come to think of it, Lucas mused, he remembered the young Livvy Macvail doing a lot of snuffling. "It was seeing you, of course, Lucky."

The Macvails had always been fond of using appalling nicknames for each other. Jonas had been Nasey and Lord Lucas Gower, a mere second son at the time, had become Lucky. He had cheerfully tolerated the label then, not having had any cause to refute his general great fortune. Now it grated like nails down a schoolroom slate.

Lucas had a few words to say to the insolent minx who had pestered him mercilessly all those years ago. First, however, he cleared the room with one imperious glance around. The Duke of Conovar requested some privacy, and Edinburgh society, as did London, scurried to accommodate him. Even Lady Leverham,

14

with one fretful look at the trio, sidled toward the door. Lucas imagined there was a hearty but clandestine dose of brandy in her immediate future. New scandal would have the lady taking to her bed; the mere revival of an old one would have her tippling.

At last only Olivia and Deirdre remained. He would have liked to dispatch the latter, but did not think she would obey. She had paid him no respect in the past, and he had no reason to think that would have changed. So he continued to ignore her.

"Your manners," he said coldly to Olivia after a moment, "have not improved. If you can see fit to address me properly, I would be very interested in hearing why the sight of me set you to such a horrendously unseemly display."

The chit had the grace to blush. At least Lucas thought she was blushing. Her face, already blotchy, could merely be signaling another imminent squall. In truth, he could not fathom why he was still in her presence. Seven years earlier, he had bitterly cursed the existence of all Macvails, vowing vague revenge on the lot. And no matter how hard he might try, nor how many times he had imagined such a scene, he could not disregard the fact that Deirdre was kneeling at his feet at that very moment.

There had been no apology before. Contrition certainly wasn't her aim in being there now.

"I am having my London Season this year, Luck . . . Your Grace . . ." Olivia raised the lacy hem of her shawl. In a gesture Lucas imagined was more reflex than anything else, Deirdre, ash-pale and silent, stopped it before it reached the girl's nose.

"God give me strength," Lucas muttered.

"And now you will ruin it all!"

Dragging his eyes from Deirdre's rigid shoulders and the thick curl resting there, Lucas demanded, "Ruin what?"

"My chances at a good match! You will be beastly and say awful things, and no earl will so much as look at me! How *could* you, Lucky? How could you be so cruel? After all the times I watered your horse and polished your boots!"

She had fed his horse enough sugared water to make the beast skittish, left dusty footprints all over his boots, and, as Lucas recalled, vomited on them once, too, after sneaking a shot of whiskey from his flask. She had promptly started bawling, her

15

brother had laughed uproariously, and Lucas's valet had resigned on the spot.

He very nearly reminded her of the fact, but did not get the opportunity.

"That is quite enough, Olivia." Deirdre pushed herself stiffly to her feet. As remembered, the top of her head reached just to his chin, as though it were meant to nestle under. "His Grace has done nothing to you, save keep you from banging your head soundly against the floor. And he will do nothing."

"But, DeeDee. He . . . you . . ."

"Quite right. *He and I.*" Now, for the first time since that moment in the hall, Deirdre met Lucas's eyes. Hers were bold but wary in a face far too thin and pale. "I had heard you did not go about much in Society, Your Grace. I should have been more diligent in my inquiries. If it satisfies you, I will relinquish my role as Miss Macvail's guardian and leave her solely in Lady Leverham's capable hands. Surely you will not impede her entrance into Society if I am not there, just to spite me. You . . . you were never . . . cruel."

No, she thought as she stared into the cold, unreadable face. Lord Lucas Gower had never been cruel, merely arrogant and thoughtless. His position as second son of the grand Duke of Conovar had made him spoiled. His good looks, money, and rapier tongue had made him wildly popular. Of course it had never occurred to him that one socially inferior debutante would not be honored by his intentions—and would be enraged by the careless ease with which he had essentially bought her from her socially rapacious father—without ever having addressed a single word to her.

No, he had not been cruel. He had been too far above her for cruelty.

His eyes were expressionless now. The silver of time-worn steel, they had widened in surprise when she had refused his suit those years ago, then glittered in laughter moments later when he had chided her for being a silly creature and informed her the matter was settled. Seven years, and she could still remember the humiliation of his amusement.

He had not laughed when she informed the vicar that no, she

would not honor, obey, and cherish Lord Lucas George deVilliers Gower. He had gaped, then snarled at her, those eyes sharpening like knives under the sleek shock of ash brown hair.

Deirdre almost would have preferred that fury to the cold blankness she saw now. Fury she could handle; she had felt it herself. But she had never felt *nothing*, and the utter lack of emotion she saw frightened her. Lord Lucas was the Duke of Conovar now, and he could, with a single word, cause Olivia a social death that Deirdre knew would, in the girl's opinion, be worse than actual demise.

"Please, Your Grace . . ." Oh, it stuck in her throat, any plea to this man, but she was willing to beg him till Doomsday if it would make a difference. "I will return to Tarbet. I will . . ."

He turned away from her.

"You have my word of honor, Miss Macvail," he announced brusquely, "that I will do nothing to sabotage your Season." As Deirdre watched, astonished, he even gave Olivia a faint smile. "I would suggest, however, that you desist with the histrionics. A gentle swoon is all the fashion, though I cannot fathom why, but screeching and blubbering will be certain to do more damage to your status than I ever could. You have grown into a lovely young lady, Brat. Red eyes only spoil the picture."

"Your Grace, thank y—" Deirdre began, but he continued as if she hadn't spoken.

"One more matter, then I shall leave you. I do think it best, under the circumstances, if we do not have any contact in Town. You will no doubt understand why. I wish you all success, Miss Macvail." With that he sketched a brief bow in Olivia's direction, spun on his heel, and left the room.

Frozen, Deirdre heard him announce clearly to someone outside, "Miss Macvail's brother and I were friends for some years before his death. I fear her delicate sensibilities were a bit overwhelmed at seeing me again. Quite understandable, and all is well now." Then there was the thud of boot heels on the carpet, and the hallway erupted once again into lively chatter.

Deirdre's knees felt like jelly suddenly. She had to sit down. Olivia squeaked as her arm got in the way, and hurriedly sat up to make room. "DeeDee—"

17

"No, Livvy, not a word."

"But, DeeDee, he said—"

"I heard him." And she could not quite believe what she had heard. Not only had he promised to let the past go, but he had left the party with an explanation that would silence flapping tongues as well. "I heard."

She took Olivia's following silence to indicate the girl had some idea of what had just transpired. It would be mortifying, certainly, having been told to stay away from him, but vastly preferable to the alternative scenario. Yes, Livvy had just gained a valuable lesson in the vagaries of the Haute Monde.

Deirdre really ought to have known better.

"I had not thought . . ." Olivia paused to wipe her nose with her shawl. "I had not remembered how terribly handsome he is, nor how tall. Did you not think he looked excessively well, DeeDee? That little bit of silver in his hair makes him look ever so distinguished, just as a duke ought. And did you hear? He called me lovely. Oh, my heart is fluttering! Do you think he will dance with me in London? I daresay he cuts a fine figure on the floor. I should quite float on air!"

"Olivia," Deirdre said wearily, "you have the sense of a goose."

The girl ignored her, choosing instead to continue her rhapsodies on the duke's bold nose and clefted chin, his obviously unpadded shoulders. And Deirdre could not dispel a single assertion.

Lucas Gower had always been handsome, certainly. But his bold jaw and silver eyes had been nothing when placed next to the visage of his best friend. From girlhood, Deirdre had always dreamed of a black-haired, blue-eyed Celtic warrior, and Jonas Macvail had been just that. She had fallen in love the moment she saw him standing beside her fiancé, her first meeting with the man she would marry and only her second with the man she would not, both of them garbed in their regimental blues. How vividly bright the coat had made Nasey's eyes. And how grandly arrogant it had made Lord Lucas's bearing.

The bearing was the same, but the uniform was gone, replaced by stark, elegant black. Deirdre imagined the color was by choice, rather than extended mourning. She knew it was three years since Lucas's older brother had died in a drunken riding accident, nearly

18

two since the old duke had passed on. No, Lucas wore black because it suited him.

She had always thought him something akin to the devil. Of course, that had been the dramatic opinion of an unhappy, dream-shattered girl. Now, as a grown woman who had known disgrace, solitude, and heartbreak, she could imagine why the ton regarded him as something of a deity. Like so many minor pagan gods, he was stunningly, unapproachably beautiful. And like those gods, he walked a step above the people around him. The Duke of Conovar had become precisely what his station demanded: curt, distant, and very much aware of the power he possessed.

She had once found him disagreeable. Now he was terrifying.

At that moment Lady Leverham pushed through the crowd in the doorway and trundled into the room, beaming smiles and wafting the faint scent of brandy. "Well, my dear," she addressed the still starry-eyed Olivia, enveloping her in an enthusiastic embrace, "you have quite done it! You will, no doubt, go into the annals as the first young lady to make her smashing debut by fainting. Oh, the approval of the Duke of Conovar! Splendid!"

She turned to Deirdre then. "And you, darling girl, are even more fortunate. Conovar could have been most unpleasant, after all. I was most distressed that whiffs of your past as a jilt might affect our Livvy's Season. But the dear, generous boy has clearly seen fit to forgive your poor, youthful indiscretion. What a marvelous man!"

As the other two commenced with their giggling plans for Olivia's London debut—where, the girl insisted, she would most certainly dance her waltz, at Almack's, no less—Deirdre leaned back against the cushions and closed her eyes. What everyone else seemed conveniently to have forgotten was that her poor, youthful indiscretion was buried in the Tarbet churchyard. And the marvelous, generous Duke of Conovar had put him there.

Lucas caught a few people staring at him as he made his way back to his rooms in George Square and realized he was muttering aloud. Then, too, the urge to scratch at the tormenting rash risen suddenly on his neck was too much to resist. But he could not be bothered by the fact that he must appear a twitching, babbling lunatic. He was too busy cursing Arthur MacDonald for talking him into attending Leverham's dismally provincial soiree—and cursing himself for weakness.

He did not regret his promise to Olivia. After all, she had been no more than a child when her brother and Lucas's fiancée had betrayed him. Beyond that, he had always had a soft spot for the girl. Having no sisters of his own, he had found her sheep-eyed adoration amusing and a bit charming. Lord Lucas Gower had been accustomed to unobtrusive adulation. It had been rather nice to be worshiped so openly.

No, he wished Miss Macvail only the best. And he assumed she would do well enough in Society if only she refrained from becoming a wailing watering pot in public. She had the Macvail looks, to be sure, and a pleasantly rounded figure. He himself had always preferred women with a decided softness to them. Which made it all the more galling that he could not get Deirdre out of his mind.

He had never intended to see her again. And to see her after seven years, painfully thin, those stunningly high cheekbones made all the more dramatic by the hollows beneath, her smoky blue eyes deep and shadowed, had given him no pleasure. He had wanted her to suffer, wanted it with a fierceness nearly equal to the passion with which he had once desired her. Now, oddly, he was finding no satisfaction in knowing his vitriolic wish had been answered.

He should never have accepted Hythe's invitation to hunt in Midlothian. As he had already chosen a young lady from the hordes and hence had no need to survey the display of the first week of the Season, Lucas had given in to the earl's persuasiveness.

He could have made his excuses to the Duke of Buccleuch and avoided the reception at Holyrood. He could have tossed a pigeon pie into MacDonald's face at the very mention of Lady Leverham's soiree. He could have jumped into the Firth of Forth and cavorted with mermaids.

"Well, damn!" he cursed aloud, startling the footman who had rushed to open the hotel's massive door for him. "I could have danced a jig with the devil in hell, but *no* . . ." He found himself nose-to-nose with the slack-jawed fellow. "Of all the entertainments in all this bloody huge country, I had to wander into *hers*!"

"I . . . er . . . yes, Your Grace."

Lucas glared. God only knew where the elite establishments were finding their staff these days. This one was vaguely green in the face, and his white peruke was tipped down, almost to his bulging eyes. "For heaven's sake, man, straighten your damned wig!" he snapped, then stalked toward the stairs.

His valet was waiting for him in his dressing room. "Good evening, Your Grace."

"Hardly!" Lucas shucked his coat and tossed it in the direction of the man's arms. "Fetch me a glass of brandy, Lowry."

"Certainly, Your Grace."

"Did I say a glass? Bring the whole bloody bottle."

"Yes, Your Gr—"

"And forget the glass!"

The valet juggled the coat from hand to hand, then hurriedly tossed it over his shoulder as he scuttled toward the sitting room.

"Lowry!"

The man skidded to a halt, nearly stumbling as his foot rucked up the edge of the carpet. "Yes, Your—"

"Not brandy. I want whiskey, good Highland stuff. I believe I am going to get sotted." Lucas jerked at his cravat, already a crumpled mess due to Lady Leverham's impressive grip, and threw it on the floor. His eyes lit on the valises stacked in the corner. "Lowry!"

"Yes, Y—"

"Pack. We depart at dawn."

The valet reappeared in the doorway, clutching a decanter in one hand and a glass in the other, the duke's black coat now dangling from beneath his elbow. "Of course, Your Grace."

Lucas glared at him. "I told you not to bother with a glass."

In the nearly fifteen years Lowry had served him, he had forgotten the occasional duty, offered his tart opinion on countless matters, and even quit at regular intervals. He had never, however, deliberately disregarded a command. At the moment he was leaning against the doorjamb, sparse hair wild and jaw tight.

"The glass is not for you, Your Grace." With that he settled the coat over his own shoulders, poured a hearty shot of scotch into the glass, and handed over the bottle. Then he bowed and tossed back the drink. The coat slid to the floor. He gave a thin smile as he retrieved it. "I will begin packing immediately."

Lucas closed his eyes and counted five. "Lowry."

"Yes, Your Grace?"

"I am on the verge of sacking you."

The valet handed him the coat and set the empty glass atop a chest of drawers. "No need, Your Grace. I resign." With that he stepped around Lucas, lifted the top valise from the stack, and began filling it with Lucas's shirts. "Was there anything else? Shall you require help in undressing?"

"No." Decanter in one hand, black superfine in the other, Lucas headed for the bedchamber. "Wake me at sunrise. Oh, to hell with that. I ought to be well into my second bottle by then. Simply pour me into the coach."

"Very good, Your Grace." Lowry slung the second valise off the stack and reached for a pile of cravats. "Ah, one small matter, Your Grace."

"Yes, what is it? Oh." Lucas tossed the coat at his valet's head.

Lowry caught it deftly. "I was thinking of your new watch fob. Should you like me to pack it with the others, or will you be wearing it on the morrow?"

Lucas glanced down at the front of his waistcoat. There, caught on a button and tangled with his gold chain, was a string of pearls. He tugged it free and swore fluently. No doubt the thing belonged to Miss Macvail, and had come loose during her swoon. In the following chaos no one had managed to notice it was no longer about her neck, nor that the Duke of Conovar was sporting a decidedly odd piece of jewelry for a man.

He dropped it onto a small, occasional table. "See that it is returned to Miss Macvail." He realized he had no idea where the Brat and her scarecrow guardian were living. "Care of Lady Leverham, Charlotte Square."

"Would that be Miss Olivia Macvail, Your Grace?"

"Indeed, Lowry. Is there a problem? I assure you, she is quite grown and unlikely to lose her breakfast over my boots again."

"Of course, Your Grace." Lowry, arms full of stockings, expression bland, was standing in the dressing room doorway. "You wish me to summon the concierge, who will in turn dispatch a footman to return the pearls to Miss Olivia Macvail through the home of Lady Leverham, from the Duke of Conovar."

"I was going to sack you, wasn't I?"

"I resigned, Your Grace."

"True." Then the man's meaning in questioning the order hit home. "Well, hell. It would look rather dodgy, wouldn't it? Fine."

Lucas retrieved the pearls and tucked them into his waistcoat pocket. Why he should care was really beyond him. He had done the Brat an immense favor already that evening. He bloody well could send off the blasted pearls, any gossip be damned. The more he thought on the matter, the more reasonable it seemed for the sins of the brother to be visited on the sister.

But that was nonsense, and he knew it. He would find a discreet way of getting the necklace back to Livvy, even if it meant facing Deirdre again. Perhaps even the following morning as he departed Edinburgh. Providing he could obtain their direction—and drink himself nearly senseless, of course. He had a single question for Deirdre, one that had niggled like a rash for quite some time.

"Damn," he muttered as his neck flamed anew.

"Don't scratch!" came Lowry's insolent reprimand. "It will fade when you've calmed down, Your Grace."

Lucas snarled at the valet and stalked to the mantel. He surveyed himself grimly in the mirror there. The cursedly familiar red patch had spread upward, nearly to his jaw. It itched. And it was all Deirdre's fault.

She could have been Lady Lucas Gower. No, damn it, she could have been the Duchess of Conovar. But she had chosen instead to live in rustic poverty with Nasey Macvail, who, when it all came down to it, had been nothing more than a smiling, clever, well-looking, traitorous sod.

In all his private fury, his viewing and reviewing of each of the few occasions he had spent with Deirdre before her defection, Lucas had never been able to comprehend precisely what had gone wrong.

3

DEIRDRE MADE HER way quietly along the upper hall early the following morning, closing her chamber door carefully and avoiding the creaky floorboard halfway down the worn runner. In a tiny house few sounds went unnoticed, and Olivia was still in bed.

Quite probably she would stay that way until noon if nothing disturbed her. She was not particularly fond of mornings on an average day, and the events of the night before would be enough to fuel her dreams for quite some time. In the wake of Conovar's departure, the guests had swarmed around the girl, petting and admiring, and making her the undivided center of attention. Not only had the charming Mr. MacDonald come up to snuff and partnered Olivia in two dances, but his dashing friends had eagerly followed suit.

True to Deirdre's expectations, the handsome fortune hunter, who had, incidentally and unfortunately, turned out to be the younger son of a notoriously spendthrift marquess, had appeared similarly smitten. And Olivia, whose desire for a title was equaled only by her reaction to a pretty male face, had done nothing to discourage his attentions.

Deirdre sighed as she crept past Olivia's door. A promise was a promise, but when she had vowed to Lady Macvail to see Livvy properly presented to Society, she had not allowed herself to contemplate the fact that the girl really might be best presented in a large glass box. Atop the frequent histrionics, Olivia had the distressing tendency to be at her most charming around those persons who least deserved it.

The empty-pocketed Lord Derik Germans was certain to be

only the first of many stunning creatures whom Deirdre would have to courteously and determinedly shoo away from her charge. How very nice it would be, she mused with no small amount of irony, if Livvy would cooperate.

Much as she hated to do it, she would have to sit her sister-in-law down and discuss the matter of inappropriate suitors. Olivia, no doubt, would alternately pout and giggle, then launch into her portrayal of what she called Deirdre's "deceased don discourses."

Deirdre couldn't help but smile at the memory of parodies past. If she put Livvy in mind of a teacher so infernally dull, so be it. Someone had to be the voice of reason in the family. Macvails, delightful though they were, were notoriously poor at that necessity.

She had just reached the first landing when a door flew open above her. Wincing, she crept down a few more stairs, knowing even as she did that she had been caught.

"DeeDee?"

"Good morning, Olivia. I had not expected you to be up for some hours yet."

The girl was not only awake, but excessively so. Deirdre closed her eyes for a weary second as Livvy came bounding to the head of the stairs, wrapper flying. "How could I possibly stay abed after such a night! Summon Betsy for me, would you? I'm famished. No, wait. I need your help in choosing what I'm to wear today."

"You are a big girl, Livvy. I have full faith in your ability to choose a dress."

"But I'm going driving this afternoon and must look my best!" Deirdre paused mid-step. "Driving? With whom?"

"Come back up, please, DeeDee. I simply cannot decide between the white muslin and the yellow."

"Olivia. With whom are you . . ."

The girl was already skipping back to her bedchamber. "Are you coming?"

"No." A faint chime from the downstairs clock told Deirdre that she was already late. "I have errands, among which is visiting Lady Leverham and retrieving my pearls. I don't suppose you would care to visit the milliner . . . since you are already awake," she added dryly, knowing perfectly well what the response would be, "and it is your hat."

"Do be serious. I am nowhere near ready to appear outside. Besides, you are on your way out anyway." Olivia reappeared long enough to admonish, "Really, DeeDee, I find it most vexing that you insist on doing the household shopping. What if Miss MacDonald were to see you leaving the candle maker's or the butcher?"

It was an old and useless argument. Deirdre had neither the time nor the inclination to explain that the meager staff was already stretched and that she was far more successful at bargaining with the various merchants than their deaf and curmudgeonly cook.

"Rest assured, my dear, that I am unlikely to run into any of your acquaintances. They won't be up and out for another several hours. Now, about your driving companion . . ." Olivia was gone again. Deirdre drew a patient breath, then called sternly, "You will not go out unaccompanied with Derik Germans! Is that clear, Livvy?"

She assumed the faint grunt was an affirmative. Staying only long enough to tell Betsy that the princess was awake and famished, and to have a brief shouting match with Cook over necessary supplies, Deirdre hurried from the house.

It was but a few minutes' walk to her first destination. The New Town was already bustling, carriages and merchant wagons rumbling along the stone streets. Deirdre stopped and allowed herself the luxury of simply watching. Warmed as she always was by these scenes, Deirdre smiled to herself. A hackney driver stopped shouting at his horse as they passed and, jaw a bit slack, lifted his hat. "A guid mornin' tae ye', ma'am."

"And to you," Deirdre replied. She clearly recalled years of her mother's admonishments against talking to strange men. If she remembered correctly, Anne Fallam had found most men strange and had talked to almost no one.

Deirdre valued what privacy she had; she valued it immensely. But she refused to keep herself at a distance from the people around her. Being lonely was something she would accept. Deliberately being alone was not.

As the hack drifted by, she hurried across the street and up the steps of a modest house. The door flew open as she reached for the knocker. "Good morning, Jennie," she greeted the apple-cheeked little maid.

"Mrs. Macvail." Jennie bobbed a cheerful curtsy. "The master'll be fair happy to see ye."

Deirdre's step quickened as she made her way up the stairs. She would be fair happy to see the master, too. These visits had been the highlight of her time in town.

A booming voice answered her knock. Inside what would ordinarily be the back bedroom, morning sunlight flooded over bare floors, cast a halo around the figure in the center, and shot blindingly off a bald pate. Deirdre smiled as she noted the smear of green paint there. Apparently something had not gone quite right, and a bit of contemplative rubbing had been required.

The painter turned to face her, effectively blocking the canvas on which he was working. "Deirdre!" He opened his arms in greeting. When she hesitated, he glanced down at his paint-spattered smock and grinned ruefully, dark eyes glinting. "Sorry, my dear. I always forget."

"And I always want to embrace you, mess or not."

Henry Raeburn accepted her kiss on his ruddy cheek and brushed hers with one reasonably clean knuckle. "You are late, lass." He deftly shifted to block the canvas again when she attempted a quick peek. "And brazen, too."

"Well, I had to try." Familiar with the routine, Deirdre removed her spencer and took her place on the chaise near the window. "This is our last sitting, you know."

"I do, and thank you ever so much for rubbing such melancholy truth in my face." He peered around the easel. "As lovely as your face is, my dear, it now possesses some distinctly blue shadows."

"I'm afraid Olivia kept me up well into the night with her rhapsodies."

Raeburn shook his head in amusement. "She certainly enjoyed herself. I wonder if we ought to warn London of her imminent arrival."

"Oh, I daresay the ton will survive."

28

"No doubt, and quite probably hail her as an Incomparable."

"Only if she ceases with the dramatics."

Raeburn chuckled as he dabbed away at his canvas. "Never underestimate the appeal of a graceful swoon to English Society."

"Well, then, I suppose we shall simply have to work on the grace bit."

"My dear, you could teach grace to Genghis Khan."

Long accustomed to the man's compliments, Deirdre gently waved this one away and settled herself in the position she had occupied several times before. "You will be coming to London, won't you?"

"Eventually."

"I don't suppose you would care to make eventually mean tomorrow?"

"Not even for you, my dear. Perhaps next year."

The painter's dislike of London was well-known—and cheerfully hailed by many of his Scots acquaintances. Deirdre sighed. "I know it is terribly weak of me, but I am expecting the very worst."

"Aye, well, no one would blame you for that." Raeburn gave her a sympathetic smile. "Ah, Deirdre. As much as your melancholy suits the canvas, it does terrible things to this old heart of mine. It will not be so bad. Conovar behaved rather well last night."

Deirdre sighed. Much as she adored Raeburn, she wished he had been a bit less well acquainted with the Macvails—and that he was a bit less perceptive. "He did, yes, which means London might be slightly less unpleasant than expected. Perhaps people will simply content themselves with sniping behind my back rather than giving me the cut direct."

"Mmm. But will you allow them to accept you again, if they are willing?"

"They won't. I committed an unforgivable crime, you know."

"Hardly, my dear. You merely jilted one of Society's young bucks to marry another. Perhaps the more intelligent among the lot will remember that Conovar was only a second son at the time, while Jonas was heir to a barony."

"To be sure. It would be far too much to expect the more

29

intelligent among the lot to understand how unpleasant the concept was of marrying Lucas Gower." Deirdre shrugged at Raeburn's raised brows. "Yes, yes, I know. I must take what I can get in the way of a pardon. The fact, however, is that the second son became the mighty duke, while Jonas died before inheriting." She looked up, knowing her anguish showed in her face, but unable to help it. "And Society will remember that he died an enlisted man, not even the officer he once was."

Raeburn put down his brush and came around the easel to take one of her hands. "We all loved him, Deirdre, as much in spite of his nature as because of it. He chose to return to service."

Oh, yes, Jonas had chosen to return, even after Conovar had had his commission revoked. He had returned cheerfully, without even a curse for the man who had once been his friend. He'd refused to blame Lucas at all.

Deirdre was not so noble.

Raeburn gently touched her cheek again. "You've been given a rough lot, but you've done all right for yourself. Don't crumble now."

She reached up to pat his hand, smiling faintly at the green smudge he had left on hers. "With Livvy to be presented? The Haute Monde would *never* forgive me should I let her loose upon it without at least token control over the situation."

"That's my lass." He resumed his place at the easel. "Now, be still. Your mouth is eluding me." He winked. "It took me nearly six years of cajoling to get my shot at it. Do cooperate."

Deirdre obediently titled her face into the light. "Will you let me see the portrait before I go?"

Raeburn squinted intently at her for a moment, then switched brushes and dabbed away with pink. Deirdre reminded herself that there was a visit to the shoemaker to be made. "I don't think so, my dear. Knowing you, you would roll your lovely eyes and say something excruciatingly polite."

She shot him a look. "Do you always speak to your subjects that way?"

"With fees to be collected? Of course not." His eyes twinkled at her over the canvas. "I simply give them discreet warts. Ah, no laughing, lass! Wistful, please."

Deirdre rolled her eyes and silently scolded the darling man for demanding sadness when he made her feel lighthearted and cherished. *Wistful.*

Well, that wasn't so terribly difficult. All she had to do was think of Red Branch Cottage with its rosy stone walls, and how long it would be before she saw it again. The rent had gone up once more—courtesy, she suspected, of the Edinburgh agent. The cottage's owner, whoever he was, took no interest in his property and would quite probably surface only if the rent went unpaid.

Yes, thinking of her precious home made her both wistful and anxious. Contemplating the tasks yet to be done before her departure would no doubt make her utterly miserable. That, insofar as the portrait was concerned, might not be such a bad condition. Deirdre thought Raeburn would be perfectly happy to accept miserable as an alternative to wistful.

There was still so much to be done before the morrow. She was due at the solicitor's by noon to try, as she had a hundred times before, to squeeze a few more pounds from a trust already stretched thin. She meant to leave no bills unpaid.

That, in itself, meant an unpleasant hour or so at the butcher's. She was certain the man had once again added some creative surcharges to the bill and would require the usual pleas, cajolings, and threats to remove them. Then there was the baker, the coal merchant, the shoemaker with his unique concept of pink . . .

The list grew as the day suddenly seemed to possess somewhat less than the customary twenty-four hours. Deirdre blinked away the image of her coins vanishing before she'd even counted them. It was a familiar state of affairs, and one she could not be bothered to worry over. Instead she tried to decide between a bottle of good wine or some of the Turkish sweetmeats Olivia liked so well—should there be a few shillings to spare. Their last supper in Edinburgh could use a bright touch.

She determinedly did not think of the Duke of Conovar at all. His Grace with the stony eyes and granite heart—

"Deirdre, lass, that scowl would frighten the devil himself."

31

"Well, I'll just have to try it, then," she replied airily, "should we meet."

Raeburn winked at her, and reached for a tube of red.

Lucas's eyes felt like hot coals and his stomach lurched along with the carriage. Lowry, he decided, chose the very worst times to follow orders precisely to the letter. He had just managed to drink himself into a pleasant stupor when the valet had come bustling into the room, bearing coffee and a damnably self-satisfied air. They were departing several hours later than planned, but they were indeed departing—when Lucas could imagine nothing better than a morning spent with the covers over his head.

Now, as they rolled their way out of George Square and into a long day of travel, he gritted his teeth and wondered if he could avoid ever coming to Scotland again.

"The hotel provided us with a splendid traveling basket, Your Grace." Across the carriage, Lowry lolled comfortably against the squabs. "Do let me know when a bit of roasted chicken appeals to you."

Had Lucas possessed the requisite strength, he would have reached out and throttled the sod. Instead he tried to discreetly press his fist into his roiling gut and muttered, "Save me the effort of sacking you and resign."

"I think not, Your Grace. I find myself most content with my position today."

Lucas vowed to banish Lowry to the outside of the carriage once they left the pearls at Lady Leverham's house. A few hours of riding with the driver might eliminate some of the smugness, and would provide the peace Lucas needed for a restorative nap. He thought he would send the hotel's splendid basket out, too.

A peddler's cart loaded with jangling tin pots rattled past. Lucas winced as light bounced off a highly polished surface and into his distressed eyes. Edinburgh at this hour was too sunny and too loud for civilized persons. There was little to be done about the noise, but he had every confidence that he could control the sun. He reached for the window shade.

The carriage was moving slowly enough that he got a very good view of Deirdre as she stepped out of a neat brick house.

There was no mistaking the too-slender form or bright curls. As Lucas craned his neck to watch, she paused and turned back toward the older man who appeared suddenly at the threshold. For a moment they were hidden by a stone pillar, but there was no missing the embrace.

Even as he dragged his watch from his waistcoat pocket, he was rapping his stick against the ceiling. The carriage shuddered to a halt. Lowry peered owlishly at him and demanded, "Is something amiss, Your Grace?"

Lucas brandished his watch. "Half-past nine."

"Indeed."

"Who pays visits at half-past nine in the morning, Lowry?"

"No one among the quality, Your Grace."

"Precisely." He reached for the door handle. "Night visits end at this hour. Morning visits bloody well aren't paid till afternoon. And women with innocent charges have no call to be paying visits at all!"

He was already on the street before it occurred to him that what Olivia Macvail's guardian did or did not do, morning or night, did not matter to him in the least. In fact, Olivia Macvail's guardian could have assignations with every balding, one-foot-in-the-grave man in Scotland for all he cared.

He tightened his grip on the door, this time to haul himself back inside the carriage. Too late. Deirdre, having reached the street, had already spied him. Her hands stilled in the process of tying her bonnet strings. Under the straw brim Lucas saw her eyes widen, the smooth brow furrow.

Cursing under his breath, he gave a terse bow as she approached. "Good morning, Mrs. Macvail."

She hesitated a moment. "Good morning, Your Grace."

A number of indiscreet questions flashed into Lucas's mind. He quashed them. Absurd as his headlong dash from the carriage had been, it would serve a purpose. A quick glare at the box had the coachman quickly averting his gaze. Lowry, to his credit, withdrew into his seat.

33

"Forgive me for accosting you, madam, but I saw you leaving . . ." He gestured behind her.

Deirdre's eyes flitted back toward the house, but she offered nothing beyond, "Yes, Your Grace?"

Lucas drew the paper-wrapped parcel from his coat pocket. "Miss Macvail's necklace came into my possession during the chaos last night. I was intending to deliver it to Lady Leverham on my way out of town, but meeting you will spare me the bother."

He had not meant to be quite so blunt, but having Deirdre standing before him had his teeth on edge. Well-honed decorum, he'd found some years before, was only worth so much in the face of a good snit.

Deirdre glanced at the parcel in his hand almost as if it contained a snake. No, he decided wryly, she was looking at his skin as if it bore scales. She reached out at last.

"Thank you. Olivia was quite beside herself when she found the pearls gone."

He could well imagine the Brat's response to finding her bauble missing, and actually chuckled before he could stop himself. He remembered an occasion some twelve years back when a lost doll had brought the entire Macvail household to a screeching halt. Well, he amended, it was young Olivia who had done the screeching—and had not stopped until he himself had organized a search. When Jonas had located the toy behind a sofa cushion, his sister had smiled brilliantly, then kicked him soundly in the shins for having carried the thing to her by the hair.

Lucas blinked away the memory to find Deirdre staring at him curiously, bronze-gold brows raised. He realized he was grinning like an idiot and brusquely composed his features. "I suggest you have the clasp examined, Mrs. Macvail. It appears to be quite old."

"It was made originally for my grandmother," she replied tersely. She pressed the parcel briefly between her palms, then tucked it into the string bag she carried. "Again, thank you—"

"See to the matter soon, madam. The next person to find the thing might not be so concerned with another's possession. I would venture to guess something so precious would be difficult to replace."

34

No, he thought, not difficult. Impossible.

Deirdre faced him for a long moment, eyes cool. Then she announced, "Everyone loses something precious in life, Your Grace. We survive. I do appreciate your concern, however."

"Think nothing of it," he muttered, knowing she would damn well do just that.

"Well, thank you again. Good day, Your Grace."

She stepped around him and headed down the street. Lucas watched her go. He would have preferred not to notice the gentle sway of her hips as she went, but noticed anyway. Then he spied several other men noticing. One nearly dropped the crate of lettuce he was carrying as Deirdre passed him. Another stopped dead in his tracks and spun for a better view.

A low whistle caught Lucas's attention, and he spun to find his coachman leaning forward on the box, eyes dreamy.

"As you were!" he snapped.

The driver hurriedly sat up straight. From the corner of his eye, Lucas could see Lowry scuttling back into his seat. One would have thought Edinburgh had just been blessed by a heavenly visitation. Deirdre Macvail was simply another woman in a city full of them, and just as flawed as any.

She was also, damn it, too bloody beautiful to be of this earth.

An overdressed dandy, complete with pink-striped waistcoat and padded aqua coat, trotted from one of the houses. He skidded to a halt at the sight of Deirdre walking by, then doffed his hat with an exaggerated flair. She did not respond. Lucas did. He stalked after her, shooting a deadly look at the fop as he went. The fellow had the further insolence to grin.

"Mrs. Macvail." Lucas very nearly grabbed her arm to stop her. "Allow me to escort you home."

Again, she regarded him as if he were a reptilian creature. "No, thank you, Your Grace. You are most accommodating to offer, but I must decline."

"And I must insist."

"Why?" she asked bluntly.

He blinked at her, not quite knowing how to explain that the continued well-being of several people nearby depended on her getting her pert bottom into the carriage. "You surely cannot expect me to leave you here in the street."

"Yes, I can expect just that. Rest assured, you have fulfilled your gentlemanly duties. I will make sure your graciousness is duly noted."

Oh, that tone stung. "Damn it, Deirdre, get in the carriage . . . *if you please*."

She turned to face him fully then. Clearly anticipating her acquiescence, the driver all but flew from his perch to open the door for her. A single, fiery look from Lucas had him slinking back up.

"Well, that certainly hasn't changed," he heard Deirdre murmur.

"I have long been accustomed to being obeyed," he shot back.

"And I have long been accustomed to being shoved about like a chess pawn. No longer." The sharp edge was gone from her voice suddenly, replaced by a soft weariness. "I am a different woman than I was when you didn't quite know me, Your Grace, but I was never an ivory game piece. Perhaps I should have told you that then. Perhaps it all would have turned out differently . . ." She gave him a brief, sad smile. "But *seas between us braid hae roared sin' auld lang syne* . . . Ah, well. Good-bye, sir."

Lucas let her go this time, but kept his eyes fixed on her graceful back until it disappeared among the colorful bustle of the street. When he could no longer see her at all, he turned away and realized he had not been alone in staring. He met the gaze of a weathered, grimy-faced street sweeper who promptly tipped his ragged cap and broke into a gap-toothed grin. He cleared his throat and asked the sweeper, "The last thing she said to me . . . Did you happen to catch it?"

"Deif, are ye? She said 'good-bye.' "

"Er, before that."

"Oh, aye. 'Twas poetry. Don't you ken our Rabbie?" At Lucas's blank expression, the old man huffed out an exasperated breath. "Rabbie Burns, you daftie! The greatest poet ever trod the earth."

"Burns. I see."

"Aye, well, the lass was but sayin' you've got broad oceans an' years atween you." He removed his cap and rubbed a gnarled hand over his bald head. "Och, lad, don't you *read*?"

Lucas thought of the several hundred dog-eared books in his library. He thought of the several hundred more that had passed through his hands during his years as a student. Thirty years of life, twenty-six or so of reading, and he was still apparently as much of a daftie as ever.

4

LUCAS STUDIED THE bay stallion's bunched muscles and tried to remember why he had requested a closer view. The purpose of attending a sale at Tattersall's was to choose a suitable means of transportation over the ground. From the look of the beast, it would have him six feet under within minutes.

A low whistle sounded beside him. "You're a brave man, Conovar. They say that animal's first three owners have four broken legs, two shattered arms, and a cracked skull between them."

Lucas silently commended himself on perceptiveness, then turned to face the new arrival. Evan Althorpe had his long form propped against the paddock rail, hat tilted in customary negligence over his brow, a faint red smudge decorating his loose cravat.

"You really ought to limit your visits to North Row to the occasional night, man. They say your mistress's last three protectors have two enraged wives and six empty pockets between them."

Althorpe grinned. "I haven't a wife, am well used to empty pockets, and for all you know, could have spent the morning with my maiden aunties in Berkeley Square."

"Well, then, I suggest you tell Auntie Wilhelmina that her lip rouge needs repair."

"Lip . . ." Althorpe's fingers drifted to his neck. "Well, bother."

Lucas managed to keep a straight face as the man rolled his eyes and rotated his jaw, trying to get a better look. "You're late."

"Yes, yes, I know. But you've never taken my advice on anything in the past, so I thought I might just as well arrive once you'd

38

made your purchase." The pair turned back to face the bay. "Twenty pounds says your cousin will be wearing the ducal coronet come Tuesday."

"I really ought to take that wager," Lucas said dryly. "Even if I lose, you'll have a hell of a time collecting your winnings from Francis."

"True. He'll get it all: lock, stock, and barrel when you kick off, won't he?" Althorpe flicked the brim of his hat, gave a cheeky grin, and turned away.

"Where are you going?"

"Off to find your cousin, of course. I can't be wasting my time making nice with you any longer. I prefer to cultivate acquaintances that will support my drinking for a long time to come."

"Very amusing."

"Wasn't it? Oh, for God's sake, Conovar. A smile won't permanently mar that splendid visage of yours. In fact, if you would consider flashing one now and again when you say something amusing, people might actually *like* you."

Lucas raised a brow. "According to our delightful daily rags, I am the most popular duke in the realm."

"No, my friend, you are simply the most *available* duke in the realm, not to mention one of the few still in possession of his hair, teeth, and wits." Althorpe removed his hat and ran a hand through his own untidy fair hair. "But that was a very good example of how you might be considered a wit if you would just be bothered to smile. It was a reasonably clever quip. The problem is that you tend to look as if you take everything you say totally seriously."

"And your point is . . . ?"

Althorpe sighed. "Must you make so little effort to be agreeable?"

"Must you make such a great one? I'm sure it's mentally and physically exhausting, being charming all the time."

Lucas signaled his acceptance of the horse, then watched as the beast almost flung the groom holding its halter into the boards. He would have to remember to warn his own stable staff. It wouldn't do at all to have the animal launching an unsuspecting soul into the hereafter on its first day in residence.

Beside him, Althorpe muttered something about ice floes for veins. Lucas hardly thought himself cold-blooded. He had, however, read Machiavelli extensively at his father's command, and was well versed in the theory that it was better to be feared than loved.

It hardly mattered that he had not loved Machiavelli in the least. He had been utterly terrified of his father.

"Shall we go celebrate your purchase?" Althorpe ambled by Lucas's side as they quitted the yard. "You must provide me with at least one bottle of something ungodly expensive before you try riding that hell horse."

"Much as I would like to practice being agreeable, I have other plans. I'm on my way to pay a visit at the Vaers'."

Althorpe promptly clapped his hat over his chest. "Methinks I hear the impending clank of legshackles."

Lucas was hearing a deafening clattering from the chute into which his new mount had just been led. He resolutely ignored it. "No agreement has been reached as yet, but I think Miss Vaer and I will suit admirably."

"Is Miss Vaer of the same opinion? Oh, don't bother glaring at me. If you will remember, I was in attendance at your wedding. One might take the bride's flight from the altar as an indication that she did *not* think you would suit admirably."

"I don't want to talk about Deirdre."

"I don't blame you. She was an Incomparable."

Lucas felt his fists clenching at his sides. "I don't want to talk about Deirdre."

"Fine. Although, I am going to have a bit of trouble explaining why you might want to postpone your visit to Miss Vaer without mentioning Mrs. Macvail."

"Try," Lucas suggested grimly.

"Well, if you paid any attention to the goings-on of the Season, you would know that Lady Leverham's luncheon was today. Apparently Olivia Macvail is fast on her way to becoming the toast of the ton, and the Great Husband Hunt has begun. The luncheon was a sort of tally ho."

Lucas wasn't surprised in the least to hear that the Brat was entrancing Society. Like a small child, the ton always seemed drawn to the flashiest, loudest, and silliest.

Thus far, he had avoided any gathering where he might run into any member of the Macvail coterie. For the past six years, his attendance at Society functions had been infrequent and unpredictable. Everyone still sent invitations, but no one could expect him to accept. The system suited him just fine. Dodging the recent round of parties had been easy enough. Not seeing Deirdre had been no hardship.

Not thinking about her, about her shadowed blue eyes and painfully prominent cheekbones, was proving all but impossible.

Everyone loses something precious in life, Your Grace. . . .

He tried to remember what Althorpe had been saying. Olivia, Leverham, Deirdre . . . The same soft mouth, but such bitter words from it.

I was never an ivory game piece. . . .

"Enough."

Althorpe blinked at him. "Enough of what?"

Lucas irately waved off the question. "Tell me what a luncheon at Lady Leverham's has to do with Elspeth Vaer. I would hardly think the guest list would include the competition."

"Not ordinarily, but Miss Vaer's brother happens to be among the eligibles. In fact, at this early date, I would say he is the one most likely to find himself snared by the lovely Livvy's charms. The entire happy party is quite probably lounging around the table now, trading thinly veiled insults and discreet inquiries into their respective financial situations." Althorpe jauntily tipped his walking stick over his shoulder. "Ah, the courting rituals of the quality."

Lucas quite agreed. The posturing and maneuvering was beyond absurd. "Why didn't Lady Leverham invite you? Title aside, I would think your wit alone would place you among the eligibles."

"Who said she didn't? I, my friend, know better than to break bread with the enemy. Besides, Miss Macvail's charms are not quite so grand as to overshadow her want of fortune, and I really must choose a wife carefully if I am to keep Alice in lip rouge."

"God forbid you be concerned for your estate."

"Oh, hang the estate. It will see to itself. Now, are you buying the grog as Miss Vaer is unavailable?"

"I suppose so, in the absence of a better option."

Althorpe grinned, unoffended. "You wear your ennui so well, old trout. I ought to be taking notes."

Lucas ignored him. Ennui was the least of his motivations for dipping into the whiskey. He would have to face the demon horse he had just purchased at some time, and sooner was always better than later. He planned to be a trifle less than fully sober when he did it.

"You know, Conovar, I've just come up with the question of the hour." Althorpe waved his hat under Lucas's nose with ill-suppressed glee. "What are you going to do if Miss Olivia marries the Honorable Mr. Vaer, hmm? Assuming you and Miss Vaer suit admirably after all, you might find yourself with the lovely Livvy as sister-in-law."

"Althorpe, you are a menace."

"Ah, but a foresighted one. Damn, but I'm clever. Ah, another plot twist in our Drury Lane farce. If I am not mistaken, and I am seldom mistaken, Francis was on Lady Leverham's guest list. Even without your fortune, he is plump enough in the pockets to marry whom he pleases. And he is a well-looking fellow."

"Oh, for God's sake . . ."

"Just think, man. You have two very good chances to end up tied to Miss Macvail. Remind me to place a wager in the book when we get to White's."

Lucas knew he wouldn't have to do anything of the sort. The man never forgot a good deed, a slight, or an opportunity to get a laugh and a quid or two at the same time.

"Well, bother it. I did try, Conovar, truly I did, but I find I cannot keep from mentioning Mrs. Macvail after all." Althorpe sped up to match Lucas's quickened stride. "Leverham's influence is beginning to work, you know. Or perhaps it's simply that Deirdre is still one of the most stunning creatures ever created. Regardless, only the pinch-lipped, crow-eyed matrons are snubbing her. The lads are poised to spring. One word from a leader—"

"You may stop there." Lucas slapped at a bag of oats with his walking stick. "I will give you the benefit of the doubt, and trust you were not going to suggest that *I* give that word."

"God forbid. After all, the woman committed the heinous crime of choosing not to marry you." Althorpe raised a conciliatory hand. "I simply thought you might want to ponder the image of Deirdre and Francis in a good coze over luncheon."

"And why would I do that?"

"Because, my friend, he was playing court to *both* Macvail ladies at the Heathfield bash. Perverse fellow, isn't he?"

Perverse was not the first word Lucas would have chosen for his cousin. It was far too polite. And Althorpe was far too perceptive. Francis had made a life's work of thumbing his nose at the man he thought had deprived him of a dukedom. Courting Olivia . . . or Deirdre would be the perfect insult.

"I believe my cousin's birthday was several weeks ago. I wonder if it is too late to give him a gift."

"Passage to Australia is always a popular choice."

"Don't be absurd." Lucas smiled grimly. "Francis detests the ocean. No, I believe I will give him the horse I just bought."

Somewhere in the stalls behind them, wood shattered.

Deirdre was becoming accustomed to the desire to be anywhere other than where she was at present. Now, rattling through Hyde Park in Francis Gower's crowded curricle, she was discovering a previously unknown affinity for the peat bogs of western Ireland. She had never seen a peat bog, but was convinced it was vastly more appealing than London's grand park in late afternoon.

Beside her, Livvy bounced happily on the seat, enjoying herself immensely. The presence of the handsome Mr. Gower certainly helped, but she was finding untold delight in the age-old tradition of seeing and being seen by everyone of consequence.

Garbed in a frothy white walking dress and high straw bonnet, she was quite the picture of demure beauty. The pink gauze wrap almost managed to hide the fact that she was sitting on her hands.

Lady Leverham's stern instruction to, as she had phrased it, "curb the understandable but unfortunate impulse to wave like a standard over the demesne" had apparently made an impact. The baroness had an understandable but unfortunate passion for all things medieval, and tended to pepper her speeches with *ye olde* aphorisms. Livvy had a surprising respect for the archaically tinged advice.

Mr. Gower was, in the lady's estimation, a bit of a jackanapes but a courtly enough fellow. Hence, Deirdre found herself playing chaperone to a courtly jackanapes and a nattering demoiselle who had, to her credit, thus far curbed her standard-like tendencies.

"Oh, DeeDee, look. Isn't that Lady St. Helier? My goodness, she is dashing! I must have a driving dress like hers!"

The young countess was dashing indeed in her brightly painted tilbury, hands sure at the reins of a sleek gray. She nodded pleasantly as she passed, and only Deirdre's quick hand to Olivia's elbow kept the girl from flailing both arms in return. Livvy's will always faltered in the face of combined elegance and title.

Deirdre hoped the enthusiasm would stop with the military-style dress. She had no idea what she would do should Livvy set her heart on a gig.

"I trust you will grant me the honor of a dance at the St. Helier ball, Miss Macvail. It will be an empty evening for me otherwise." Francis turned his attention from his driving to flash a stunning smile at Olivia. Deirdre eyed the crowded path ahead and debated telling him to save the flirtation for another occasion.

Livvy didn't seem to mind their imminent collision with any number of fast-moving vehicles. She fluttered her eyelashes and blushed prettily. Lady Leverham's instructions, no doubt. "Of course, sir. I will be certain to save a minuet for you."

Deirdre closed her eyes wearily. Their estimable hostess had done rather too good a job. Livvy was becoming an accomplished coquette. And Francis responded precisely as he was supposed to. "A minuet with you would be the height of delights, mademoiselle, but I entreat you to allow me more time than that. The *ecosaisse*, at least."

As the two commenced with a debate on the very best length for a dance, Deirdre decided she had spent worse afternoons catering to Livvy's whims. Silly as Gower was, Deirdre could not help but like him. He was certainly appealing to look at, with his curling brown hair, warm hazel eyes, and slender form, but he was also unfailingly pleasant and, in those moments when he was not blathering like the typical dandy, quite clever. Beyond that, it was no secret that he was not impressed in the least by his cousin.

After nearly a fortnight of reading the London papers and listening to conversations whispered just loud enough at parties for her to hear, Deirdre's longtime opinion of the ton had not improved. Like a band of weak-willed children, it never failed to bow to the bully. Conovar, despite being remote, cold, and vain, was still greatly in favor. Francis, childlike in the standard dandy's manner, at least showed some adult discretion.

He would be a perfectly decent match for Olivia. Even if he never inherited the Conovar estates—and gossip decreed that was growing more unlikely by the day—he was wealthy enough to support Livvy's extravagance, and seemingly even-tempered enough to tolerate her dramatics.

Unfortunately, Olivia's heart was still set on snaring an earl or higher.

Even worse was the fact that the girl, assured of her own great prospects and in perfect accord with Lady Leverham, was now determined to see Deirdre married off as well. Had the concept not been so unappealing, Deirdre might have been amused by the irony of it.

"There is Lord Hythe, DeeDee. Rumor has it he is looking for a wife, and he's far too dull a stick for me." Livvy prodded her with a plump elbow. "Smile."

"Really, Olivia!"

"Oh, now you've gone all prune-faced, and Hythe is riding away! Turn this contraption about at once and follow him, Mr. Gower."

"*Olivia!*" Deirdre offered a quick prayer for patience. "Mr. Gower, you will do no such thing."

It was too late. Grinning broadly, Francis swung his pair into a tight arc and, heedless of pedestrians and riders scrambling to get out of the way, drove the curricle right over the raised path border and back toward the center of the park.

Olivia quickly lifted her posterior from her hands to cling to the seat. "Faster, sir. He is escaping!"

A trio of matrons scattered, screeching and waving their parasols in frilly indignance. Francis waved cheerfully back, then saluted smartly as he nearly ran down a pair of strolling hussars. He did lose the grin for a moment as one wheel clipped a bench, but shook his driving whip an instant later, sending his cattle into a jerky lope.

"We'll catch him!" he cried. "Tallyho!"

Lord Hythe was clearly heading for the gate. As the curricle sped toward him, Deirdre silently willed him to move faster—and not to look behind him. "Mr. Gower . . ." she began. A corner of Livvy's gauze wrap flew into her face. She shoved it away. "Mr. Gower . . ." They skidded onto the north drive, turf and gravel flying. *"Francis!"*

He finally turned to face her. "Hmm? What was that?"

"Stop this at once!"

"Sorry? Can't hear—"

Hythe had halted his horse in front of the gate. Behind them, Deirdre could see another rider on a massive, sidestepping bay. They were close enough now that she could just make out the tassels on Hythe's boot and the granite face of the new arrival. "Of course," she muttered on a sigh, then braced herself against the seat and leaned over Olivia, as close to Francis's ear as she could. "I said *stop*! Before I remove that whip from your hand and crack it smartly over your head!"

They stopped. Francis hauled the pair to a shaky halt some ten yards from the gate and turned to gape at her. Olivia gave a single, nervous giggle. Deirdre slowly unclenched her fingers from the side of the vehicle and held out her hand. Francis's eyes widened further, but he passed over the whip.

"Thank you." Deirdre carefully set it on the floor at her feet. Then she opened the door and climbed to the ground. "Livvy?"

"But, DeeDee—"

"Olivia."

The girl sullenly joined her, trailing several yards of gauze wrap and a wounded air. "How are we to get home?"

"We will walk. Good day, Mr. Gower."

Head high, trying to ignore that fact that her hair had slipped its pins beneath the loose bonnet and was now in a tangled mess about her shoulders, Deirdre took a firm grip on Olivia's arm and marched toward the gate. They had not gone more than ten steps before the curricle rattled up beside them.

"I say, Mrs. Macvail, I am sorry. Just a lark, you know."

"I know, Mr. Gower. Good day."

"Please, allow me to see you home."

"Yes, DeeDee, please . . ."

She silenced Olivia with a sharp look, then spared Francis an even glance. "Good-bye, Mr. Gower."

He pulled his team to a standstill, and Deirdre silently commended him for at least having the grace to concede. She then turned her attention to the mounted pair ahead. Lord Hythe's handsome face, as always, bore no expression whatsoever. The man was a model of austere propriety, and Deirdre could not quash the faint flare of amusement as she considered Livvy's relative wisdom. It was a very good thing indeed that the girl thought him a dull stick. Had she possessed any hope of becoming Lady Hythe, she could not possibly have killed it more effectively if she had launched herself from the curricle and into his lap. Far less diverting was the thought that the earl would probably let slip a few words about the incident at the very next party he attended.

The stern visage might conceal his disapproval, but everyone knew Hythe was a scourge on indecorous behavior.

The Duke of Conovar's face, on the other hand, hid nothing. His dark brows nearly met the brim of his hat, and there was a dull flush creeping toward his cheekbones. Deirdre met his fierce gaze for a moment before his mount jerked into a skittery dance and his attention turned to controlling the beast.

Hythe pulled his own horse back a few steps and raised his hand to his hat. "Good afternoon, Mrs. Macvail. Miss MacVail."

"Lord Hythe." Chin aloft, she managed, "I trust you have enjoyed your ride. The air is"—Damp, she thought—"delightfully cool."

She ignored Conovar's snort.

"Indeed. Splendid day for a stroll." Hythe nodded politely.

"Take care across Park Lane. The carriage flow is never light at this time of day."

"Thank you, my lord. Come along, Olivia."

She had thought to pass the duke with no more than a brief word. To be honest, she had hoped his skittish mount would prevent even that. She really ought to have known better.

He rode forward until he was mere feet away. "Good afternoon, ladies."

Deirdre's warning squeeze was completely wasted. Olivia smiled brilliantly and gushed, "I am so very glad to see you, Lucky! Where on earth have you been hiding? We've been here a fortnight, and I did so hope to see you. You were ever so kind to return DeeDee's pearls, and—"

"Olivia!" Deirdre said.

"Well, he was! I shall be wearing them tonight at the St. Heliers', so you will see how very well they look, Luck—Oh, I am sorry, Your Grace. You will be there, won't you?"

Deirdre tensed, waiting for the inevitable blast. It had been so *promising*, Conovar's continued absence from the social whirl. She had actually allowed herself to hope that they would be able to get through the Season without another Scene. She had played and replayed the last one countless times in her head. And come to the conclusion that, for some inexplicable reason, the points she had scored were empty.

Now Conovar had every opportunity to snub her—and Olivia. Right in front of the lofty Lord Hythe.

"I do not think I will be attending the St. Helier fete, Brat. But I am certain you will not notice one less admirer in the crush."

Livvy positively beamed. Deirdre felt her jaw going slack. Conovar inclined his head and looked ready to speak again. He did not have the chance.

"Damn me, Conovar, isn't that Kettering's horse?" Francis had left his curricle and was now standing behind them. "I thought the beast was on its way to becoming paste at the knacker's."

The duke's mouth, relaxed but moments earlier, tightened again. "Tattersall's. I purchased him today."

Francis let out a low whistle. "Always were the daredevil, weren't you? Bold as fire and cool as ice. I hear Kettering will be in bed for the rest of the Season. Well, hail to the foolhardy." He gave a mocking salute, then announced, "Must be off. Ladies, do allow me to see you home."

Deirdre silently counted five. "Thank you again, Mr. Gower, but we do not care to drive."

"Drive? Certainly not. We shall walk." He lifted one hand, displaying the lead ribbons there. "Splendid thing about wheeled conveyances. They can be pulled behind as well as driven."

The image was simply too much: the three of them strolling through Mayfair with horses and empty carriage rolling behind. "Francis," Deirdre said wearily, "go home." She nodded to the others. "Lord Hythe, Your Grace. I hope the remainder of your day will be equally diverting. Gather your wrap, Olivia. It is trailing in the dirt."

Conovar's face bore the same expression it had when they had first approached, brows dramatically arched. Deirdre straightened her shoulders and led her sister-in-law toward the gate.

"Crack him over the head with his own whip, was it, madam?" he murmured as they passed. "You quite terrified *me* with that threat."

Stunned, Deirdre looked up. And, before she could stop herself, returned the wholly unexpected smile. "Really, Your Grace—"

A sharp snap of leather had her spinning about. Francis, reins in hand, gazed back placidly from beside his curricle. Then Conovar cursed, and Deirdre was forced to jump aside, Olivia in tow, as his horse lifted both front hooves several feet off the ground before shooting forward.

As Deirdre, Olivia, the faintly smiling Francis, and wide-eyed, lofty Lord Hythe watched, the beast thundered off. The duke's violent epithets trailed in their wake. Over a bench they went, down a gentle slope, and directly into a copse of hawthorn, where they disappeared from sight.

Without a single polite farewell, Hythe kicked his own mount into motion. Moments later he, too, vanished into the shrubbery.

"Off to the rescue. Once a *chevalier* . . ." Francis shook his head dolefully. "Six years in the cavalry, and my cousin still doesn't know a thing about choosing a horse. Heartbreaking. Now, do get in, my dears. Those clouds are beginning to look ominous."

5

TRUE TO EXPECTATION, the St. Helier ballroom was full to bursting. Deirdre eyed the lacy confection in her hand and wondered what fool had decreed such useless fans to be de rigueur. The one she held was as likely to create a cooling breeze as the wings of a moth.

A few feet away Olivia was putting her own fan to its intended use, alternately peeking over the top and thumping the arms and shoulders of the young men surrounding her. Deirdre winced right along with Teddy Vaer as Livvy smacked at his wrist. The girl did nothing in halves, and would probably be astonished if one of her eager swains let out an understandable protest. For his own part, Vaer bore the assault bravely, and was rewarded by one of Livvy's dimpling smiles.

Deirdre had to admit that her sister-in-law was behaving herself very well. With the exception of such lapses as encouraging Francis Gower to thunder through Hyde Park like a drunken gladiator, she was quite earning her status as a Diamond. She sparkled, dazzled, and made everyone around her feel rather special.

There had not been a tantrum in days. Deirdre had felt safe in leaving Lady Leverham's that night without the requisite handkerchief-bearing reticule. With her adoring circle of young men and ladies alike, Olivia was in heaven.

For her own part, with each successive fete, Deirdre was certain she was getting a view of hell: being absolutely alone in the midst of a very hot, very crowded space populated by half of the politicians and most of the nobility of England.

True, no one was shunning her outright, and a few men had

even requested dances. She had declined each. She took no more pleasure in being a slightly scandal-glossed novelty than she had in being a scandalous outcast.

What she missed most—so much that the ache was palpable—was the company of giggling, teasing, encouraging friends. One of the few pleasures she had found in her own Season was the afternoons with other girls. How nice it had been to have a respite from the silly posturing and flattery of the young men—and the endless quizzing of their protective mamas.

Now she had nothing in common with the joyful debutantes. And the women who had been her companions were married, with their grand titles, indulgent husbands, and pampered children. Those who were in Town had not bothered to communicate or approach her at social gatherings. Not one of the cards she had left with pinch-lipped butlers had been reciprocated.

Apparently the cloud of being a jilt still lingered over her—darkened, no doubt, by the fact that the man she had jilted was the Duke of Conovar. Then, too, she had decided, a young widow was far more dangerous to a matron than a headstrong young lady. Without many of the strictures heaped on the girl and wife, a widow was free to indulge her whims. Apparently those whims were expected to include wealthy, not necessarily unmarried men.

To be fair, Deirdre supposed she understood. She envied her former friends, but not as they might have thought. She did not covet their houses or carriages or glittering jewels. In truth, she coveted nothing they had. Especially not the husbands, who quite probably spent far more time away than at home.

She envied these women the children they had, or would have, with all her heart.

Oh, she and Jonas had wanted children, had planned the number and the fine Scottish names they would give them. But Jonas, like so many of his brave and bright-eyed peers, had assumed their marriage would last forever while the war would not.

Olivia's giddy laugh carried through the crowd then, and Deirdre smiled. Perhaps Jonas had not given her a family of her own, but he had given her his. She had been as heartbroken as Livvy when the elder Macvails had died in a carriage accident, less than a year after their son fell on a Spanish field. And she had clung to Livvy as fiercely as the girl had clung to her.

There was nothing on earth she would not do for Jonas's . . . *her* sister.

"DeeDee, you must come with me! This very instant."

She blinked as Olivia bounded from her knot of admirers and reached out to snare her wrist. "Where, dearest?"

"To the Jermyns', of course!" The girl rolled her eyes at the very stupidity of the question.

"Of course," Deirdre repeated tartly. "This very instant." She smiled and resisted as Livvy began tugging. "Perhaps we ought to invite our considerate hostess along."

"Yes, yes. I'll find Lady Leverham! Do move your feet, DeeDee. We haven't time to spare." She bounced with cheerful impatience as the baroness excused herself from her own circle of friends. "We must go."

"Go where, my dear?" Lady Leverham, resplendent in an embroidered gold gown that she'd had painstakingly copied from a portrait of Eleanor d'Aquitaine, nodded her head in time to Olivia's bouncing. "My goodness, love, you are old enough to find a garderobe on your own."

Deirdre couldn't stop the laugh that bubbled out. Delighted, Lady Leverham laughed with her. "No, madam. Apparently Livvy has decided the Jermyn fete is necessary to her continued existence."

"Well, why didn't you say so?" The older woman's gaze swept over the floor, then met Olivia's. Her brows rose, Livvy nodded emphatically, and suddenly Deirdre found herself being hustled toward the door by two solid and determined escorts. She had no idea what message she had missed, and decided she really ought to recommend the pair to the War Department. Silent communication would be ever so useful behind enemy lines.

Within minutes they were all settled in Lady Leverham's carriage, rolling their way toward a house that could have been reached twice as quickly by walking. "Now, do you care to share the secret? What is at the Jermyns' that is so important?"

"Mr. Vaer, of course. He promised his sister to escort her, and they left just ahead of us. Oh, do hurry!" Livvy urged the driver through the solid roof.

"Mr. Vaer?" Deirdre's brows rose. "Mr. Vaer, if I am not mistaken, is the son of a relatively young, very healthy viscount. Your earl . . ."

"Is, at present, the son of a viscount who, in turn, is the son of an ailing earl." Lady Leverham smoothed her skirts contentedly. "Lord Vaer will soon be the Earl of Otley."

"Ah. I did not know there was an Earl of Otley."

"I did," Livvy announced with satisfaction. "He is not at all well."

Deirdre rolled her eyes. "Honestly, Livvy, listen to yourself, hastening the demise of an old man."

"I am doing nothing of the sort. I am merely stating facts."

"Very well, dear, if you say so. Olivia Otley." She wrinkled her nose in affectionate ridicule.

"Lady Otley to you, madam." Livvy peered anxiously out the window. "Oh, why are we not there yet? Arabella Seanan is angling after Mr. Vaer, too, and she has such a ghastly large fortune!"

"Compose yourself, love." Lady Leverham patted the girl's hand. "I am certain both the Seanans and the Vaers are caught in this dreadful crush, too. Besides, Miss Seanan is a shrew. The Vaers have a ghastly fortune of their own and need not marry where they are not inclined."

No, Deirdre thought. The stunning Elspeth Vaer would marry whom she pleased. And the current *on-dit* was that she was well pleased with the Duke of Conovar. An announcement was expected by the end of the Season.

Deirdre pitied the girl excessively. No title, status, or impossibly handsome face was worth living with the arrogance and basic disdain for anyone else's feelings. Of course, the duke had been rather kind to Olivia, and if he smiled at Miss Vaer as he had smiled that afternoon . . .

No, it was simply not worth the rest.

"Livvy"—she reached out to clasp her sister-in-law's hand—"Livvy, do you truly care for Mr. Vaer? I mean, you scarcely know him. Is he really the sort of man with whom you wish to spend your life?"

Olivia blinked at her. "How could he not be? He is handsome, wealthy, and will have a very nice title someday."

"Oh, Livvy."

"Really, DeeDee, you cannot tell me you did not think of these things when you married Nasey. And you were engaged to Conovar. Of course, were Nasey not my brother, I would have thought you an utter noddy. As it is, I would wager you expected much the same as I do."

"I loved your brother," Deirdre said simply.

"I daresay I shall love Mr. Vaer exceedingly well once he declares himself. Besides, and I do feel badly saying this, DeeDee, really I do, but you were a widow at twenty-two. Your choice ended badly."

Deirdre smiled sadly as the carriage came to a halt in front of a teeming stairway. "You are quite right, dearest. It ended badly indeed." And, she added silently, had not progressed perfectly, either. "Mr. Vaer seems a very good sort of fellow."

"Oh, he is." Olivia was already bounding from the carriage. "A bit of a dull stick, and I do wish he were somewhat taller, but a very good fellow."

Waiting only until the others had joined her, Livvy began to squeeze her way toward Mr. Vaer and into his future as Earl of Otley.

Deirdre lost both companions quickly in the crush. Livvy moved with impressive speed when she wanted something badly. Well, there was nothing to be done for it but wander around until she encountered someone who would talk to her. Which meant she needed to locate Eleanor d'Aquitaine amid the crush of modern London's most crowded ball.

She had not gone more than ten feet before a hand snared her elbow. Startled, she spun to face the grinning visage of the very first man she had danced with in London. He had been clownish and irreverent, and had helped banish the nerves that had all but rendered her a frozen statue. The tousled, pale hair was the same. The slightly askew cravat was the same. The delighted,

55

lopsided grin was as familiar and welcome as it could possibly have been.

"Greetings and salutations, Mrs. Macvail."

"Lord Althorpe!"

"What, so formal? We were friends once, or was that merely the wish of my besotted heart? I believe I met you even before your husband did. How quickly you forgot me." He clapped a hand over his heart, closed his eyes, and gave a sigh that would have had tomatoes pelting him had he been onstage.

"Evan," she greeted him again with a laugh. "You were as besotted with me as the king himself. And you have not changed a whit."

He grinned. "Between us, I have heard the king's madness was brought about by your refusal to so much as look his way. It's dashed good to see you, Deirdre." He paused, grin fading. "I am sorry about Jonas. So sorry. We've lost too many good men to infernal war."

Deirdre nodded her thanks for the condolence. "It has been nearly four years, and I miss him. But Waterloo gave us peace, and we should be thankful for all the brave young men who survived." She managed a bright smile. "So tell me, which young lady are you sweeping off her feet tonight?"

"Why you, of course. I do believe I hear the beginnings of a Scottish reel."

"Oh, Evan, I do not . . ." Why? Why shouldn't she dance? "I would love to."

The lively dance allowed little opportunity for conversation, so Deirdre simply gave herself up to the sheer pleasure of the music and motion. She had not danced in so many years—since the round of rustic parties after her wedding when the people of Tarbet had opened their homes and arms to their dashing lad's new wife.

She had loved the reels, even more so when Jonas had swept her in such fast, giddy circles that she had laughed and gasped, trying to catch her breath. They had been so wonderful, those days, and had gone by so fast that she had nearly come to believe they had never actually happened. Now, with Evan Althorpe skipping and winking, and making her laugh anew, she remembered. And cherished the memory.

The music ended with a ringing flare. Evan, hair mussed further and eyes bright, guided her from the floor. "They made a true Scot of you, didn't they?"

"Aye, they did that. 'Tis a bonny place, wi' braw hert, Argyll."

"And you are a bonny lass with a grand heart, too, Mrs. MacVail." He tucked her hand firmly into the crook of his arm. "You really do look marvelous, my dear, but so damned sad. Yes, even now when you are smiling. Our very own Deirdre of the Sorrows."

She groaned softly. "Why does everyone feel the need to evoke that silly tale? For goodness' sake, you shouldn't even know it, English as you are."

"Ah, an insult against the English. You really have become a Scot. Give us some credit, Lady Macbeth. Everyone born in the Isles knows the tale, and no one with half a brain could fail to make the connection. Heartbreakingly beautiful woman runs from the evil warrior king and into the arms of her true love. Jonas died, Deirdre. Don't you die before your time, too."

"Evan, please. I am hardly going to will myself into the grave."

"No, I'm certain you won't, but the spirit can die long before the body." He squeezed her hand and winked. "And you had such a splendid spirit, my girl. Every poor sod in England was half in love with you. We'll all fall again if you'll let us."

Warmed, cheered by the good humor of an old friend, Deirdre laughed. "You'll never fall for anyone, Evan. It would quite ruin the line of your coat."

"Too true. I'll just lean a bit, then. Will that do?" He paused suddenly and murmured, "Well, well, the evil warrior king himself. Is this going to be awkward for you? You can slip away into the woods."

She looked up to find Conovar standing not five feet away. Dressed again in stark black, his sable hair combed severely back from his proud brow. He could have been a warrior king, perhaps, but he did not look particularly evil—simply grim.

"No, but thank you, Evan. It will be fine." With the duke's good

57

behavior to Olivia, and that brief moment of teasing that had so astonished her, in mind, she offered a tentative smile.

He did not return it. Instead he gave a terse nod. "Mrs. Macvail. Althorpe."

Deirdre bit her lip, then said, "Good evening, Your Grace. I did not . . . I did not expect to encounter you tonight."

"Oh, my friend here leaves his ramparts when it suits him. Do excuse us, Conovar. I have promised to procure Mrs. Macvail some refreshment."

The duke nodded again, then turned away, leaving Deirdre certain that the man she had encountered mere hours before had been some stranger who simply bore a staggering resemblance to the Duke of Conovar. She allowed Evan to guide her away.

"He's a proud fellow, you know."

She silently accepted Althorpe's defense of his friend. When they reached the door to the refreshment room, she stopped. "Thank you for the dance. I cannot tell you how much I enjoyed it. I think perhaps I will . . ." She gestured vaguely to the side.

"Of course." He chucked her gently under the chin. "She's back, my dear. The beautiful, Incomparable Deirdre Macvail is back in Town. Do not forget that, and do not let anyone else deny it."

"Thank you, Evan." She touched his sleeve briefly, then turned back to the ballroom.

She had been to the Jermyn house once before, three days before she had climbed into a carriage with her gloating parents and driven north to the grand Conovar estate. A sennight before she had driven madly to Gretna Green with Jonas Macvail.

Jonas had been in this house, too, on that night. And he had quietly directed her through the ballroom and onto the balcony she was heading for now. Stuck almost carelessly onto the back of the house, its door hidden by a large plant and filmy drapes, it had been isolated, private, and ultimately fateful.

She had followed the directions almost immediately. While her fiancé played cards in the game room, she had crept away to meet the man who was his friend—and who had become hers over the past week.

Deirdre slipped past the same plant and through the same

curtains. This time, however, no one waited for her outside. Wisteria that had been deep even then now swelled in an arch, several feet deep. It would have been the perfect place for a first kiss.

She and Jonas had not needed more than simple moonlight.

"You will have a choice, Deirdre, though you haven't so far."

His hair had been so black, his hands so gentle as they held her face.

"You can come away with me now. No, don't say anything. I will go wait in the side garden. If you don't come to me, I will come to you in Northumberland. I'll wait outside the chapel. All you have to do is walk out the door . . ."

A single tear slid down her cheek as she remembered. He had kissed her once more, sweetly, then vanished back into the house. She had not possessed the courage to follow him then, but she had run from the Conovar chapel, heart bursting, into his arms a sennight later.

She had been convinced Lord Lucas Gower would follow. She hadn't cared, not at all, but had expected to hear his voice, that deep, powerful voice, come through the door of each posting house where they made their brief stops.

"Here it is. The best escape portal in England, and I discovered it years back."

Despite the fact that she had every right to be there, and was committing no wrong, Deirdre's heart galloped in her chest. Instinctively she ducked back into the wisteria as the duke's deep, powerful voice came through the window. Too busy trying to calm her pulse to ponder that fate was certainly having its laugh now by throwing her time and again into the man's presence, she made herself as small as possible. With any luck he and his companion would inhale a bit of fresh air and take themselves back to whatever lofty pursuit they had left.

"Convenient little corner." Hythe followed Lucas onto the stone balcony.

"I've always found it so." Lucas accepted a thin cheroot and leaned forward as the man plied his flint. "Much as I like Jermyn, his wife's parties always reduce me to some sort of temporary flight. And I have yet to find this spot already occupied by a pair of trysting lovers."

He had been more than ready for a respite from the party. Seeing Deirdre laughing in Althorpe's arms had been quite sufficient to snuff out the faint feeling of enjoyment he had worked up through the evening. He did trust that his friend's basic common sense would keep him from making an imprudent attachment. Of course, simply looking at Deirdre could make a man forget even his own name. Some poor fool would probably end up handing over his heart, and Lucas, in the simple interest of brotherhood, seethed at the idea of one more baffled, jilted bridegroom.

Hythe's offer of a companionable smoke away from the crowd had come at the perfect time.

"Dare I ask if the bay is still alive, Conovar? I feared for it on its return to your stables."

"Very much alive. The beast and I understand each other. He will not break my neck, and I will not turn him into a sofa."

Hythe chuckled. "I fully expected to find you with something broken today. Damn me. Who taught you to ride like that? Not a man in a hundred could have stayed in the saddle."

"My father saw to it that we could sit any animal."

"Practical."

"Indeed." Lucas remembered the mean-tempered mule the old duke had once led into the stable yard. He supposed his father had found the entertainment of watching his second son go headfirst into three different gorse bushes sufficient cause for the little exercise. "You missed a prime auction at Tattersall's today. Paiseley sold off half his stable. The matched blacks went for a song."

"Ah, the squeeze of debts. Did he have to let the Arabs go?"

"Three."

"And yet you bought the beast from the bowels of hell. I cannot help but wonder why."

Lucas was not about to explain. "I like a challenge," he said easily. "And by the way the beast took three benches and a hedge today, I know he'll do well in the country."

Hythe took a leisurely puff of his cigar. "Planning on rusticating, are you? Rumor says you're looking for a wife." He smiled faintly at Lucas's noncommittal grunt. "Rumor also says the pack has been narrowed to one. She's a lovely creature, Miss Vaer. I daresay she'd make a splendid duchess."

"Or countess? I've heard she is on your list, too."

Hythe shrugged. "If, as you say, I even have a list, I assure you it would hold more than one name. I can think of a good four or five young ladies in Society who would suit me as well as the next."

"Can you?" Lucas leaned his elbows on the balustrade and studied the glowing tip of his cheroot. "I can only contemplate one at a time."

"As I said, she is a woman well worth contemplation." Both men turned as another figure stepped through the window. "Ah, Althorpe. Followed us, did you?"

Althorpe's teeth flashed in the faint light. "Smelled you, actually. I don't suppose you'd have another of those nasty cigars, would you?" Out came Hythe's case, and soon Althorpe was puffing away contentedly. "Heaven," he murmured. "Between the two of you, I could become the most indulgent fellow. Do stop me before I reach utter decadence."

"Would that I had known you when we were in short pants," Lucas returned dryly. "I might have saved myself these past years of curiously high drink bills at White's."

"Just look at it this way, old trout: You saved yourself a fortune in candy bills." Althorpe blew a string of perfect smoke rings, poked cheerfully through the last of them, then faced Lucas with an uncustomarily subdued expression. "I don't know if you're aware of it, Conovar, but Mrs. Macvail's reappearance has got tongues flapping about you again."

Lucas winced. "Like bloody cows with already chewed fodder. Haven't the fools anything better to discuss?"

"Well"—Althorpe took another appreciative drag on his cigar—"the story of Chloe Somersham shooting Gramble is rather tasty . . ."

"Chloe *shot* someone?"

"Indeed. Dead in the foot. Seems he was chasing her a bit too ardently at some country do. Splendid chit's only apology was that her aim was low . . . Ah, but you've distracted me from the

61

topic at hand. Someone is apparently spouting some rot about that fight you had with Macvail when he returned to service."

"Good God," Lucas muttered. "That was nearly four years ago."

Althorpe shrugged sympathetically. "We Society types are short on decent entertainment and long on memory. And one's heart cannot help but be touched by simply looking at the fair Deirdre. She quite inspires lofty sentiments . . . before the more visceral ones, of course." It was his turn to wince. "Sorry, old man. I didn't mean . . . I . . . well, I just thought you might like to know."

Lucas grunted and waved away the unnecessary apology. He was all too aware of what simply looking at Deirdre could inspire a man to do. He forced a relaxed grin. "I don't suppose we could persuade Chloe to have another go at Gramble's . . . other foot, divert the gossips."

"Unlikely." Hythe tossed his cigar into the depths of the garden. "I've heard Gramble has retired to Humberside for the remainder of the Season."

"Pity." Althorpe gazed sadly at his cheroot for a moment before flicking it after Hythe's. "He owes me ten pounds. Now, Jermyn was just getting ready to raise the stakes at his table when I wandered out here. What do you say, Hythe? Do you think you could stand to join Conovar in losing a quid or two to me? I like fleecing fellows who are sure to pay up."

Lucas wasn't surprised when Hythe hemmed for a moment. The man was a fierce opponent, but invariably had to be coaxed into the frivolity of party card play. "Come along, Hythe, unless you'd rather go back to leading simpering debutantes around and around the dance floor."

"Ah, but Miss Vaer has promised me the final cotillion."

"Fine," Lucas replied affably. "We will empty your pockets in plenty of time for you to make that dance."

"Grand!" Althorpe clapped a comradely hand on Hythe's shoulder and guided him back through the window. "Now, which of you fine chaps is going to lend me a tenner?"

Lucas ground his cigar against the balustrade before flicking it into the wisteria. A flutter of white caught the corner of his eye as he followed his companions. How very like Lady Jermyn, he mused, to keep doves in her garden. No doubt she clipped their wings to prevent escape. Women, he decided amusedly, really went to the most extraordinary lengths to keep their possessions.

Dismissing the unfortunate bird, he followed his companions back into the house.

6

DEIRDRE TOOK ADVANTAGE of a free afternoon to read in the parlor. Olivia was off with Lady Leverham, shopping for more flimsy, pastel items, leaving the house uncustomarily silent, calm, and empty of fawning suitors. Deirdre had waited only until the door closed behind them to slip into the parlor, kick off her shoes, and curl up on the sofa with a pot of tea and plate of biscuits in easy reach. She did not plan on moving for at least an hour.

The elegant copy of *Emma* was a new addition to the household, having arrived the day before in the company of Francis Gower. In the sennight since their hell-for-leather dash through the park, the young man had arrived daily, bearing the usual assortment of suitorly gifts for Olivia. The roses had earned him a sweet if vague smile, the chocolates a slightly sticky one. Deirdre had taken pity on the fellow and mentioned her sister-in-law's love of Turkish Delight. Olivia had accepted the parcel with a charming thanks, but had not opened it. She had been too busy trying to charm Mr. Vaer out of the discussion of Epsom Downs he was having with George Burnham.

Unfortunately, fluttering eyelashes and stirring sighs had not surpassed the fascination of the Turf. Nor had Livvy's tart comment that such conversation, like the dirty horses who ran the races, hardly belonged in a drawing room, done more than to earn her a few pitying male glances. In the end she had lapsed into a mild sulk before accepting Clarence Reynolds's stammered invitation for a drive.

She'd required a cold compress on several abused body parts later, including her aching head. Everyone knew that Reynolds, beyond being a crashing bore, drove the most poorly sprung gig in Town.

The following day Francis had come bearing the book. Olivia had actually laughed, then turned back to the now-attentive Mr. Vaer with the airy comment that one really couldn't be bothered by such dull stuff as reading when there was news of the Turf and the Four-in-Hand Club to be discussed.

Francis had merely given her a tolerant smile and set himself to enjoying Cook's renowned strawberry tarts.

Now, well into the book, Deirdre decided she quite forgave him for the dismal adventure in the park. She decided, too, that she would see Livvy reading *Emma* if it meant bribes, threats, or sitting on the girl to hold her down.

The talented authoress had created the most charmingly, delightfully unlikable heroine yet to grace a novel. Emma was spoiled, misguided, and as woefully dim about life around her as a clever young woman could possibly be. "How could she help it with that name?" Deirdre commented cheerfully to the furry bundle in her lap. "I've always thought 'Emma' sounded like someone stammering over what to say next."

A black-mustachioed face peered up for a moment, let out an unsubtle yawn, and disappeared again in the folds of her wrap.

"I quite agree." She chose a biscuit and nibbled at it. "You know, I do believe I have met Mr. Elton recently. . . . Well, of course. He is Mr. Vaer."

She glanced up reluctantly when the butler appeared in the doorway, a calling card in his gloved hand. "Have we another overeager swain, Peters? I really do not care to entertain him, no matter how determined he is to wait for Miss Macvail's return."

The retainer's lips twitched. He had already turned away three young men who had declared they would be willing to visit with Mrs. Macvail until her charge returned. "Lord Althorpe, madam, would like to know if you are at home."

"Oh, certainly! Do show him in." Deirdre hurriedly brushed crumbs from her bodice and groped about under the sofa for her shoes.

Moments later Evan Althorpe strolled through the door. "The

65

first truly temperate day in weeks, the sun is shining, soft breezes are blowing, and where do I find you?"

Deirdre smiled as he bent over her hand. "Inside with a book, and thoroughly content."

"Thank God." Evan dropped into the facing chair. "I was terrified I would have to offer a stroll in the park, and I simply cannot abide a sunny day. One feels compelled to do something productive. I would much rather be confined to my home or club, where I am not expected to move about more than is absolutely necessary. Do ring for some refreshment, my dear. I need to revive my strength."

"Of course." She removed Lady Leverham's pet from her lap and rose to reach the bellpull.

"Good heavens, that is an ugly cat!"

Deirdre laughed. "Evan, really. Galahad is a perfectly lovely monkey. Lady Leverham dotes on him."

"No accounting for taste." He withdrew a quizzing glass from his waistcoat pocket and leaned forward to get a better look. "What on earth possessed her to obtain a monkey? I . . . oh, I say! Deirdre . . ."

She turned back to find Galahad seated contentedly in Evan's lap, his little mouth distorted into a saucer shape. Evan was tugging ineffectually at the chain dangling down the animal's chin. "Oh, Galahad."

"He *ate* my glass!"

"Not at all. He is merely tasting it. Glass and silver are among his favorites." By tickling the monkey's sides, she got him to release the glass, which fell damply into Evan's hands. "We believe he actually swallowed one of Olivia's earrings last night."

Evan, his face contorted in comical distaste, was gingerly wiping off the glass with a silk handkerchief. "I wish you the joy of waiting for it to reappear." He paused and sighed before resignedly tucking the dried object back into his pocket. "Here, hand the beast over."

"Why do I doubt you intend to make friends with him?"

"Wise woman. I intend to give him a firsthand taste of that window."

Far more intelligent than many of the people who came in and out of the parlor, Galahad shook a furry fist at Evan and chattered his own shrill insult. Deirdre chuckled as she set him on the floor. He promptly scuttled under the sofa, muttering simian invectives as he went. "How on earth do you deal with children?"

"I don't," Evan grunted. "I once found it rather amusing to bounce my sister's spawn and watch them turn pink, but inevitably all children do is piddle on one's feet, which quite defeats any entertainment in the venture. Troublesome creatures."

"You were a child once yourself, you know."

"Never. I sprang into the world just as I am now." His eyes lit up as a buxom little maid arrived with fresh tea and pastries. "Heaven. I have been positively craving something sweet." He attacked the strawberry tarts almost before the plate touched the table and popped one into his mouth. "Do forgive my appalling manners, madam. I fear I am rather too much at ease with you."

Deirdre smiled as she poured, then shook her head in amusement as he held up three fingers for sugar. "We are not half so formal in Scotland. I miss it terribly." She passed him his cup and waited before he took an appreciative sip. "Evan, I . . . well, since we are such good friends . . . Would you answer a question for me?"

"Certainly."

"It is about something I've heard recently . . ."

"Slander, I tell you. Pure fiction. I *never* carry rats into the House of Lords, and most certainly did not place one in Castlereagh's wig." He waggled his fingers over the pastries, debating his next choice. "It was a frog."

"Oh, Evan." Deirdre would have liked very much to hear the story, but she had far more serious matters on her mind. "I want you to tell me about the argument Conovar had with Jonas before he shipped out for the last time."

Althorpe paused with a chocolate biscuit halfway to his mouth. "Argument? I have no—"

"Don't, please. I need to know."

"Deirdre." He sighed and returned the biscuit to his plate. "You know better than to listen to idle gossip."

Yes, she did. And the subject had indeed been passed through Society in gleeful whispers during the past week. Had that been the extent of it, she might have thought it merely a typically pitiful act on the part of gossips to revive an old scandal, and let it go. But she had first heard the matter discussed by the duke himself, that night on the balcony.

She needed to know.

"Did they fight, Evan, or not?"

"I . . . For heaven's sake, Deirdre. It is a silly piece of ancient gossip . . . I really wish you wouldn't look at me like that. I am having the sudden and thoroughly unpleasant urge to slink off to church."

"It seems an odd choice for idle gossip," she said tersely, "especially four years after it is supposed to have happened. I am not stupid."

"No. No, you are anything but. You must have heard that ignorance is bliss when 'tis folly to be wise."

"Don't spout Shakespeare at me, Evan, especially incorrectly. It is beneath you."

"I suppose it is. Very well. They argued just before Jonas enlisted in the foot corps and shipped off for the Peninsula. I don't know what was said; I wasn't there. All I know, all anyone knows, is that they exchanged angry words."

Deirdre nodded, believing him. Evan's ethics skirted the outrageous at times, but she had never heard that he was a liar. "Why has this come up now, so long after?"

Althorpe lounged back in his chair and regarded her thoughtfully. "A very good question, my dear, but I would venture a guess that you simply haven't provided a satisfactory show."

"What on earth does that mean?"

"It means, Deirdre, that everyone expected an entertaining display of wounded pride and righteous anger. You and Conovar have been rather disappointing on that count. Come now, don't look so astonished. You know a scandal is hardly a scandal if it does not become public."

"So unless I choose to make a scene in front of half the ton," she demanded wryly, "people will create one?"

"Not half, my dear" was the blithe retort. "A good scene in

68

front of three or four old biddies will suffice . . . Well, damn. I am sorry. I do not mean to make light of any of this." He gulped at his tea. "None of this is distressing Conovar. You must try to be similarly unaffected."

Deirdre felt her jaw dropping. "*Unaffected? My husband was drummed from his regiment and forced to reenlist as a foot soldier! The mighty Duke of Conovar might well be unaffected, but I am living with what he wrought."*

"Deirdre, sweetheart, believe me; I feel for you. But Jonas made his own choices. Conovar's influence was only strong enough to—Well, hell."

"No, by all means, continue. Strong enough to what? See Jonas so disgraced that he had no choice but to resign his commission? I reasoned that out years ago. What else, Evan? Is he laughing about it now? Gloating? Dropping insidious little hints to Lord Vaer that, should Elspeth not come up to snuff, he will—God, what could he not do? Drive the man into debt; see him expelled from his clubs . . ."

She felt her hands clenching painfully in her lap. "And this whole blighted town is so shallow that such disgrace would seem like the ultimate fall. I will not have it, Evan. I will not have him thinking he can use his lofty position and damnably impressive pride to pave his sorry way any longer!"

"Now, Deirdre, I just left him at the club with Vaer, and I must say, he was hardly—" Althorpe juggled his saucer and rose awkwardly as she sprang to her feet. "I haven't the foggiest idea what is going through your mind right now, but I do not like that expression in the least. I feel responsible for it, and I, for one, loathe being responsible for anything calamitous."

"Rest assured, Evan, I shall not mention this conversation. Now, I am sorry to be so rude, but you must excuse me." Stalking to the door, Deirdre called for the butler. "Peters, summon me a hack, please. And fetch Lord Althorpe's hat. He is leaving, too."

Evan was slumped miserably against his chair, saucer still in hand. "Wherever you are going, I shall escort you."

"I would prefer that you not, but I am grateful for the offer."

"Don't be silly. I have a feeling I might be needed, though I do

69

wish you would reconsider whatever scheme you have brewing. I do so hate scenes. I always seem to end up in the midst of them."

Deirdre gave a thin smile. "I will be certain you stay completely uninvolved, so you may cease rattling the china. You've already spilled tea on your foot."

She was in the hall, collecting her wrap from a confused Peters, when Evan came after her. "Ah, Deirdre, I don't suppose you have a gun on hand."

"Please, sir. I am hardly so lacking in control that I would resort to violence."

"That reassures me somewhat. I, however, would not object to having a weapon. Your perfectly lovely monkey piddled on my boots. When we return, I intend to turn the little beast into a dust mop." He accepted his hat and sighed as he shoved it onto his head. "Very well, so you are not to be diverted by a bit of desperate humor. Deirdre, please . . . Oh, dash it all. Peters, has the hack arrived?"

Deirdre did not argue as he followed her down the outer stairs and to the door of the waiting hackney. She seized the door and snapped, "Oh, bother. I left my gloves in the hall!"

Evan helped her into her seat. "Of course. No challenge must be given without gloves," he muttered. "Very well. I shall fetch them."

By the time he reached the street again, Deirdre and the hackney were already turning the corner onto Berkeley Street.

Lucas was in a bit of a hurry. Vaer had dropped the sly information that his daughter was presently at home. Lucas intended to call by three. Miss Vaer's parlor had become damnably crowded of late, and he loathed the feeling of being one more salmon in a competitive upstream struggle. It was bad enough that he suddenly felt compelled to observe even the smallest of courtship rituals, far worse when he was forced to do so in the company of men who were years younger and aeons dimmer.

Only two days before, Ricky Granville had all but made a flying leap from his horse in order to reach the Vaers' door first. Lucas had promptly walked right past the house and straight to the unchallenged sovereignty of his own library. On the preceding day, he had arrived bearing a delicate posy of pansies only to learn that Miss Vaer was out driving with Lord Aubert. He had passed the pair on his slouching way to his club. Elspeth had looked very well indeed on the high seat of Aubert's phaeton, a dozen red roses held in eye-arresting contrast to her white dress.

This time Lucas was going to arrive before the crush, and he wasn't carrying a damned thing. His already ambivalent desire to impress Elspeth had been completely replaced by the simple intention of ascertaining whether she had half a brain to go with her lovely face and glossy brown curls.

He had just reached the hallway and was ready to call for his hat and stick when he was waylaid by a pink-faced Thomas Kettering. "I am very glad to see you, Your Grace!" the fellow declared, bowing so energetically that his already strained coat buttons nearly popped. "My father has been most desirous to hear of your health."

Lucas studied the young man's red face, rather an alarming shade beneath the shock of copper hair, and refrained from commenting that Kettering would be far wiser to be concerned for the health of his heir. Instead he replied, "As you can see, sir, I am perfectly well."

"Good, good. Dashed glad to hear it. It is just that . . . Well, not to put too fine a point on it, Your Grace, but my father was quite distressed to hear that you had purchased the bay. Quite distressed. He came halfway out of his bed when he heard the news, and the surgeon specifically told him not to move for at least another fortnight. The bones in his leg are not healing as quickly as was expected." Young Kettering withdrew a handkerchief from his pocket and mopped at his damp brow. "Quite distressed."

"I paid the asking price," Lucas said mildly.

"Of course, Your Grace. I certainly did not mean to imply otherwise. It is just that my father had hoped the beast . . . er, animal would go to someone less . . . less . . ."

Important, Lucas finished silently. He could well imagine Kettering's horror upon learning that his murderous horse had gone to one of the premier peers of the Realm. "You may assure your

71

father that the animal fully meets Conovar standards. I would not have made the purchase otherwise."

"I . . . I see . . ." Thomas swallowed nervously. "I did hear that he balks at the West Mews gate."

Lucas cursed silently. Was there any news so dull that the ton would not stoop to chew on it? "Yes, we have taken to going over the railing instead. The horse is a champion jumper."

"Ah . . . well. And his propensity to charge across the street whenever there is a fast-moving carriage approaching?"

"Gross exaggeration. I daresay Lady Winslow was given quite a start when her coachman drove into Ramsden's hedge, but it is well-known that the fellow drinks." Lucas suddenly found he was rather enjoying himself. The bay afforded some amusement—when he was not in the saddle. "Tell your father that I commend his taste in cattle. Not every man could hunt down the single most resolute horse in England."

"I am certain he will be pleased—er, resolute at what, Your Grace?"

The hall clock chimed. Lucas saw that Thomas had begun to wring his hands and decided some decisive action was needed if he were to get out the door before supper time. "Sir, the gallant Kettering nature is a grand thing. Allow me to buy you a drink." With one hand he gave the man a light shove toward the reading room. With the other he signaled to a waiting footman. "If you would care to trot ahead."

"I do not . . . Yes, certainly, Your Grace." Thomas tottered away.

"A bottle of Madeira," Lucas hissed at the footman. "And do not let him up from his seat for at least half an hour." His hat and stick appeared, just ahead of another liveried servant. "Well, damn. What is it now?"

"I beg your pardon, Your Grace, but your presence is requested outside."

"By?"

"I do not know, Your Grace. Shall I inform the hackney driver that you are unavailable?"

"Hackney driver?"

"Indeed, Your Grace. It is his passenger who sent the request."

Lucas glanced wearily at the clock and debated escaping through the kitchen door. Quite probably Althorpe had returned from whatever assignation had demanded his attention, and was now ready for a jaunt to some other entertainment. Sighing, Lucas waved off the footman and headed for the street. He had no intention of accompanying the bounder anywhere, but he would make use of the vehicle. Perhaps he would even send Althorpe inside to coax young Kettering into a contentedly drunken stupor. The fellow would do anything for a free bottle.

The hack's door was open, and he had one foot inside before spying a flow of pale blue skirts that most certainly did not belong to his friend. He gazed up past tightly clenched hands to an unfashionably demure bodice and then to a lush mouth that was altogether too familiar despite being set in an angry line.

"Mrs. Macvail?"

"Get in, please, Your Grace. I would rather not have all of St. James witness this meeting."

He did, his knees brushing against hers as he took the opposite seat. She hurriedly scooted aside. He quashed the flaring impulse to follow. "This is a most unexpected encounter, madam. To what do I owe the honor?"

"Do us both a great service and refrain from the polite blathering," she snapped, and for a fleeting moment, Lucas was reminded of the fiery creature he had pursued all those years ago. But this was not the lovely young girl who had stirred him with her spirit. This was a mature, icily beautiful woman who looked ready to have his blood. "I have a few words to say to you and will not have them defused by false courtesy."

Intrigued, Lucas leaned back against the worn seat. "Fine. I'm listening."

"How very predictable you are. Cool, distant, *amused*. Well, I am not here for your amusement, Your Grace. I never was. I am here to make you face the past. No, to face yourself." Her eyes blazed at him across the dim cab, blue fire in her pale face. "You epitomize everything I always hated about Society. You do nothing for the world, yet expect everything from it. You honestly believe the rest of us are here in order to serve you. You have monumental pride, and when it gets bruised, you salve it by

73

crushing anyone and anything that cannot strike back. That is petty, Your Grace. Worse, it is cowardly and wholly devoid of *honor*."

Oh, the words stung. Lucas had flattened men for saying far less. But this was not a man; this was Deirdre Fallam Macvail, the only woman who had ever flattened him. He was not about to give her the satisfaction of doing it again. He would be damned before he would allow her to gloat over his helplessness—or his bewilderment.

"You slay me, Mrs. Macvail." He tried to sound as indifferent as possible, and cursed the rash he could feel creeping inexorably toward his jaw. "I must say, it is a novel experience, being taken to task for an absence of honor by a woman who left her fiancé standing at the altar."

"Of course," she hissed at him, "you would use that as ammunition. Or is it defense? I'm certain you have never once even tried to comprehend why I did what I did."

On the contrary. He had tried more times than he could possibly count. "Is that what this is about, madam? You wish to enlighten me at last."

"This is not about why I fled. It is about the despicable way you avenged yourself. And the complete lack of remorse you are showing even now."

"Enough!" Incensed now, though no less bewildered, Lucas sat forward and rubbed angrily at his neck. "Whatever nonsense brought on this insulting little tirade—"

"*Nonsense?* My God, you call the heartless act that lost a far better man his life nonsense? Jonas might have betrayed your friendship, you arrogant cretin, but no court on earth would condemn a man to death for that. And now you publicly dismiss the truth, debasing even his memory! *Nonsense?*"

"Condemn . . . Well, damn me. I should have known, should have expected it. You are finally blaming me for Jonas's death."

"Not finally, Your Grace. I have always blamed you for my husband's death. Unlike you, however, I am not of a vengeant nature. Or I wasn't until people began whispering about your fight with Jonas and you chose to laugh the matter off." Her chin went up, and even its trembling could not diminish the simple

74

grandeur of the picture. "You *are* to blame. For all of it. God help you, Lucas Gower, because no honorless deed goes completely unpunished."

Her voice broke then, and she waved blindly toward the door. "Get out."

Lucas did not move. He couldn't. "Do you really want the truth about Jonas, Deirdre?" he demanded gruffly. "I am not certain you do, nor that you will believe it once you have it." She glared at him, tears beading her lashes, but clearly refusing to break. "I will give you the truth, but hear me well: You will never again accuse me of being without honor."

7

"JONAS DIDN'T RESIGN his commission, Deirdre. He was stripped of it, days before he married you."

"*What?*" Stunned, disbelieving, she gaped at him. "What sort of fool do you think I am, to tell me such a thing?"

"I do not think you a fool at all. On the contrary, I trust in your intelligence to see what is before you and recognize the truth in it."

Deirdre did not think she wanted to hear whatever he had to present after all. She would not have believed he could sink lower in her estimation than he already was, but this cruel, cold attack on the name of a man she had loved, a man who could not defend himself, had her seething.

She narrowed her eyes and studied his face intently, searching for any sign of remorse. What she saw was a tense, undeniably stunning countenance, his gaze unreadable beneath the bold brow. He looked weary, perhaps, but Lucas Gower had often looked weary—if only about the eyes. Ennui was so very fashionable among the obscenely wealthy and boundlessly influential, after all.

"Did you enjoy seeing my husband hand over his uniform, Your Grace? Was it a satisfying moment? I daresay three months isn't so very long a time to wait for revenge."

He rubbed a hand slowly over his eyes. "I am wasting my breath here, aren't I? Just tell me this: When was the first time you saw Jonas out of uniform?"

The memory of a soft brown wool coat flashed into her mind. She had snuggled against it during the drive to Gretna Green. "No," she said flatly. "I cannot countenance that as proof of anything other than common sense. We would have attracted far too much attention had Jonas traveled in his uniform coat."

"That was certainly a good explanation on his part." Conovar rested his elbows on his knees and regarded her intently. "How did he explain his extended absence from the regiment?"

Truly indignant now, Deirdre snapped, "Three months after we were married, he told me he had received a *request* for his resignation. That seems as understandable a reason not to return to service as any!"

"Before that, Deirdre. Think. What regiment in wartime would allow an officer to simply disappear for three months? In most camps that would constitute desertion, wouldn't you say?"

"I know very little of military protocol, Your Grace, but that hardly seems unreasonable for a newly married man."

Not true, she was forced to admit. It hadn't seemed very reasonable at all. But Jonas had been so cheerful during those months, so wholly unconcerned with the mess they had left behind, with the constant want of money. And she had been so happy, so dazzled by her dashing new husband that she had carefully avoided asking any questions that might diminish their bliss. Any questions, she realized now, whose answers might have been distressing.

"What I know, Your Grace, is that Jonas was a brave man with a great love for his land. When he grew restless and was unable to serve as he had in the past, he enlisted in the only way he could."

"Damned foolhardy, hubristic idiot!"

Startled by the sudden, harsh emotion in Conovar's voice, Deirdre could only gape at him.

"Yes, Deirdre, Jonas and I fought. Plenty of people know that. It was, to put it mildly, an ugly scene. Plenty of people know that, too, even as no one knows precisely what was said." He lifted his jaw then, and Deirdre could see pain clear in his eyes. "To hell with whether you believe me or not. I hated Jonas Macvail in the end, but I never wished him dead. In fact, I did all I could to convince him not to go back into service. He . . . wasn't suited for it.

"Oh, I'm not blasting his dedication," he continued bitterly. "The bloody fool was a one-man crusade against the Empire. The solitary scourge. Yes, we fought. I told him he would make a damned poor martyr. The foot corps he chose was nothing more than a collection of human goats, being sent off for noble sacrifice. And do you know what his response was, Deirdre? After the rather impressive string of curses, of course. He told me he was going to march all the way to bloody Moscow and shoot Bonaparte himself. Then he turned on his heel and walked away. I let him go. God help me, I was still angry enough to let him go. But what else could I have done? Damn it, *what else could I have done?*"

Deirdre sat in the closed carriage in the middle of a sunny spring day and was chilled to the bone. Conovar couldn't have known, could not possibly have known that he'd described exactly the same scene that had transpired between her and Jonas just before his departure.

"Don't be silly, darling. How could I not return? As soon as I've marched to bloody Moscow and put a lead ball in the Little Corsican, I'll come whistling home to you."

She had let him go. He had been so determined, so bright-eyed with anticipation and zeal, that she'd let him go. There had been nothing else for her to do.

Shaken, dizzy, she clutched at the worn leather seat beneath her. "Dear God. Oh, Jonas."

She was not aware she was crying until Conovar reached across to her, offering his handkerchief. Shaking her head mutely, she groped in her reticule for her own.

"I am sorry, Deirdre," he said softly. "Please believe that."

Perhaps she did believe him. At the moment it didn't matter. "What did he do? To lose his commission?"

There was a long pause before he replied, "I don't know."

Deirdre gave a choked laugh. "Now, finally, you're lying to me. But I expect I do know."

Jonas had not always been where he was supposed to be. The wanderlust of the Loch Lomond lad, he'd called it. Time on the open road. For two years Deirdre had believed him, wanted so much to believe him. Eventually, however, even her formidable will had not been able to keep images of hills and heather from being replaced by those of lush female forms and linen sheets.

"It was impossible to condemn him, wasn't it?" she said sadly.

"It was. Always. And I did try, very hard ultimately."

She looked up, fought proudly against the gentle tug of his sympathy. "Forgiveness shouldn't be a struggle, Your Grace."

"I don't disagree with that. But we're only human. It's very hard to pardon a man who betrays honor and trust, and steals something costly from you."

"He stole nothing," she replied bitterly. "He won *me*. I know you don't see matters this way, and I suppose I understand, but the betrothal contracts never made me yours."

There was a long moment of silence. Deirdre expected Conovar to argue, to insist that yes, the costly agreement he had made with her father had made her just that: his possession. When he frowned, she waited resignedly for the words.

"I never thought to own you, Deirdre."

Years of resentment, more than disbelief, had her retorting, "You purchased me!"

"I . . . Yes, I suppose it appeared that way. I suppose I chose to let it appear so." He ran one hand wearily through his hair. "I don't think I could have articulated my intentions then, even if I had wanted to."

"I don't understand."

His smile was slow, sad, and disturbingly affecting. "You thought me arrogant and spoiled from the beginning. True enough. What would you have thought had I been able to tell you that from the first moment I saw you, I felt that you would make me *less* than I was? That I wanted to be lessened so much it ached." He chuckled humorlessly at her expression. "You would have thought me a babbling lunatic. I would have thought myself a babbling lunatic."

Baffled, she stared at him, trying to understand. "Perhaps had you talked to me, made even the slightest effort to know me, we might have avoided some of the trouble that followed."

"Well, we'll never know, will we?" He shrugged and reached for the door handle. "No matter. I suspect you don't need to, but go speak to Viscount Tarrant if you wish to confirm what I've told you about Jonas. He was our captain. And don't be concerned that he will follow me in speaking ill of the dead. He will merely tell you what truth he feels is appropriate."

79

He stepped from the hack then, one hand remaining on the door frame. "Are you . . . Will you be all right?"

Several tart retorts died on her lips. "I will be fine."

He nodded once, and again. "Good-bye, Mrs. Macvail. Rest assured, I will not trouble you again."

She almost stopped him, ready to protest, to say it had been she who had troubled him. Instead she raised an unsteady hand in farewell.

Lucas bowed, closed the door gently, and walked stiffly back toward the club. Althorpe was there, rump settled firmly against the rail, arms braced against his thighs. His face, what Lucas could see of it, was a brilliant red.

"Good God, man, what happened to you?"

"Never mind me," Althorpe muttered. "I merely ran the entire way from Berkeley Square. Are you bleeding? In possession of all your limbs?"

"No and yes." Lucas bent over to see the man's expression. It was slightly pained and decidedly guilty. "Allow me to hazard a guess here. You were aware that Mrs. Macvail had a bit of a bone to pick with me."

"I tried to stop her. Then I tried to tag along. Would've done it if she hadn't scarpered on me."

"Mrs. Macvail is difficult to dissuade when she sets her mind to something."

"Mrs. Macvail," Althorpe said grimly, raising himself slowly to lean against the rail, "would have routed Boney a good five years earlier than our intrepid military had anyone bothered to give her a chance."

"Quite probably." Lucas passed over the handkerchief Deirdre had refused. The one Althorpe was clutching looked like it had been dropped in a puddle. "Now, would you care to tell me what you said that set her off?"

"What *I* said? How did I become the villain of this piece? Review the facts, old chap. I came dashing to the rescue." He gazed mournfully down at his feet. "My boots will never be the same."

"I beg your pardon." Lucas shifted to lean beside him. "I have little experience with being rescued."

80

"Well, you shall have to practice with someone else. My days of spontaneous gallantry are over."

"Understood. Now, what did you say to her?"

Althorpe shuffled his desecrated boots. "I really don't know, but I assume whatever it was had something to do with the rumors flitting about. Apparently she had no idea you and Jonas fought."

"Well, she does now. And she knows the true story."

"Splendid. Good for you. I don't suppose you'd care to tell *me* the true story."

Lucas shook his head. "I think not. It doesn't really matter."

"I had to ask." Althorpe mopped at his jaw with Lucas's handkerchief. "How did she take it?"

"I am not bleeding, and I am still in possession of all my limbs."

He had lost something, however, and was having a damnably hard time accepting the loss. He no longer felt any of the bitterness for Deirdre that had fortified him for six years. And without it, he was left with very much the same feeling he'd had as he had watched her flee down the chapel aisle and away from him, bits of her shredded bouquet trailing behind her.

He felt as if he had lost his one chance at heaven.

"So are you and Mrs. Macvail going to play nicely now and further disappoint the gossip-hungry masses?"

"Longing for a good fight, are they?" Lucas smiled humorlessly. How well he remembered the endless stream of gleeful consolations he had received in the wake of his unsuccessful attempt at matrimony, remembered equally well the ill-suppressed frustration when he had failed to show the appropriate indignation. "I believe Mrs. Macvail and I have come to an accord of sorts. She will forgive me for not particularly liking her husband in the end, and I shall forgive her for not particularly liking me."

"Well, that sounds portentous."

"Does it? I rather thought it sounded final."

Althorpe gazed thoughtfully at the spot Deirdre's hack had occupied. "I don't know. Attachment born of adversity is dashedly popular in romantic novels of late."

"We really must do something about your reading habits.

Besides, a man who pursues a woman who loathes him is fated for disappointment—if not a nice, quiet cell in Bedlam."

"Oh, you make this much too easy, Conovar." Althorpe grinned broadly, then swept one arm in a dramatic arc. Lucas ducked to avoid being smacked in the nose with the damp handkerchief. "Who, certain of his fate, loves not his detester . . . who dotes, yet doubts, protests, yet strongly loves!"

"Thank you, Iago," Lucas said dryly. "I assure you, I am awed, but the Bard is no doubt rolling in his grave at your appalling alteration of his words."

"Poetic license," Althorpe retorted.

"Poetic carnage, though that is hardly my greatest complaint."

"Fancy that. What is?"

Lucas levered himself away from the railing. "Your choice of fodder. Next time you feel inclined to misquote Shakespeare at me, do try to choose a play where everyone doesn't end up dead."

"Fine. I'll limit myself to *A Midsummer Night's Dream*. You can be Petruchio, with his mule's head."

"Puck, you dolt," Lucas muttered under his breath as he walked away.

"No need for that sort of language, old man." Althorpe caught up with him and strolled cheerfully alongside. "I could have made you Falstaff. Now, where are we going?"

Lucas paused at the corner of Piccadilly. He had been heading toward the Vaer residence. Suddenly that seemed about as appealing a prospect as an afternoon of listening to Althorpe mangle tragic drama. He really would have to pay a formal visit to Elspeth Vaer sometime soon. Soon, he decided, would have to be later.

"I am going home. Where are you going?"

"With you, of course. My cupboard is bare."

Lucas was hardly in the mood for company, but he supposed he would do well to accept some. He had a strong urge to get stinking drunk, and he tended to do foolish things when he was drunk. No, better to crack a bottle with Althorpe present. That way he could be certain of consuming only a meager glass or two. His companion would commandeer the rest.

Several minutes later Althorpe announced, "I say, Conovar, you're going the wrong way."

Not precisely the wrong way, Lucas corrected as he realized they were walking up Berkeley Street, but certainly the long way. To his house, at least. The current path would lead right past Lady Leverham's residence. Cursing silently, he turned about. And groaned aloud.

Strolling toward them at a jaunty clip was his cousin.

"Good afternoon, gentlemen." Francis was looking even more colorful than usual in a brilliantly yellow waistcoat and emerald coat. "Off for a bit of delightful stupor at your club, are you?"

Althorpe eyed the man's getup with interest. "Well, we hadn't heard the circus was in town. I suppose we could alter our plans for the afternoon. What do you say, Conovar?"

Lucas grunted. He had had his skirmish for the day and was feeling somewhat less than victorious. Francis, too, seemed disinclined to spar. He replied blandly, "I am just coming from the Royal Academy exhibit."

"Is that so?" Althorpe tilted his hat back and scratched his head. "I thought they did not allow the tasteless in without an educated escort."

"How very droll you are, Althorpe. For your edification, I am a patron. Oh, don't look so surprised. I appreciate a publicly naked woman as much as the next man, and I must say there is a splendid amount of fair flesh on display this year. Interesting representation from Scotland, too. You both really ought to go have a look. You have a Ramsay or two, don't you, Conovar?"

Lucas sighed and resigned himself to participating in the conversation. "Three. Of great-aunts Lorrie, Coralie, and Mona."

"Ah, poor Auntie Mo. She did rather resemble a cod in her later years."

Lucas couldn't disagree. "I trust you aren't suggesting I go to the exhibit to see anything by Ramsay. Word has it the man has been dead some twenty years."

Francis smiled thinly, then busied himself with straightening his pristine cuffs. "The Scots connection came to mind. You really must go see the Raeburn entry. It is causing quite a stir. He is the true successor to Ramsay, you know. This particular work could very well have come from your walls."

"A portrait of someone else's cod-like aunt, I expect."

"Your fault," Althorpe interjected airily. "I have told you to find some abundantly naked ladies to replace the dour bats you have. Perhaps the addition of the Raeburn would help somewhat."

Lucas shot him a look. Abundant nudity and his ancestresses was too distressing a combination to contemplate. "I hardly think Mr. Raeburn is displaying an odalisque."

"Pity" was the sad reply.

"Go see it anyway," Francis insisted. "It is a portrait of an utterly stunning blonde."

"Wearing a tartan and tam, I suppose," Althorpe muttered with distaste.

"Not at all. She is wearing some drapey stuff and the most heartbreakingly heartbroken expression I have ever beheld. You know, I would have taken her for the Virgin Mary or perhaps Lady MacFarquhar, who I hear is quite broken up over the death of her pug, had the face not been too familiar to mistake. Stunning piece. The painting, I mean, though the same can be said of the subject."

He yawned and went on, "I suppose I ought to be discouraging your attendance, Conovar, as you'll no doubt do precisely the opposite of what I suggest. Fine, then. Do *not* visit the Academy this Season. And when you do not go, refrain from asking the location of Raeburn's entry. Of course you can always simply *not* head toward the wall with the largest crowd in front of it." Francis twirled his stick in a jaunty arc and stepped past the silent pair. "Most importantly," he called back over his shoulder, "do *not* under any circumstances, even should your life depend upon it, ask after a painting called *Deirdre of the Sorrows*."

"Oh, DeeDee, I have heard the most distressing news!" Olivia was perched on the very edge of her seat, picking at the braided trim of the smart, military-style spencer she had worn for her drive with Mr. Vaer. "I do not quite know how to tell you. I am terribly overset!"

The two were presently in Lady Leverham's solarium, where

Deirdre had fled to think on her meeting with Conovar. Life always seemed perfectly manageable when she had her hands in the earth.

Simple, indeed. In the space of five minutes, she had admitted the undeniable merit of Conovar's words, accepted them as truth, and shattered two of her hostess's earthenware pots against the tile floor. Then she had turned her full attention to rescuing a collection of sadly neglected dahlias.

She was not ready to mourn again for her husband.

Losing him had been so painful that she had half expected to die herself. She had wandered through countless weeks, unable to stop the silent flow of tears and unable to draw a full breath. Slowly, with the love of Jonas's grieving family and the endless flow of warmth from the people of Tarbet, she had learned to breathe easily again, to get through a day without tears.

Oh, she had grieved, and grieved anew for the man she had married. She was simply not ready to do it again for the man she hadn't fully known.

In the end she had opted for saving the dahlias. They were in danger of imminent demise. When Olivia had slipped into the room several hours later, Deirdre had been dusted to the elbows with potting soil and fully recovered from the brief weepy bout brought on by the loss of one irredeemable plant.

She was mildly surprised when Livvy did not scold her for mucking about in the dirt. She was startled enough to drop another pot when the girl seized her in a quick, forceful hug before dropping heavily onto an iron bench.

Now she wiped her hands on her apron and sat down. "What on earth could you possibly have heard to bring this on?"

She had a very good idea she already knew.

"There was a terrible fight! Oh, DeeDee, the scandal!"

Olivia commenced with a very familiar snuffling. In the absence of a handkerchief, Deirdre handed over an unused gardening glove. "Dearest, I think you are being overly dramatic here. The situation is unfortunate, but hardly scandalous."

Livvy lifted red-rimmed eyes. "You know, then?"

"For a few days now."

"And you do not *mind*? I would not be able to bear the whispering. I cannot bear it!"

Deirdre stroked the girl's tumbled curls. "I've borne worse. And I cannot think that any absurdly old and meaningless gossip about the duke, Nasey, and I will touch you—"

"What on earth are you talking about?"

"Why, the rumors about the fight Conovar had with Jonas four years ago."

Livvy flapped the damp glove miserably over her lap. "Please, DeeDee! That is horribly old news. And everyone knows Lucky would never have said anything unkind to Nasey. This is infinitely worse!"

Deirdre seized the girl's hand and held it still. "Olivia. What are *you* talking about?"

"The *painting*, of course!"

"What painting? Where?"

"At the Royal Academy. I was just there with Mr. and Miss Vaer. Oh, wait until their mama hears of this! She will quite forbid them to have anything further to do with me!"

Deirdre forestalled another round of tears with a swift tug at Livvy's hand. "What painting?"

"How can you not know? It is of *you*!"

Realization dawned with a flash. "Why, that wily old fox. He told me he was not exhibiting this year!" She bit her lip, remembering how Raeburn had refused to let her see the work. No, she could not believe he would . . . He had far too much honor, far too much fondness for her to do anything improper. "Livvy, is there something about the portrait that should concern me?"

The girl blinked away tears and actually smiled. "Not at all. It is a perfectly splendid picture. You are absolutely beautiful. Terribly sad-looking, but quite the most beautiful creature I've ever seen." Her face crumpled again. "*That* is the problem. Oh, DeeDee, do you have to be so lovely?"

Annoyance at Raeburn's deception aside, Deirdre was losing her patience. "I am sorry if my face has injured you, dearest, but I cannot see how!"

"Do pay attention! There was a terrible fight. DeeDee, they are fighting over your picture! Lord Fremont bloodied Mr. Montgomery's nose in the middle of Piccadilly, and Mr. Burnham says there are already a dozen wagers in White's betting book. How am I to bear it?"

"I do not ... Are you saying that two gentlemen argued over who would purchase the painting?"

Olivia moaned and buried her face in her makeshift handkerchief. "It is far more than two." Her voice rose, despite being muffled by the glove. "Half the men in Town are trying to ... to ... buy you!"

Much to the girl's promptly wailed chagrin, Deirdre laughed. She simply couldn't help it. Stunned, only half able to believe the utter stupidity of the male species, she kept laughing. And did not stop even when she had to borrow the glove from the weeping Livvy to dry her own cheeks.

8

L UCAS WAS NOT amused. In fact, his mood was verging on murderous.

Arms crossed over his chest, he scowled at the tight knot of men crowded near the far wall. Periodically one would break away, and his place would be filled in an instant. Lucas had not even bothered to try to get closer. He could see just fine from where he was.

The portrait was stunning. Just as Francis had reported at their meeting several days before, the subject was draped in some filmy fabric that was both modest and seductive, modern yet bringing to mind ages long gone. More alluring still was the expression of epic sadness on the exquisite face. Reluctant as he was, Lucas had to admit that no red-blooded man would be able to resist the grand, primordial challenge: To replace that look with one of sublime delight.

No less than twenty men were huddled in the midst of the Royal Academy gallery, quite probably envisioning precisely how they were going to do it.

Althorpe was beside him, head tilted and eyes intent. "Breathtaking," he murmured. For the fourth time.

Lucas shot him a look. "Try drawing air through your nose, then. You will find it much easier to regain your breath when you cease panting like a hound."

"Oh, for heaven's sake, Conovar. Are you blind? She is magnificent!"

Lucas certainly was not blind. And Deirdre was beautiful enough to make any man's heart flail about in his chest. In the portrait she was depicted sitting beneath a tree, her hair spilling like molten bronze over her shoulders, her hands clasped gracefully over her heart. Her astonishing beauty radiated from the canvas; her palpable sorrow struck with unnerving power.

Affected though he was, Lucas did not find her sadness nearly half as jolting as any of the rare, fleeting smiles she had given him since the day they had met.

Beyond that, he was appalled by the display. Not the painting, though the thought that she had posed for something so intimate as this staggeringly emotional work made his gut feel a bit hollow. No, he was annoyed by the spectacle *under* the portrait. In fact, he was bloody furious.

"Damn, but wouldn't she look grand in my bedchamber," came one fervent comment.

"I'd rather have her in my study," chimed in another voice. "Waiting for me with my brandy each night when I get home."

"Daresay I'd set her up in my country place." This announcement was accompanied by a lusty chuckle. "Don't suppose my wife would much care for it, but a fellow's got to have at least one fine piece to show off to his chums."

Lucas growled and stepped forward, fully intending to show this particular fellow the knuckle side of his fist. Althorpe moved in front of him. Lucas was ready to bellow at the man not to interfere when he realized intervention was the last thing on the man's mind. Althorpe was on his way to have a closer look.

Reluctantly deciding that violence was not the answer, Lucas opted to display a different sort of clout. Leaving Althorpe to join the slavering pack, he stalked off to find someone with the power to negotiate.

He nearly collided with Lord Hythe as he entered the second gallery.

"Seen it, have you?" the earl asked dryly.

"From a considerable distance."

Hythe gazed over Lucas's shoulder. "It was worse when I arrived. I feared lives would be lost."

"Damned idiocy," Lucas grumbled.

"Perhaps. But you must admit it is spectacular work. If I were the artist, I wouldn't be able to see it go into another's hands."

Lucas peered at the man sharply, trying to decide if he had just received a pointed message. Hythe merely smiled cordially and announced, "I have forgotten my manners. My mother is here and will certainly wish to have a few words with you. Allow me to fetch her."

Lucas groaned, then tapped his foot as he waited for Hythe to return with the dowager countess. The woman had been close friends with his own mother, and he always suspected she accosted him occasionally to determine just what a disappointment he had become. He also suspected that Lady Hythe kept his mother informed of his shortcomings—despite the fact that the duchess had been dead for nearly a decade. There was a fey, otherworldly quality about Lady Hythe that could very nearly make one believe she conversed with the departed.

She was floating toward him now on the arm of her son. As far as Lucas could tell, the woman had not changed in twenty-five years. She was still tiny, fair, and garbed in a pale gown the color and consistency of a spiderweb.

"Ah, Your Grace." She held out a languid hand. "I would not have expected to see you here."

"Good afternoon, my lady." He debated repeating his cousin's quip about appreciating a naked female form as much as the next man, but decided that was not the sort of report he wanted getting back to his mother, departed or not. "I try to attend the exhibition each year."

She did not look as if she believed him. He didn't blame her. "So what do you think of it?"

He glanced around the walls, crowded edge-to-edge with paintings. "It is certainly . . . colorful."

"I am not speaking of the exhibit, young man. I wish to know what you think of *Deirdre of the Sorrows*."

Lucas gritted his teeth and looked to Hythe for assistance. The earl's attention appeared to have been captured by a particularly dull painting of grazing cattle. "It is a formidable piece," he admitted grudgingly.

"Yes, it is." The countess's mouth thinned. "One must be sorry that such a lovely young lady should have been made so desolate."

"Must one?" Lucas was tempted to remark that most artists'

90

models could affect contentment while sitting on nails if it increased their fee, to snap that *Deirdre of the Sorrows* was merely a melodramatic Celtic folktale meant to discourage foolish men from falling in love with beautiful women. It would be a petty retort, and he knew it. He held his tongue. And heartily regretted the choice a moment later.

"*One* must, but from all I hear, he is not in the least contrite." Lady Hythe lifted her pointed little chin, elevating her nose to somewhere around the level of Lucas's top waistcoat button and continued, "It is amazing, is it not, what despicable behavior can be overlooked when the one who commits it is of a certain position?"

"Madam—"

"That did not require an answer, Conovar. Now, my son said he detained you on your way out. Good day, sir." She dismissed him with a fluttering hand and summoned Hythe. "I am ready to see the final room, dear. I have heard there is a Reynolds depicting Mrs. Drummond Burrell as one of the Furies."

She all but dragged her son away from Lucas and toward the expected Reynolds. Reeling slightly from the attack, Lucas could still not help but respect the effort. The earl was a good foot taller than his mother and outweighed her by at least six stone. And Sir Joshua Reynolds was far more likely to be exhibiting his celestial work to the Duchess of Conovar than the living beau monde. He, like Ramsay, was quite dead.

Lucas had always felt Lady Hythe possessed the attention span of a gnat. He thought he recalled hearing that, minutes after being informed of the victory at Waterloo, she had commenced a conversation on when that delightful boy Arthur Wellesley would fulfill everyone's expectations and defeat the nasty French. Apparently, more recent news about that spoiled Duke of Conovar had stuck firmly in her mind.

Lucas watched the pair stroll away and tried to ignore the uncomfortable feeling in the pit of his stomach. He had no idea what nonsense was being spread about. No idea why or by whom. Nor did he have time to care overmuch. He had more important business to attend to.

He rubbed absently at his neck as he went in search of a porter.

Deirdre surveyed the parlor and wondered if there were a cut flower left for purchase in London. They bloomed on every available surface in Lady Leverham's house. The last vase had been filled the day before, so the staff had become creative. A bunch of marigolds sat in a glass cruet that usually held vinegar, violets leaned over the lip of a massive silver sauceboat, and gladiolas fountained from several of Lord Leverham's decanters.

Deirdre had a very good idea she now knew how a tropical jungle looked. She disengaged the fringe of her wrap from the sticky fronds of an as-yet-unidentified, slightly feral-looking flowering plant and fled for the door. It had been an interminable afternoon, and she needed to get outside for a refreshing walk among brick, stone, and mortar.

She would very much have liked to take Olivia along, but the girl had slipped away an hour earlier, smiling smugly, and was now off somewhere with their hostess. Scheming, no doubt, Deirdre decided wearily. The pair was taking an unseemly delight in the steady stream of visitors—all male—asking for Mrs. Macvail. After three days Mrs. Macvail was ready to decamp for the Highlands.

She had refused to go see the portrait. There was no need, really. She'd received descriptions of it in minute detail from at least a dozen guests. If the piece looked anything like the narrations, she would no doubt be terrified by an actual viewing. According to Lord Newling, the eyes had brought to mind the image of how the sky must have looked above Joan of Arc's pyre. Mr. Farringdon-Smythe had disagreed, invoking instead the soulful gaze of his favorite hound. Deirdre's hair, in the words of Mr. Reynolds, flowed across the canvas like whiskey spilt from an ivory vessel. Sir Percy Gowdge had likened the melancholy curve of lip to that of the world's most magnificent bass, now mounted on his library wall.

Deirdre could not decide whether she preferred having the eyes of a dog or the mouth of a fish. The Joan of Arc image was better left uncontemplated.

Lady Leverham had gone quite starry-eyed when one man invoked the epic anguish of Guinevere. Olivia's firm approval had gone to the fellow who mentioned the deep blue of his mother's sapphire ring. Beyond the fact that the girl sparkled herself at the mention of jewels, she naturally took such a comparison of Mama's ring to Deirdre's eyes as a hint that said ring would look perfect on Deirdre's hand.

On three successive days Deirdre had endured several hours of fawning, fatuous visitors. She had, however, gently declined each invitation to walk, drive, or dance at upcoming fetes. She had not been so polite in turning down Lord Fremont's whispered offer of a house in Hays Mews and endless nights of inexpressible joy. She had quietly expressed how joyous his headfirst tumble into the Thames would make her, then discreetly tipped a Derby cream jug filled with snapdragons into his lap. She would have liked to follow with his own, earlier offering of bloodred roses, but Galahad had eaten them.

As she left the oppressively fragrant parlor now, she wondered what the appeal was, what these men truly desired from her. Had the portrait been of a lonely looking nude, she might have understood. But from what she could tell, it was nothing more than a melancholy, fully covered woman who just happened to have her face.

"Absurd," she muttered to herself as she donned her bonnet.

Peters, standing at attention beside the door, appeared ready to offer his agreement. The steady stream of visitors was no doubt stretching both his patience and ingenuity to their limits. Instead he gave a faint nod and announced, "Allow me to summon a footman and your maid, madam."

The maid was presently trying to remove charcoal smudges from the dress Deirdre had been wearing earlier. Sir Percy's gift, an enthusiastic but clumsy depiction of Deirdre in a field of daisies, had been rather messy. A footman might be available, but would be a nuisance.

"Thank you, Peters, but I prefer to go out alone." She opened the door for herself and scooted out before the butler could protest.

What she really needed was a brisk, head-clearing walk in Hyde Park, but opted against it. The last thing she wanted was to encounter any of her hapless swains—or anyone, really, who might look closely at her face and speculate on the bit of canvas and paint hanging in Somerset House. Grosvenor Square was hardly likely to be deserted, but it was close and a grand, open space. Anyplace without walls would do.

Much to her delight, she found the Square's elegant paths nearly empty. A couple wandered along the Duke Street side, heads close together and blind to the world around them. A red-faced footman dragged a trio of fat pugs toward Upper Brook. He paused and waited cheerfully while two equally plump children tormented the dogs for several moments before being recaptured by their panting governess.

Deirdre strolled toward an empty bench at the far end of the promenade. Perhaps, with a bit of peace and quiet, she would be able to solve the problem at hand. Which had absolutely nothing to do with the portrait. No, she had to decide what she was going to do about Olivia.

The girl had recovered admirably from her tantrum. The fact that the number of invitations for various affairs had doubled in the past three days had certainly helped. Lady Leverham's decision to turn the quiet evening of chamber music she had planned into a full-scale ball had sealed the matter. The Vaers' ready acceptance of that invitation had her walking on air.

Apparently Lady Vaer was not so high a stickler as to pass up what promised to be the most crowded fete of the Season. Apparently, too, she was not wholly against her son making an alliance with Olivia.

Deirdre was not so approving. Oh, Teddy Vaer was a nice enough fellow, but he was no match for Livvy. They might entertain each other during the brief, public entertainments of the Season, but Deirdre knew that a mere fortnight of suppers *à deux* would have Teddy bolting himself in his library and Olivia in fits of frustrated tears.

Creating a successful marriage was a matter of hard work and constant compromise. Deirdre did not care for the odds that the pair would succeed. Not when the most exertion Mr. Vaer put out was choosing which races to attend and Miss Macvail's idea of compromise was tucking a minuscule bit of lace in her bodice when Lady Leverham insisted on a full fichu.

Trying to discuss the subject in an adult manner with Olivia would be of little use. Trying a sterner tack would be a huge mistake. Deirdre knew only too well what effect adversity had on young lovers. She also knew how painful it was when reality eventually smacked one of those young persons square in the face.

Perhaps she could simply pop her sister-in-law over the head, haul her back to Scotland, and make sure she stayed there until her thirtieth birthday or she gained some common sense—whichever came first.

Deirdre smiled wryly to herself. The entire purpose of leaving Scotland had been to find Olivia the husband she wanted so much. The problem, of course, was that Livvy was choosing the wrong one. The ray of hope was the fact that she changed her mind nearly as often as she set it on something. With any luck she would tire of Mr. Vaer before the poor fellow actually got around to proposing.

Once the offer was made—and accepted—it was too late for a change of mind. Almost, anyway. Deirdre closed her eyes wearily. No matter which direction her thoughts took, they seemed determined to envision Olivia making one of the same mistakes she had. The path of love required a detailed map and expert guide, she decided grimly, and wondered where she had been when the requisite supplies had been disbursed.

"Mrs. Macvail."

She knew before she opened her eyes. There was no mistaking the voice. "Good day, Your Grace."

He was standing not three feet away, the sun behind him. Deirdre suddenly remembered the first time she had seen Lord Lucas Gower. Or rather not really seen him at all. She had been enjoying the fresh air at Lady Heathfield's garden party, sitting facing the sun. For a moment he had blocked it. Then he had stalked away. Only later had she learned his name. And it had been but the first of several occasions when he had stood near her and not spoken a single word.

"May I join you?"

She blinked as he took a step forward and gestured to her bench. "I . . . of course."

He flipped up the tails of his coat and lowered himself to sit beside her. "I would not have intruded, but . . ." He shrugged and

95

gave a half smile. "For two people determined to avoid each other, we're doing a rather poor job of it, aren't we?"

"I would hardly say we are determined . . ." Deirdre found herself smiling as well. "A poor job indeed. Shall I leave?"

"You were here first. Shall I?"

He had a little crease to the right of his mouth. Another woman, looking at another man, might have called it a dimple. But Deirdre, gazing bemusedly at the Duke of Conovar, somehow wouldn't have dared. Odd that she had never noticed it before. But then, in their brief encounters, she had rarely seen him smile.

"I am glad to see you, actually, Your Grace. I wanted to speak with you."

"Ah, Mrs. Macvail, I am not certain I am up to another one of our conversations."

She flinched. "Yes, well, that is precisely why. I wish to . . . I wanted to . . . Oh, bother. I'm very good at knowing when I've behaved badly, Your Grace. It seems I'm not half so good at apologizing for it."

His eyes, pewter gray in the bright light, met hers evenly. "What do you feel you must apologize for?"

"For what? Good heavens, where to start? I wish to apologize for thinking the worst of you, expecting the worst from you, and saying appalling things to you nearly every time we've met. I am not . . . Well, you couldn't know it, but I am not ordinarily a spiteful person."

"I have never heard you called so," he replied politely. It was hardly an emphatic demurral. "Thought of me, expected from me, said to me. What of speaking about me, Mrs. Macvail?"

"I beg your pardon?"

"Speaking about me. What have you said when you've spoken of me to others?"

Confused, slightly annoyed by what was certainly powerful pride, Deirdre frowned. Then she gave him a perfectly blunt answer. "I really don't speak of you much at all, Your Grace."

She nearly lowered her eyes at the force of his, but managed to keep both gaze and chin up. He stared at her for a long moment, then, apparently finding whatever he sought, nodded and looked away. "I didn't think it suited you, but I needed to be certain."

"Certain of what, Your Grace?"

He removed his hat and ran one hand in what was now a familiar gesture through his hair. "Do you suppose you could find something else to call me, Mrs. Macvail? I have never much cared for the address, but I find it even harder to hear from you."

"I cannot imagine why. The title is yours by right."

"And all the grace is yours by nature."

Deirdre sat back, stunned. And charmed. "Thank you, Y—"

"Lucas," he said simply. "My name is Lucas, and I am having a very hard time remembering the last time I heard it."

Not since before his brother's death, he thought. Even in his grief at losing his firstborn and heir, the old duke had still called him "boy." And even then, had invariably preceded it with "damn it."

"Thank you. Lucas."

How sweet the words were. He imagined Deirdre could curse at him and still sound like an angel. No, he amended, Deirdre *had* essentially cursed at him nearly every time they'd met, and she had always sounded like an angel.

"Will you tell me now," she asked softly, "what it was you needed to hear from me?"

"Ah, yes. It seems news of my appalling behavior to you is making the rounds. Hythe's mother nearly flayed me at the Academy exhibit."

"Appalling behavior?" Her cheeks flushed, and Lucas found himself thinking of autumn damask roses. "I thought we had settled that I was the one who behaved badly."

"Debatable, when one looks back," he murmured, "but we don't need to argue the point now. Apparently I am a black-hearted knave who has treated you in the most beastly manner."

"Lady Hythe said *that*?"

"Not in those exact words." No, the dowager's phrasing had been a bit more subtle, if her meaning had not.

"But you—" As Lucas watched, Deirdre's lashes swept down to cloak the smoky blue. "Oh, dear. You've seen the portrait."

"I have," he replied smoothly. "It is a stunning work. Raeburn should be delighted by the response to his talent."

Deirdre grimaced. "According to Olivia, it is causing chaos akin to Helen of Troy."

"Well, the Brat always did go for the dramatic. And I rather like the comparison."

"Oh, please! This is hardly a face to launch a dinghy, let alone a thousand ships."

How wrong she was, Lucas thought. The kingdom of Troy would spring back to life fully armed and fighting for her if it only could. He did not think she would appreciate the sentiment, however, especially from him, so he forced a grin and said instead, "You are too modest, madam. I have no doubt that, at the very least, your fair visage is capable of launching a sloop. Perhaps even a schooner."

Her laugh was quick, lovely, and gone far too soon. "You are very kind. But about what people are saying—"

"The ton must gossip about something. It does not concern me and will pass." Lucas took some comfort in knowing half of that statement was not a lie.

Deirdre did not appear to be convinced—at least by the half that was, in fact, true. "It should never have started. Is there anything I can . . . I mean, would it help if I were to tell people what really happened with Jonas?"

Lucas was speechless for a moment. "Why on earth would you even consider doing anything of the sort?"

"How could I not? People are speaking lies of you. It would be dishonorable of me to keep silent."

"Oh, Deirdre." Awed, he shook his head slowly. "It would be foolish. You and I know the truth. That's enough. There's no need to dishonor Jonas's memory now."

"I would say he did that himself," she replied, her eyes nearly as sad as those in the painting. "The truth will—"

"Remain between us."

"But, Lucas—"

"Don't argue with me, Deirdre. Not on this, please."

She seemed ready to do just that. Lucas braced himself for a fight, for an end to the unexpected, peaceful accord they had somehow reached. Instead she sighed and demanded, "Who would possibly want to spread malicious gossip about you?"

Thank God it isn't you, he said silently. "I have no idea. And it doesn't really matter. Someone else will be the sacrificial lamb by tomorrow. The only thing in this town more pitiful than the affinity for gossip is the attention span of the persons who indulge in it."

"I suppose that's true enough." Deirdre pulled her wrap about her shoulders. "I should probably be getting home."

Lucas sighed inwardly, unwilling to let go of the moment. "Allow me to escort you."

"Oh, no. Really, that isn't necessary."

"Don't want to be seen with me, do you?" he murmured, only half in jest.

"It isn't that at all." She sounded reasonably convincing. "I don't want to inconvenience you."

He shrugged cheerfully and propped one elbow on the back of the bench. "Do I appear otherwise occupied? It would be my pleasure."

She gazed at him thoughtfully, then smiled. "Very well. Thank you. I have . . . This has been most pleasant, Lucas."

That, he decided, was an understatement for the annals. "Are you in a very great hurry?"

"Well, no, I suppose not a very great one. Why?"

"I spend so little time sitting and doing nothing but absorbing the sun like a lizard. I find I rather like it. Will you . . . Would you care to join me in lizard-dom for a few more minutes?"

Deirdre said nothing for a moment, and Lucas found himself holding his breath. Then she announced, "I think I would like that very much," and tilted her face toward the unquestionably dipping sun.

9

"TRAGEDY," LADY CASTLEREAGH announced forcefully, "is what separates us from the fishes!"

With that she gave an approving smile and trundled off in the direction of the first tier boxes. The tiny pine branches she had tucked into her hair bobbed in time with her steps. Deirdre bemusedly watched her go. The lady was well-known for her eccentric appearance. By all appearances, the lady was eccentric in her behavior as well. She had offered no greeting, merely strode forward through the theater crowd, patted Deirdre's cheek, and delivered her emphatic comment.

Shakespeare, Deirdre decided, had not lost his appeal. He was still able to quite overset ladies' sensibilities—even before the curtain rose.

The Royal Opera House was filling rapidly in anticipation of a spectacular performance. Margaret Porter was to play Juliet. The critic Hazlitt had recently announced in *The Morning Chronicle*, "From this day, no theatergoer with a modicum of sense and self-respect will accept a Shakespeare tragedy without Mrs. Porter leading the cast." The Haut Ton, resolutely asserting its unimpeachable sense and self-respect, was flocking to the gilt-trimmed boxes. The more common folk, in simple anticipation of a good night's entertainment, took seats in the gallery and pit.

Deirdre stood in the lobby with Olivia and Lady Leverham, waiting for Francis to return with their programs. The baroness was twittering in gleeful anticipation. Livvy gazed listlessly around the ring of alcoves with their painted Shakespearean scenes. While not precisely pouting, she had made her wish to be elsewhere abundantly clear. Mr. Vaer was not attending the play; Mr. Gower was no longer an acceptable alternative.

Deirdre suspected his refusal to fawn over the girl of late had a great deal to do with his fall from favor. He still called frequently, but had taken to arriving with gifts that did not suit Olivia's taste in the least. Deirdre had quite enjoyed reading Byron's *The Corsair*. The Leverham library was divided fairly evenly between Lord Leverham's political tomes and his wife's gothic romances. Deirdre was perfectly happy to read anything in between.

Livvy had been quite put off by the gift, declaring, "How could any gentleman be so dense as to suppose a lady would prefer a *book* to roses or chocolates?" She'd thrown a small tantrum—and the book—when Francis, understandably annoyed, had tersely suggested that a sensible gentleman was far more likely to be entertained by a young lady whose mouth was as adept at intelligent conversation as it was at devouring candy.

Deirdre had been appropriately stern with the pair for their poor behavior. Quarreling children, she'd declared, did not belong in polite company. Livvy had promptly stomped out of the room. Francis had apologized to Deirdre, then had remained comfortably ensconced in a wing chair for another hour while they discussed *Emma*.

He had sent over a pot of daisies for Olivia the following day and had been grudgingly forgiven. It was clear, however, that the girl was not going to express any gratitude for an evening at the theater. When Francis returned, programs in hand, she folded hers in half and fanned herself idly with it.

Francis, apparently unconcerned with her disinterest, offered Lady Leverham his arm. "Shall we go in, ladies? I would not want to miss a moment of the glorious Mrs. Porter."

Livvy's languidly raised hand did not quite cover her yawn. "I cannot see what all the fuss is about. Margaret Porter is thirty if she's a day. Should she not be playing one of the witches rather than Juliet?"

"The witches are in *Macbeth*, dearest," Lady Leverham said dreamily. "What a splendid man, Shakespeare. I do so love his ladies' costumes."

"Well, she'll just get hers all wet when she drowns herself," Livvy muttered.

"That is *Hamlet*, dearest." Lady Leverham smoothed her own embroidered skirts as they started for the stairs.

"Not a bad thought, Mrs. Porter as a dampened Ophelia," Francis commented sotto voce. Lady Leverham swatted his arm with her fan. Olivia snorted.

"How talented must one be to fall down and play dead all the time?"

"One must never underestimate the appeal of well-played silence," came Francis's cheerful retort. "Its uses go well beyond a Shakespearean tragedy."

Deirdre decided it was time to end the childish spat. "Just remember that tragedy is all that separates us from the fishes," she said blandly, and urged a lead-footed Olivia into their box.

She took her own seat and scanned the crowd. Mrs. Porter's impressive talent notwithstanding, she expected the entertainment to come from the seats as much as the stage. Already a crowd of drunken dandies was roistering in the gallery. One stood on his seat, pantomiming a Hamlet-like soliloquy to the appreciative crowd. Another juggled a collection of overripe vegetables. Deirdre assumed they would be thrown at someone other than Mrs. Porter.

Above, in the boxes, quizzing glasses and gemstones flashed in the light. Courtesans sat mere feet from toplofty Society wives. Considering the fact that plunging bodices and expensive jewels abounded on both, one could best tell the difference by the men present. Those who had bothered to attend with their wives looked hopelessly bored. Their counterparts were a very contented-looking lot indeed.

A familiar blond head bowed over the hand of a beautiful brunette in red silk. Deirdre's brows rose as she watched Evan Althorpe take his seat. So he had a ladybird. Hardly surprising for a handsome young bachelor. The question was how he could afford to keep her in those diamonds.

Deirdre was not quick enough with her inner defenses to forestall the painful clutch near her heart. Men, she knew, found funds for the matters they could not live without. Jonas had.

102

She had never allowed herself to speculate too deeply on the women who had entertained her husband in Edinburgh. Now she couldn't help but wonder if they had looked anything like Althorpe's companion: lush, inviting, and stunningly exotic. She wondered if he had escorted them to the theater.

Perhaps she had never been forced to sit stiffly in a box, pretending to watch the performance while her husband slipped quietly into a seat beside another woman. But she had spent numerous nights at Red Branch Cottage, waiting for him to come home.

He always had, swinging her into his arms before he'd even shucked his coat. Sometimes those coat pockets had borne gifts. Deirdre unconsciously reached up to touch the silver locket above her bodice. Jonas had always come home, always melted her with his blazing grin and heartstoppingly skillful touch. And she had never been able to demand that he not leave again.

She started as a hand pressed hers where it rested on the gilt divider. Lady Hythe was leaning across from the next box, eyes soft with sympathy. "You poor child," she murmured. "Why, I could just weep at what you've endured!"

Deirdre blinked at her. "I . . . I beg your pardon, madam?"

"Disgraceful, how some men are allowed to behave! Lying, brawling, manipulating . . . And who suffers for it? We women, of course. Tragic, my dear. Simply tragic."

Hythe's mother nearly flayed me at the Academy exhibit. Lucas's words flashed into Deirdre's mind, followed by Lady Castlereagh's. *Tragedy is what separates us . . . Tragedy.*

She scanned the boxes until she located a tuft of pine. The ordinarily pinch-faced patroness smiled sadly and repeated the brisk nod of earlier. Deirdre's eyes flitted over more boxes. Faces that had only days before held vague disapproval now looked back with patent sympathy.

Then her gaze fell on a single figure, and she felt her hands clenching. Lucas, garbed in his standard evening black, handsome face shadowed by the low sweep of a velvet valance, was seated amid five empty chairs.

Dear God, she thought dazedly, they truly were blaming him for Jonas's death. Four years late and completely, bli

Not knowing what possible aid she could give him there, she nonetheless rose halfway from her seat. Francis's hand on her wrist drew her back down just as the curtain rose.

Lucas passed the first act of the play watching Deirdre. She was garbed once again in some grayish, extremely modest dress, her hair pulled back in a severe knot and her only ornament a silver pendant. She was, without a doubt, the most dazzling creature in the theater.

He grinned when she silenced Francis's chattering on several occasions, chuckled aloud when she reached out and grasped Olivia's chin to turn the girl's gaze from the wall to the stage. He sighed with her when Romeo professed his undying love for a woman he did not really know.

A draft caught the back of his neck. He turned as Althorpe entered the box. Lucas did not particularly want company, but was nonetheless helplessly pleased to have some. Lady Vaer and Miss Vaer had canceled their plans to accompany him at the last moment. He had a very good idea why.

"I will give you the benefit of the doubt, and assume you bathed this week," Althorpe murmured as he surveyed the empty seats.

"Well, damn," Lucas returned dryly, "I knew I forgot something. What removed *you* from the luscious Alice's side so soon? She's certainly in fine looks this evening."

"Isn't she? Gorgeous creature." Althorpe took a seat. "A diamond bracelet hustled me out, actually."

"Well, you always knew she had expensive taste. This demand should come as no surprise."

"You mistake me, my friend. She doesn't need me to purchase a new bauble for her; she's already wearing one."

Lucas whistled softly. "Any idea who he is?"

"Not a one. I thought I'd plant myself here and see if the fellow shows himself." Althorpe leaned back and draped one arm casually over the seat beside him. "Not that it matters, really. I was beginning to tire of the situation anyway."

"You're taking her desertion rather too well."

"Do you think so? Perhaps. I will dash out a note when I get home tonight."

"To Alice?"

The first piece of fruit was launched at the stage, smacking the rotund Papa Capulet on his rump. Althorpe smiled faintly. "To my man of affairs, canceling the lease on the house, the servants' wages, and the household accounts. I will write to the modiste myself in the morning. Not bad timing at all. I believe Alice ordered several new gowns only yesterday."

Lucas pictured the ladybird suddenly finding herself out of her home, staff, and wardrobe. He imagined it would not be a pretty scene. He had always known Alice to be greedy, but he'd never have thought her stupid enough to flaunt another man's gift in her current protector's face. "I don't suppose there's a chance the bracelet was a gift from some chap who came before you."

"Oh, I suppose there is. Unlikely, though, and of course I didn't ask."

"Of course you didn't." Lucas shook his head wryly. "Remind me never to anger you. You go for the swift and brutal strike."

Althorpe shrugged. "Suits the crime here." He turned and regarded Lucas thoughtfully. "I would say you've angered someone rather greatly. They're saying rather nasty things about you, you know."

"I've figured as much." Lucas glanced at the empty chairs. Recalled several slightly frosty greetings from ladies he had encountered on his way to the box. "What have you heard recently?"

"Besides the information that you have horns and a pitchfork, you mean?"

"Yes," Lucas muttered. "Besides that."

"Oh, where to begin? Let's see." Althorpe began to tick the list off on his fingers. "You had Macvail stripped of his commission, demoted into the foot ranks, and placed at the front of the line. You purchased the Raeburn portrait and have been using it for dart practice. Ah, and there is my personal favorite: You are planning to charm Mrs. Macvail into another engagement . . ."

"Let me guess. I will then abandon her at the altar and ride off with a famous courtesan."

"Too trite, man. No, you will abandon the lady at the altar, then flee for Gretna Green with Miss Macvail."

Lucas smacked his fist against the railing. "Bloody hell! Is there no level to which gossips will not stoop for their entertainment?"

"Not to put too fine a point on it, old man, but the debate is over the level to which *you* will stoop for your injured pride."

"Oh, well, thank you very much for the clarification. You're finding this rather amusing, aren't you?"

Althorpe's eyes narrowed. "Careful there, Conovar. I would never find amusement at Deirdre's expense. I knew her value well before you did."

"You should have tried to marry her, then," Lucas grumbled.

"Yes, well, you beat me to that one."

"Am I meant to apologize now?"

"Apologies, to the best of my knowledge, have never been part of your repertoire. And don't get snippy with me, old trout. I'm not the one who got everything he wanted in life, then threw a fit when he lost out once. Nor am I the one who nearly throttled an Academy porter last week."

Lucas cursed quietly. "How do you know about that?"

"I'd come looking for you. We went to Somerset House together, if you recall."

"I suppose you heard the exchange, then."

"I do not eavesdrop," Althorpe replied blandly. "Besides, anything the poor fellow said was well muffled by your grip on his throat."

Lucas flinched at the memory. He had not handled the situation well at all. "Twenty pounds bought forgiveness."

"I'm sure it did. How much bought the painting?"

"I offered a thousand."

Althorpe's jaw dropped. "A *thousand*? For a dartboard? I certainly hope you're throwing gold-tipped darts."

"Very amusing. As it turns out, the painting has already been sold."

"To whom?"

"I have no idea," Lucas muttered. "But I intend to find out."

Althorpe studied him for a long moment before quietly asking, "I suspected as much, but you still want her rather badly, don't you? It won't do, you know, trying to assuage your bruised pride by luring Deirdre into some sordid alliance. She doesn't deserve that."

"Sometimes I think you have a very low opinion of me, Althorpe."

"Sometimes I do." The man rose to his feet. "Enjoy the performance."

"Where are you going?"

"Off to sit with the Hythes. They have a better view."

"Must you go? Parting is such sweet torment," Lucas drawled.

"Sorrow. Not torment. Really, man, if you're going to quote Shakespeare, you must make an effort to get it right."

Lucas did not turn to watch Althorpe leave. Instead he gazed back at the Leverham box. Deirdre was leaning forward slightly in her seat, her face illuminated by the candlelight. God, but she was lovely. He was too far away to be certain, but Lucas was convinced he saw her lips trembling.

On the stage a pair of foolish, star-crossed young lovers emoted their way toward their sorry fate.

Deirdre excused herself at the end of the play and headed for the ladies' retiring room. She sat quietly until the lump in her throat faded away. Given the choice, she would not have stayed for the closing farce, but Lady Leverham would not miss it. Mr. Blanchard was to play the Knight, Mr. Liston the Deaf Minstrel. A departure at this point was unthinkable.

Mrs. Porter's performance had been quite moving. Deirdre had never much cared for *Romeo and Juliet*—even before she'd had her own ill-fated love. She had never possessed much tolerance for people who abandoned all hope in the face of tragedy, and Shakespeare's pair were a prime example of wasted lives.

She was decidedly annoyed with herself for having wept her way through the final act.

After dabbing a bit of rose water at her temples, she resolutely straightened her shoulders and strode back to the lobby. One more

107

sympathetic glance was liable to make her scream, but facing them with bowed shoulders and lowered eyes would be worse. She had no idea what she was going to do about the dismal situation. There was no question, though, that she would do something.

For all the times she had silently cursed Lucas Gower, she was finding a vast irony in the fact that she was prepared to loudly defend him now. "Thereby hangs a tale for you," she announced to the unattractive marble Shakespeare who graced the largest alcove. "I suppose all the primary players will end up in a heap at the end."

"Interesting image."

Deirdre jumped, then flushed. Lucas came away from the wall to her left. "Must you do that?"

"Do what?"

"Pop out of the air when I'm least prepared for it."

He chuckled and came to stand beside her. She was forced to tilt her head back to see his eyes. They were amused—and warmer than she had ever seen them. "This time *I* was here first."

"An interesting spot to lounge."

"Ah, caught. Very well. I saw you leave and followed. Do you mind terribly? I wanted to speak with you."

"I'm glad, actually. Shall we go back to your box? I . . . saw you were alone."

"Yes, I was," he replied grimly. "Which is a very good reason for us to remain out here."

Deirdre bit back a sardonic laugh. "I am hardly likely to be compromised by sitting in a theater box with you. A perquisite of widowhood, you know."

"You might be surprised by what the flapping tongues would say regardless." He gestured toward a low bench in a nearby alcove. "Will this do?"

Once again, Deirdre found herself occupying a small space with a very large man—whose presence inspired several very disquieting sensations inside her. She opted against trying to decide precisely what they were. "What was it you wished to discuss, Your Grace?" He raised his brows. "Lucas."

"The tales are getting worse."

108

She did not need to ask what he meant. "I was rather afraid of that. I've been receiving condolences."

"Good."

"What? It is *not* good! It is silly, rather rude, and a thumping bore. I do not know what people are saying about you, Lucas, but I can guess. The possibilities are alarming."

It was the first time he had seen her eyes spark for him, rather than against. And he felt something twist in the vicinity of his heart. "Nothing so terrible," he lied gently. "Deirdre, I want you to promise you will simply accept the sympathy."

"Don't be silly! I am not about to do anything of the sort. Why, I—"

"Please." Without thinking, he reached out and grasped her hand. It felt very small in his, and the instant decision not to let go was fully conscious. "You deserve a bit of sympathy."

"Oh, please!" She tugged sharply, but he did not release her hand. "I am not one to be pitied, Your Grace!"

He swore inwardly at himself. That had been clumsy. "I didn't mean to imply you were. I simply meant the ton owes you some . . . respect. Take it."

Her eyes narrowed, and he expected another blast. Then she sighed and relaxed her clenched fingers. "I do not like the ton," she said tartly. "A flock of chickens has more sense."

"I agree. But you have Olivia's future to keep in mind. If not for you, accept the approval for her sake."

"That was low, Lucas," she shot back, but smiled. "Low and terribly effective."

"I thought it might be."

She gazed at him intently for a moment. "You are rather scrupulously honest, aren't you? I wish I had known that . . . before."

He knew he ought to set her straight on the matter, but couldn't. Not with her beautiful, gracious face gazing up at him like that. All he could manage was, "Thank you."

"Oh, don't. I am sorry I accused you of being dishonorable. It was unforgivable, and I feel terrible about it."

"It was understandable. Completely."

109

"Mmm. If you say so." She slipped her hand from his then, before he could stop her. "I wish Olivia's instincts about other men were as good as they've been about you."

"And what does that mean?"

"She thinks you are quite the most princely fellow in Britain."

Lucas chuckled. "I rather doubt that. She has told me precisely the opposite countless times. But no, I was asking about her instincts elsewhere."

The lush mouth tightened. "I think she might marry Teddy Vaer."

"And that is a bad thing? He's wealthy, affable, and not wholly stupid. She could do far worse."

"Faint praise. But yes, he's a good enough man. I just think . . ." She shrugged. "I suppose I should watch my tongue. It is your future brother-in-law I am insulting, after all."

"My . . . ? Ah, yes. Nothing is settled as yet." He watched her face carefully, searching for . . . something. She merely nodded pleasantly.

"Nor has anything been settled between Livvy and Mr. Vaer. Time will tell."

"Deirdre . . ." Lucas reached for her hand again.

"I say, Deirdre." They looked up to find Francis standing at the foot of the stairs. He looked, Lucas thought, like someone had tied his drawers in a twist. "Lady Leverham told me to come fetch you. The farce is about to begin." His eyes settled coolly on Lucas. "Good evening, cousin."

"Francis." Lucas cursed family, farces, and a lifetime of bad timing under his breath as he stood. "I will detain you no longer, Mrs. Macvail. It has been a pleasure."

She accepted his hand and rose to her feet. "Thank you, Your Grace. I . . . am certain we shall see each other again about Town." She turned to join Francis.

"Wait," Lucas said quietly so the words would not carry. "Come driving with me tomorrow." From the corner of his eye, he saw his cousin tapping his foot impatiently. "Please. I will come for you at four."

Deirdre hesitated, and his throat constricted.

"Yes," she said at last. Then she hurried away.

Lucas had to sit down again. His legs were shaky, his chest tight. He had not felt quite this way since his adolescent school days. He drew a deep breath and let it out in a heady sigh. "Yes!" he repeated triumphantly, and thumped the cushion beside him.

10

DEIRDRE HAD A headache. She and Olivia had visited most of the shops in Bond Street, half in Oxford Street, and Livvy was not even close to being ready to stop. Deirdre was tempted to leave the girl to root through the present pile of ribbon and take herself quickly home. She did not want to make Lucas wait. She had no idea if he would.

She could not leave her charge, however, and resigned herself to a few more minutes of sifting through pale fabric objects. London, she had decided, really had not changed at all since she had left. Men still sported appalling, peacock-embroidered waistcoats, and young ladies were expected to wear pastels. At least she was blending in.

"What is your opinion on this one, DeeDee?"

She turned her longing gaze from the sunny street to her charge. Olivia was holding a length of satin ribbon against her pale yellow walking dress. It was the color of the inside of an egg—not the yolk—and would no doubt shred with the first washing.

"It is . . . very fashionable, dearest," Deirdre said wearily.

"That is precisely what you said about the last three!" Olivia pouted and dropped the ribbon back onto the counter.

"Which only goes to show, you have impeccable fashion sense."

Slightly mollified, Livvy turned her attention to a selection of white gloves. Deirdre watched the bustling street through the window. A passing gentleman raised his hat. He did not look especially familiar, but Deirdre nodded her own greeting. Whether due to Raeburn's painting or the absurd whisperings about Lucas, she had become something of a celebrity. The present shopping expedition had been slowed dismally by the constant stream of greetings—and sympathetic hand pats.

Deirdre supposed she ought to be grateful. The last of the cloud had been lifted from her reputation, and many of the greetings now included previously unattainable invitations as well. Livvy had bounced happily at the one from Lady Heathfield, and blushed profusely when Lady Vaer had almost smiled. No doubt she would swoon should an Almack's voucher make its tardy appearance.

Deirdre sincerely hoped the girl wasn't holding her breath for that one. Lady Castlereagh's fishy approval aside, there was no guarantee of an invitation into the hallowed halls of the Wednesday night Assembly. Nor could Deirdre regret its absence. From her own Season, she recalled uncomfortable chairs, appalling refreshments, and interminable hours of being perused through quizzing glasses.

She nodded again, this time in reply to Richard Granville's enthusiastic wave. Then she winced as he, not looking where he was going, smacked into George Burnham, who was not watching where he was going, either.

"He is handsome, isn't he?"

"Hmm?" Deirdre turned to find Olivia at her side, gazing speculatively out the window. "Who?"

"Ricky Granville, of course. And he's ever so besotted with you."

"Rubbish," Deirdre retorted, but without much conviction. Apparently, Mr. Granville had been ready to offer two hundred pounds for the portrait, only to be swiftly curbed by his older brother. Deirdre had not yet met Viscount Tarrant, but she commended his common sense. "Have you finished here? I really must get home."

"Oh, yes, I suppose so . . ." Livvy was still staring after Mr. Granville. "He might suit, you know."

"For you? Whatever happened to Teddy?"

"Oh, I have every intention of marrying Teddy, when he asks. No, I was thinking of Mr. Granville for you. He is from a very important family and not a bad fellow at all, even if he hasn't a title."

113

Deirdre rolled her eyes. True enough, Ricky Granville was not a bad fellow, was from an important family, and did not possess a title. He could be a princely member of the royal family for all she cared. "You may give it up, Olivia. I am not interested in finding a husband."

"Are you quite certain, DeeDee? Half the gentlemen in Town are very interested in marrying *you*."

Deirdre rather expected marriage was not foremost in many of those admiring minds, but she wasn't about to correct Olivia's assumption there. She was amused by the girl's hapless match-making attempts and by the speed with which the portrait had gone from being a disaster of epic proportions to something akin to divine favor.

"Since you seem so inclined to discuss impending marriages, dearest, perhaps we could discuss yours."

"What of it?" Livvy tossed her dark curls. "I know you do not approve, but Mr. Vaer is precisely what I came to Town to find."

"It isn't that I disapprove. I simply wish . . . You said *what* you came to find, Livvy, not *whom*. That concerns me."

"Oh, piffle. Grammar." In that moment, eyes flashing, Olivia looked very much like her brother. Deirdre knew from experience that, whatever came next, there would be no arguing against it. "I tell you, DeeDee, I am determined to be Lady Otley, and I will not be dissuaded by you or anyone."

"Sweetheart, I only mean to say that you do not really know—"

"Don't you go spouting nonsense about time, DeeDee. How long did you know Nasey before you eloped, hmm?"

Deirdre knew she ought to have taken her own counsel and not bothered with any form of debate. "You're right, Olivia. Sometimes time means nothing, but sometimes it makes all the difference in the world."

She saw Lucas, close beside her on the theater bench, his eyes soft on her face. Yes, time made all the difference. It had brought her from hating a man as she had hated no one before to . . . quite liking him. And she did like him. Very much indeed.

He would have arrived at Lady Leverham's by now. If she could get Livvy out of the shop and on the path home, perhaps he would still be there, waiting.

"All I wish of you, Olivia, is that you follow your heart. Listen carefully to it, and never stop listening. Will you promise me that?"

Livvy promptly gave her an affectionate hug and chided, "You do worry so, DeeDee. You really must try accepting things as they come. You will feel ever so much better about life." Incredulous, amused, Deirdre watched her sister-in-law stroll toward the door. "Now, are you coming? You were in such a hurry before."

They had not gone more than ten paces down Oxford Street when Olivia muttered, "Well, bother. I had so hoped not to see *him* today."

Francis rolled up beside them in his curricle and tilted his fashionable beaver hat. "Good afternoon, ladies. Have you left a flounce or furbelow for the rest of the Diamonds, Miss Macvail?"

Livvy tilted her head and saucily retorted, "Have you left a smidgen of wit for the rest of the dandies, sir? I vow you have so much more than your share that it quite escapes the rest of us."

Francis smiled indulgently. "I see you have been sharpening yours. A commendable endeavor, my dear. Dare I hope you have been reading as well?"

Deirdre contemplated stepping in. The bantering between the two tended to exhaust her. Olivia, however, was in prime form.

"I did pick up *Emma* several days ago, when I had nothing better to do. I was quite astonished to find that this was the heroine you so admired. She is terribly spoiled and frightfully dense. I could not relate to her at all."

"Fancy that," Francis muttered.

Another familiar carriage rattled up the street, and Livvy seized Deirdre's arm. "Look, DeeDee. There is Lord Hythe with Miss Vaer. I feel rather frightfully sorry for him."

"Why? I thought you liked Miss Vaer."

"Oh, I like her very well indeed. So does Lord Hythe, which is why I pity him. She has quite settled on Lucky, and what woman"— she shot a delicately pointed look in Francis's direction—"could possibly fail to be smitten by such a man as the Duke of Conovar. That bearing, those estates . . ."

"That nasty habit of stepping on people," Francis added blandly.

Deirdre sighed and turned her attention to Lord Hythe, who had halted his vehicle nearby. At his side Elspeth Vaer looked very satisfied. And very lovely. "Good day, my lord. Miss Vaer."

Elspeth nodded graciously. Hythe tipped his hat. "Good day, Mrs. Macvail. This is a familiar and delightful sight."

She could not tell if he was being ironic about the latter bit. The scene must certainly be familiar: she and Olivia on foot beside Francis's curricle, Francis smiling like a well-fed cat.

"Perhaps you will allow me to escort you home this time," he said, right on cue.

"Thank you, Mr. Gower," Olivia said promptly, "but we are quite determined to walk—"

"Thank you, Francis, we would be happy to accept," Deirdre corrected. "I am terribly late and would be glad of the ride."

"Late?" Francis sprang from the vehicle. "We mustn't have that."

"Late? Good heavens. I have, as usual, arrived at the wrong moment."

Deirdre turned to see Evan Althorpe sauntering toward them. Well, she mused, one more person and the jolly party would be complete. Of course, that person was no doubt presently tapping his elegantly shod foot, waiting for her to appear.

"Lord Althorpe. How very nice to see you. I wish I could stay and chat . . ."

"But you are late. I am not in utter despair, though. We shall have ample time to have a good coze tomorrow night." Evan's gaze drifted over the assembled party. He bowed. Hythe nodded pleasantly. Francis grunted something inaudible and pulled the carriage door open wider.

Livvy paused with her foot on the step. "What *are* you rushing for, DeeDee? You haven't said. If it is merely to take tea with Lady Leverham, I am certain she will understand. There was that reticule back in Bond Street that I believe will suit me after all. You know, the pink silk with—"

"It will be there tomorrow." Deirdre planted her hand firmly under the girl's elbow and pushed. "I am engaged to . . . ah . . ." Well, why not? Why shouldn't she announce her plans? Lucas needed all the public support he could get. And perhaps it would wipe that smug little smile off Miss Vaer's face. "I am going driving with Conovar, and I am late. Francis, shall we go?"

Francis didn't move. Miss Vaer's smile faltered. Lord Hythe's face registered nothing whatsoever. Olivia gave a quiet gasp, and Evan let out a low whistle.

"You, my dear, are a brave woman."

Deirdre scowled at him. "Really, Evan. Not you, too."

"Not me?" Althorpe grinned ruefully and shook his head. "I merely say it as I see it. Poor fellow's been taking a bit of a drubbing lately. I simply thought you might want to . . ."

"Revel?" she said quietly, leaning toward him. "I thought you held me in higher esteem than that."

"I hold you in the highest esteem," he replied, just as quietly. "What I meant to say is that you've taken your own drubbing. I wouldn't expect you to welcome more."

Deirdre was ready to snap at him, but remembered their audience. Francis, Livvy, and Miss Vaer were at unsubtle attention, trying to catch every word. Lord Hythe was perfectly composed and apparently completely unconcerned.

"I really must be off, Evan. We shall speak tomorrow night."

"Of course." He held out a hand and assisted her into the carriage. "I would not detain you. Do give Conovar my best regards."

"I will." She glanced around, waiting for others to add their greetings to Lucas. No one did. "Well. Ready, Mr. Gower. I don't suppose you would mind going at a quick pace."

"Through these streets?" Francis replied uncertainly. "We would not wish to cause any accidents. But, I assure you, I will go as quickly as I can."

Deirdre eyed the whip on the floor at her feet and tried not to groan when Francis guided the pair slowly into the stream of carriages. At this rate Lucas would be sprouting gray whiskers by the time she arrived. She vowed the next time she saw Francis's carriage anywhere in the vicinity, she would turn and run in the opposite direction.

At Davies Street, unable to endure the snail's pace any longer, she got a firm grip on his sleeve. "Francis," she said calmly, enunciating each word, "please don't think me ungracious. I am very grateful for your assistance here. I am also very much afraid that

117

if you don't get this miserable contraption moving, I will be forced to do something rash."

Francis's brows shot up, and he blinked at her in surprise. Then his eyes darted to the whip under her feet. "Of course, madam," he replied, and slapped the reins smartly across the horses' rumps.

"I simply cannot comprehend it," Lady Leverham said fretfully as she passed him a tiny, lace-edged napkin. "You must have done *something*, Your Grace. There is no other explanation."

Lucas shot her a grim look. All he had done was arrive on time, expecting to find Deirdre waiting, then accepted her hostess's twittering excuses and offer of tea. During the succeeding minutes, he had said little, listened politely, and sat as still as his rising impatience would allow. As far as he was concerned, Lady Leverham deserved as much; she hadn't snubbed him or greeted him with a suspicious eye. He'd received more than his share of fish gazes in the past several days.

Whether or not there was a rationale for this slip from grace, he most certainly had not done anything to cause the present situation.

"These things happen," he replied far more graciously than he was inclined, and unfolded the napkin to its fullest, negligible extent. It was hardly likely to be sufficient, but he would be damned if he would use his own handkerchief.

He turned the full force of his now-baleful gaze on the monkey, who was perched nonchalantly on Lady Leverham's shoulder, shredding a piece of apple. No one looking at the blank-eyed little cretin would guess it had just thoroughly wetted one very expensive, painstakingly polished Hoby boot.

"You must have intimidated him, Conovar. Galahad is a most sensitive creature."

Sensitive as a goat, Lucas thought, as the monkey, having finished off the apple, pulled a silver pin from the lady's hair and began chewing on it. "If I did so, I am most heartily sorry," he managed as he dabbed gingerly at his boot with the napkin.

"Did you hear that, Galahad? His Grace has apologized. Now, wasn't that good of him?"

Lucas might have been mistaken, but he would have sworn the

monkey gave a little simian belch. Lady Leverham, however, was duly pacified.

"I always did think you a knightly fellow, if a bit rash," she continued. It took Lucas a moment to realize she was speaking to him rather than her pet. "I must say, you do choose the most daring crusades. One was forever nibbling at one's nails in your youthful presence. Terribly bad behavior, of course, but unavoidable."

"My . . . er . . . crusades?"

"The nail-nibbling, dearest. Your crusades were merely curious."

"Curious." He had the disconcerting feeling he was about to receive a lecture. "I see." The idea of enduring a harangue from this twittery woman left him slightly twitchy. He would endure far worse, however, if it meant seeing Deirdre.

"Why, we all know about Kettering's horse, dear boy. And no one could possibly forget the year you raced that funny little boat from Margate to Brighton. You could not have been more than twenty at the time."

He had been sixteen, and the funny little boat had been a stiff-ruddered, creaking sloop belatedly retired from the Duke of Kent's collection. Lucas's father had purchased the thing for pocket change, then waited comfortably in Brighton for his younger son to pilot it around the coast. The Prince of Wales had cheerfully handed over ten pounds when Lucas made port.

Lucas had been sweaty, nauseous, and jelly-kneed for the following sennight.

"The follies of youth," he commented dryly.

"Mmm." Lady Leverham gave a brisk nod, hampered in the act, no doubt, by the fact that the monkey was now seated atop her head. The first hairpin had disappeared, and Lucas supposed the beast was poking about the lady's elaborate curls for another. "And, of course, there was your splendid run to Salt Hill several years later. I do believe you set a record, did you not?"

If he had set a record in the carriage-run so popular with the Four-in-Hand Club, it had been for near misses. According to Colonel Berkeley's report to the old duke, Lord Lucas had done nearly every curve after Binfield on two wheels. This dashing accomplishment, unbeknownst to all but Lucas and his terrified tiger, had been due to the fact that he had lost hold of two of the ribbons just after Newell Green. He had tied the things around his wrists for the return journey—and fortified himself with a bottle of port.

Galahad ceased his poking and returned to Lady Leverham's shoulder. He was now eyeing Lucas's watch fob with interest. Lucas placed a protective hand over his waistcoat pocket. The idea of having the creature on his lap was too much to contemplate. With his watch temporarily unavailable, he darted a glance at the mantel clock. Half-past four.

She wasn't coming.

On hearing that Deirdre was out shopping with Olivia, Lucas had been philosophical. No doubt the Brat would delay their return, he'd mused, but Deirdre wouldn't allow them to be too late. Not when she had accepted his invitation.

Now he was almost ready to believe that she wasn't coming. Almost. He was not quite ready to remember just how he had felt as he'd watched her run away from him those years ago, back down the aisle, white silk skirts lifted nearly to her knees. It had been a nasty sensation, right up there with the time his brother had accidentally thwacked him below the belt with a swinging cricket bat. Worse, actually. Watching Deirdre flee had been more along the lines of having a red-hot poker thrust into his breast.

At present he was experiencing a very unpleasant twisting, knotting sensation in his gut.

"I have taken up enough of your time, my lady . . ." He braced his hands against the chair arms and began to rise.

"Do sit down, Your Grace," Lady Leverham commanded with a sharp tone and angelic smile. Lucas sat. "More tea?"

"I . . . No, thank you, madam."

"Another piece of cake, then."

"Thank you, but no. I really must—"

He broke off as his hostess turned her head and whispered something to the monkey. "A moment, please, Your Grace," she addressed him briefly, then was back to whispering. To Lucas's astonishment, the beast saluted, scampered to the rug, and ran out the door. When he looked back, Lady Leverham was patting her hair back into place and gazing at him expectantly. "I thought it best if we have a bit of privacy for this discussion."

The conversation, to the best of Lucas's recollection, had involved a list of his crazed, youthful "crusades." The audience had been a small monkey. He was fast coming to the conclusion that Lady Leverham had more bats in the rafters than York Minster.

"As you wish, my lady." Better, he thought, to humor her for a few minutes, then skulk off to ponder the fact that Deirdre had abandoned him again. "Was there something else you wished to discuss?"

"Were we not talking of your brash endeavors? Of course we were. Have I already mentioned how very impressed I was when you sparred with John Gully, John Broughton, *and* Gentleman Jackson all within the space of a weekend?"

Lucas groaned quietly. "I did not have the honor of fighting with Jackson at that time, madam." If the truth were told, it was that man, whose sobriquet was well deserved, who had halted the bout with Broughton and then assisted the battered, reeling, twenty-year-old Lord Lucas to bed where he had remained for the next two days.

"No? Well, everyone assumes you did. Quite a popular tale with the ton bards, you know."

"Regrettably, I have no control over the tales."

"I suppose you don't. You are the stuff of legends, nonetheless, dear boy."

"Really, my lady, I hardly think—"

"More popular still, though I quite blush even to mention it, is the legendary evening at the Velvet Cord. I believe the number reached above ten—"

"Madam!" Lucas snapped, shocked and mortified.

Lady Leverham giggled and pressed bejeweled fingers to her lips. "Inexcusable for me to even speak such words, I know. But a lady is given such liberties when she reaches a certain age and position in life. Oh, dear, I really have offended you, haven't I? How very careless of me. It is simply that you are such an epic figure, Conovar. One cannot help but be awed."

Lucas's skin felt as if it were being scorched. "That tale," he ground out between clenched teeth, "is pure fiction."

He did not believe it necessary to inform her that he had never been inside the infamous brothel. When a man had spent somewhere around seven years living with the absurd reputation of having bedded ten acrobatic *filles de joie* in a single evening, the matter of location was unimportant.

"Inexcusable," Lady Leverham repeated, then nibbled for a moment at a morsel of rum cake. "Oh, don't scratch, dearest. You will get blood on that splendid cravat knot."

Lucas's fingers dropped away from his neck. "Lady Leverham, I really must be going. I am expected at . . . at . . ."

"Must you go?" She pouted expertly. "Well, if you must. Do allow me to apologize again, Your Grace. I do so hate to offend by repeating untrue gossip."

"It is quite all right." His voice sounded strangled even to his own ears. "I am happy to be able to refute . . . ah . . . a spurious tale."

"Mmm. Yes. A man must defend his honor. Though I must say, as much time as I have spent on this earth, I am still deplorably unclear as to what many men consider matters of import. The list does seem to vary so."

"Indeed." Lucas rose in a single motion, lest she try to stop him again. "Thank you for the tea and the pleasure of your company, my lady."

She beamed up at him. "Oh, the pleasure was mine. I do believe the last time you were in this house was with your dear mother. And now you've grown into such a legendary figure. I am utterly awed."

Lucas closed his eyes for a weary moment. "As I said, madam, many of the tales are grossly exaggerated."

"Ah, but accepted as gospel truth. Would you take a bit of advice from a silly old lady, Your Grace?"

He thought he might take a bit of hemlock if it would hasten his departure. "Of course."

"A good knight's honor is his true strength and sometimes must be defended—shall we say—emphatically."

"I . . . see. Well, thank you, my lady. I will take that advice to heart."

"Will you? I am so glad."

Lucas nodded a bit vaguely and took a hopeful step toward the door. "Good day, Lady Leverham. I shall see myself out."

She stopped him just as he was reaching for the door handle. "What shall I tell Deirdre, Your Grace?"

Well, damn. "I . . . er . . . Please tell Mrs. Macvail I regret having to depart before she returned, but that I had . . . business to attend to."

"Certainly. Ah, Your Grace . . . ?"

Lucas's fingertips brushed the brass handle. "Yes, madam?"

"What are *you* going to tell Deirdre?"

He studied the pleasantly wrinkled face through narrowed eyes. The woman was beaming at him again. "I will tell her much the same when next we meet."

"After that, dear boy."

"I am afraid I do not understand."

Her smile softened into one a parent might give a slow child. "You have not been listening, have you? Well, I shall try to explain in simple terms." She sat up very straight and folded her hands in her plump lap. "You have a very good character, Conovar. I have always thought so. But you also have a regrettable tendency toward remoteness. This time around, use the brains and voice God gave you. The form and title you inherited from your father are certainly impressive, but won't help you attain the Grail."

As he gaped at her, she reached for the teapot and refilled her cup. "I do hope you will attend my little soiree tomorrow night. I have always said every good crusade begins with a party."

"Lady Leverham . . ."

"Good day, Your Grace. I will not keep you any longer. If you would do me a great service on your way out, however . . ."

"Of course."

"Thank you. You will find Galahad somewhere near the door. Do inform him that eavesdropping is *not* worthy behavior for a monkey."

Speechless, Lucas plodded from the room. And very nearly

tripped over the monkey, who was sitting in the middle of the hall, casually grooming his long tail.

"Eavesdropping," Lucas heard himself mutter, "is *not* worthy behavior." Then he stepped around the beast and headed for the door.

Several minutes later he climbed into his cabriolet and guided the matched grays toward Oxford Street. He'd meant to take Deirdre to the old Marylebone Park. It was a bit of a mess due to Nash's sweeping alterations, but it was still pleasant enough—and removed from the prying eyes and flapping tongues that filled Hyde Park at this time of day.

Lucas needed to think. And Lady Leverham's words were far better fodder than why Deirdre had not been there. He rather suspected that if he set his mind to it with dedication, he would make some sense of the blathering about knights and honor. No, he amended. He already had.

He did not think Deirdre would have honored the betrothal even if he had spoken to her more all those years ago. Not once she'd met Jonas Macvail, certainly. He was getting a very good idea, nonetheless, of how he must have appeared to her then: a brash, arrogant, remote figure whose only cares seemed to be for useless adventure. Real or false, the image had been an unbecoming one. No wonder she'd disliked him from the beginning.

Come to think of it, he mused, he hadn't much cared for himself, either.

He wondered what Deirdre would have done all those years ago had he told her that, from the very first moment they'd met, she had made him feel like a simple man with simple, blood-stirring desires. That he'd completely forgotten the lifelong task of pleasing his father and had been consumed with thoughts of how he could please *her* once they were married. That he'd fallen in love with her without ever having exchanged a word.

All of that, he knew, was useless speculation. He'd lost the chance. The real question now, and he couldn't help but be irked that Lady Leverham of all people had been the one to express it so succinctly, was whether he would make use of the brain and voice God had given him.

He wanted Deirdre Macvail, probably more desperately than he had seven years earlier. And he figured he had half the likelihood of winning her.

"Bloody hell," he cursed, and jerked his team to the side of the street. He had no idea what he was going to say to Deirdre, but he wasn't about to skulk off and sulk when he could be saying something.

He would park himself in front of Lady Leverham's house, and when Deirdre arrived, he would . . .

The curricle rattled past him at a rapid clip, but not so fast that he missed seeing its occupants. His cousin was at the reins, Olivia Macvail seated several feet away. Between them, face shadowed by a deplorable straw bonnet, was Deirdre. One small gloved hand was wrapped firmly around Francis's arm.

All in all they looked like a very contented party indeed.

11

"I'M NOT GOING."

Lucas tugged the cravat knot loose, unwound the linen from about his neck, and dropped it defiantly on the bed. He then scowled down at his valet, silently daring the man to say a single word. Lowry merely scooped up the mangled cravat and, with a resigned sigh, returned to the dressing room.

"Why should I?" Lucas continued ill-temperedly to himself as he stalked across the room in search of his abandoned brandy glass. "She obviously didn't want to see me yesterday." He found the glass atop the bureau, tossed back the inch that remained in the bottom, and glared at Lowry who had reappeared in the doorway. "I might be a fool," he muttered, "but I am not a stupid fool."

The valet's brows rose, but he murmured an appropriate, "Of course not, Your Grace."

Lucas squinted at the man's hands. "What is that you have there?"

"A fresh cravat, Your Grace. The last one seems to have lost its starch."

"Lowry, you're dismissed," Lucas snapped, then told the man in no uncertain terms what he could do with the cravat.

"That sounds most uncomfortable, Your Grace, and you do not pay me enough to endure such distress."

Lucas grabbed the brandy decanter from the bedside table and refilled his glass. Dropping heavily onto the mattress, he prepared to drink himself into a better mood. The first two glasses hadn't done much along those lines. "A man has a right to change his mind, damn it."

"Of course he does." Lowry stepped forward, cravat extended.

"Come any closer, and you will be looking for a new position."

"A worthy threat." The valet leaned forward and removed the glass from Lucas's hand, replacing it with the linen. "I recommend a Waterfall."

"What for? I told you I am not going."

"True. No, no. Right over *left*, Your Grace. Here, allow me."

Lucas released the ends of the cravat and reclaimed his brandy. "Why on earth do we need women, Lowry?"

"Continuation of the line, Your Grace."

"You don't have a *line*."

"Ah, quite right." The valet efficiently, and tightly, began the knot. "I suppose it must have something to do with their smell, then."

Deirdre always smelled faintly of roses. Lucas's body tightened, and he cursed. "I cannot marry simply because the witch smells nice."

"Perhaps not, but you do have a line to continue."

Lucas grunted and pushed himself to his feet. "Francis can do that. God, what a thought." He stalked across the room and dropped into a chair. "So there we have it. I don't need the woman at all."

Oh, but he did. He needed her to make him feel that he was fine the way he was. And Deirdre did just that, without trying at all. Amazing, he thought bitterly, that seven years after making him feel an inch tall, her simple presence could now convince him that he was the biggest man on earth.

He had fumbled his way through the day, alternately longing for and dreading the evening. He would see Deirdre; she would explain her absence of the day before and melt his rigid bones with a smile. He would see Deirdre; she would cut him off at the knees with cool indifference.

"Damn it, Lowry, how old am I?"

"You will be one-and-thirty at your next birthday, Your Grace."

"Damned right." Past thirty and behaving like a carbuncle-faced schoolboy. "When do we grow up?"

"I have no idea, Your Grace." The valet proffered two stickpins.

127

"Sapphire or ruby? I am afraid the diamond's setting was bent somewhat when you . . . er . . . removed the last cravat."

Lucas, deep in his ponderings of adulthood, petulantly shoved Lowry's hand away. "I don't want either one. I'm not going."

He wasn't coming.

Deirdre scanned the crowd once again, and once again saw no sign of Lucas. Of course, it was hard to see much of anything in the crush. Almost from the moment the first guests had stepped across the threshold of the Leverham house, there had barely been room to breathe. How ludicrous, she thought, what a bit of paint and some silly gossip could do for a hostess's reputation. No doubt Lady Leverham's staff would be pulling empty glasses and half-eaten foodstuffs from every corner for days to come.

The house was filled to bursting. Deirdre kept looking, however, for one towering ash brown head. Lucas had been gone by the time she'd rushed up the steps and through the hallway the preceding day. Lady Leverham, comfortably working her way through a plate of biscuits, had been vague as to how long he'd waited, and even more vague as to any message he had left.

Now Deirdre set her gaze resolutely on the ballroom entrance and willed him, as she had since the party began, to walk through it. By this time she had very nearly mastered the art of watching the door while listening to whatever bit of tripe was being imparted by her present companion. In the past hour the place beside her had been occupied by Lady Hythe, Francis, Evan, and several persons who had never spoken to her before.

At present George Burnham was standing rather too close and speaking entirely too loud. "Splendid fellow, your husband. Always thought so. Can't say the same of Conovar. Too full of himself by half, even at Eton."

Deirdre briefly surveyed the man's ornately styled hair, cheek-brushing collar points, and raised quizzing glass. Everything about him was overdone by half, except perhaps his speech. That was consistently half formed. "I did not know His Grace at Eton, of course," she said mildly, "but I imagine he was not so different from now—"

"Quite. Pompous, thoughtless creature."

"Actually, I was going to say that the duke impresses me as being a very fine man."

"Does you proud, your graciousness." Burnham squinted approvingly through his glass. "Fellow doesn't deserve it, I say. Not after all he's done."

"Really, sir—"

"No demurrals, dear lady. Always mean what I say."

Deirdre sighed. "Yes, I'm sure you do."

A pox on her promise to Lucas. She was determined to put an end to the ridiculous gossip. Unfortunately, each person to whom she tried to assert his honor had been equally determined not to listen. Even more frustrating was the fact that they seemed set on lauding her saintly nature.

Her saintly nature was being sorely tested. Gentle rebuttals of the jibes directed at the duke clearly were not going to work. She was ready to try pounding some sense into dense heads with a brick.

Unfortunately, there were no bricks at hand. There was champagne, however, and she grabbed a glass from a passing tray. Perhaps a saint would not have indulged in three glasses, but she was hardly in a holy frame of mind. She was annoyed, impatient, and slightly giddy.

In short she did not feel at all like herself, and it was most disconcerting.

She drew a deep, fortifying breath and heard Mr. Burnham murmur, "I say. I do say . . ."

This time, when she glanced at him, she did not meet his eyes. They were fixed on her bodice. "Oh, for heaven's sake," she snapped, and had the satisfaction of seeing a dull flush creep up the man's cheeks.

She had no idea why she had allowed Olivia to coax her into commissioning the dress in Edinburgh, even less as to how she had ended up in it now. The emerald silk was lovely and lush to the touch. She was convinced the seamstress had left a necessary piece out of the bodice. The pattern had certainly looked modest enough in the book. The finished product had made her gape at herself in the mirror. Had Livvy not thrown a foot-stomping fit when she tried to remove it, she would have relegated it to the depths of the wardrobe.

Sighing, she tried to discreetly shrug the bodice up a few inches. Mr. Burnham cleared his throat. Deciding enough was enough, Deirdre swallowed a good portion of her champagne, thrust the glass in the direction of her leering companion, and, not waiting to see if he caught it, struck off toward the door.

It was slow-going as the floor, beyond being terribly crowded, appeared to be sloping upward a tad. Her skirts, too, seemed determined to wrap themselves around her legs. All the more reason, she decided, to wear muslin. Silk was ever so clingy. Brushing one hand down her hip, she realized she was wearing only a single petticoat and wondered where the other had gone. Back into a drawer, she thought. Lady Leverham's doing. Something about fair ladies and the proper flow of the *bliaud*.

She took a few more careful steps and found herself face-to-face with Lord Hythe. Or rather, face-to-cravat, but it only took looking up to remedy the situation. It was a very attractive face, she decided, but far too stony. In fact, it rather reminded her of a sculpture from her mother's garden. Anne Fallam had been a very pious woman and had preferred biblical figures to their mythical counterparts.

"Saint Paul?" Deirdre speculated doubtfully.

Hythe's vividly dark brows rose a fraction. At least Deirdre thought they had. Perhaps not. Her vision was slightly wavery, and the earl was not known for his illuminating facial expressions. "I beg your pardon, Mrs. Macvail?"

"Saint Paul," she repeated. "Or was it Simon Peter? Someone who faltered a bit but ultimately got his head on straight. You remind me of him. Whoever he was."

"I see." Hythe appeared to ponder the matter. Then he lifted his chin and regarded her down the length of his formidable nose. "I trust you will inform me when you decide which I resemble."

"It would be my pleasure, my lord, but I fear it unlikely. He is settled in Somersetshire, you see, and I have no idea when I shall return there, if ever."

"I see," the earl said again. "May I be of some assistance, Mrs. Macvail?"

She was surprised—and slightly appalled—to hear herself giggle. "I do not think so, my lord, but thank you. It is a matter of choice that I do not visit Somerset, rather than a matter of ability."

"Ah. Well, I was referring to a glass of lemonade, actually. You seem a bit . . . overwarm, perhaps."

"Oh, not at all. I am perfectly comfortable. But thank you again. You are very kind." Deirdre spied Lord Fremont approaching from behind the earl, and decided it was time to be moving along. "I do hope you enjoy the rest of the evening."

She started to duck away, but he halted her with a firm hand on her wrist. "Do take care, Mrs. Macvail."

"Of course I will. And for what it's worth, I am usually far more reliable in my comparisons. I think it *was* Saint Peter. Good evening, sir."

It occurred to her as she wended her way toward the door that perhaps she'd had a bit too much champagne. It always muddled her brain. Well, she would simply stop with the next glass. It wouldn't do at all to get sotted. Not with Olivia to look after and Lucas to look for.

A footman trotted by, and Deirdre deftly snagged a glass from his tray. Rather pleased with her dexterity, she raised the glass for a celebratory sip. It was not until the rim bumped against her nose that she realized there was no champagne there.

"What perfect timing I have for once."

She peered over the rim of the flute. Evan, resplendent in a celestial blue coat, stood grinning at her, two glasses in hand. He smoothly replaced the one in her hand. "A toast," he said cheerfully, raising his flute, "to the worst crush of the Season."

Deirdre lost some of her champagne when someone jostled her from behind. "I must keep reminding myself that that is a good thing."

"The very best. I daresay our hostess is beside herself."

A quick glance across the room showed Lady Leverham to be beside Lady Vaer. The two looked equally content with life. "Evan," Deirdre said, surveying Lady Leverham's embroidered skirts and decidedly conical headdress, "I have a rather important question to ask you."

"By all means."

"Just what is a *bliaud*?"

"A what?"

Deirdre shook her head. "Oh, never mind. I was merely wondering if I were wearing one."

Evan tilted his head and gave her a long look. "What you are wearing," he announced finally, "is, in a word, a hazard."

"I quite agree. It has been trying to hobble me all evening. I should like to see you gentlemen wearing breeches sewn together at the knees. A hazard indeed."

"That is not precisely what I meant, my dear. When I said 'hazard,' I was implying the ability of such a dress to make a man trip over his own jaw."

"Really?" Inordinately pleased, Deirdre beamed at him. "What a lovely thing to say."

"Actually, it was a shocking thing to say." Evan leaned forward and captured her jaw with his free hand. "Good Lord. You're foxed, Mrs. Macvail."

"Mmm. I don't think so. Not quite. But I really ought to give this back to you before I become so." She held out her glass and was astonished to find it empty. "Well, bother. Did I do that?"

"I fear so. Come along, madam lush. I believe a bit of fresh air is called for."

Deirdre dug in her heels when he tried to guide her toward the windows. "I cannot go anywhere, Evan. I must stay right here." She pointed at the floor for emphasis.

"And why is that?"

"I am waiting."

"Waiting. Of course. Silly of me." Evan smiled faintly. "And you are waiting for . . . ?"

"Lucas. He didn't wait yesterday, so I am waiting now."

"I take it there was no drive."

"No." Deirdre breathed out a melancholy sigh. "How long would you have waited, Evan? How long would you wait?"

"Good heavens. What a question. I . . . Deirdre?"

She barely registered the fact that she had grasped his arm. Tightly. "Well, it is about time."

Lucas stood in the doorway. Even from where she stood,

Deirdre could see that his expression was as grim as his stark black clothing. His eyes met hers, cool and impassive, dousing some of the champagne's rosy glow. "Oh, dear," she whispered.

Evan turned to follow her gaze. "So the king arrives," he murmured. "Doesn't look terribly cheerful, does he?"

"No, he doesn't."

"I . . . ah, Deirdre, perhaps we ought to go have a dance."

She lifted her chin and managed a smile. "Thank you, but no. I can handle this."

He nodded, then brushed her cheek with a knuckle. "I'm here if you need me."

"I know."

"Deirdre." He stopped her as she stepped away. "In answer to your question . . ."

"Yes?"

"I would have waited a very long time."

"Thank you, Evan." Warmed, heartened, Deirdre made her slightly shaky way toward Lucas.

He was having a rather difficult time remembering that he was angry with her. In fact, as she walked toward him, all ivory skin and emerald silk, the very idea seemed absurd.

Ah, but he did have a reason, he reminded himself sternly. She had been off cavorting with his cousin when she should have been cavorting with him. She had been snuggled up against the bounder in his carriage when she should damn well have been snuggled up against him in his carriage. And now she was crossing the floor, a vision of far too much ivory skin and far too little emerald silk, and she was smiling . . . hesitantly . . . at him.

"Well, hell," Lucas muttered, and went to meet her halfway.

Her smile widened as he closed the gap between them. It was a brilliant greeting, and a welcome, and Lucas nearly tripped over his own feet. He heard soft strains of music, thought he truly had gone a bit mad until he realized it was coming from the next room.

A dance. Yes, that would do very nicely. He would simply sweep Deirdre onto the floor, her hand in his, and let explanations wait till later.

He almost tripped for a second time when a trim little figure stepped right in front of him. The half bottle of brandy he'd consumed and his haste to get to Deirdre joined forces against his equilibrium, and only the abrupt locking of his knees kept him from plowing right over Hythe's tiny mother. As it was, he rocked forward on his toes before coming to a jarring halt.

"I am most sorely disappointed in you, Conovar!" the countess announced without preamble, jabbing a delicate finger into his chest. "I had hoped you might suffer a twinge of conscience, but it appears you are quite without a conscience."

"Madam, I do not . . ." He darted a helpless glance over the lady's head. Deirdre had come to a standstill several feet away and was watching the exchange with wide eyes. "I am afraid I do not . . ."

Lady Hythe appeared to grow several inches, and he realized she was now standing on her toes. With her out-thrust jaw and snapping eyes, she looked like a vengeant fairy.

"Have you not done enough already, young man? Have you no shame?"

Lucas closed his eyes and prayed for patience. The countess poked him again. "Lady Hythe, I understand that you are upset—"

"*Upset?* I am utterly enraged!"

"—but it really would help if you would be so kind as to tell me what I have done this time."

"I am less concerned at the moment, Conovar, with what you have done," she snapped, "than with what you are going to do."

As always, Lucas did not have a difficult time imagining the woman indulging in such an act as seeing into the future. He, however, possessed no such talent. "Tell me, madam. I am going to . . ."

"You are *not* going to lure that poor girl into a sham engagement! Not if I can possibly stop you. Do you hear me?"

"I believe everyone heard you, my lady."

Lucas blinked. Deirdre, who had been standing behind the countess only moments before, had somehow slipped between them and was now planted firmly there, hands on her hips. "Ah, Deirdre . . ."

"Don't you dare tell me to sit back and take this quietly, Lucas," she snapped. "This is my concern. Now, Lady Hythe, I do not know where you get your information, but I assure you, it is *not* reliable."

To his great surprise, the countess's face promptly softened into an apologetic smile. "Oh, my dear girl. I am so sorry for all of this. But"—the steel returned to her eyes—"I fear my source is most reliable. Conovar has every intention of charming you into an attachment and then . . ." She spread her hands expressively. "Well, you cannot doubt his intentions after that."

Lucas heard Deirdre mutter something that, if he were not mistaken, was one of Jonas Macvail's favorite lurid curses. The following, "Rubbish!" was louder.

"I'm afraid not, Mrs. Macvail." The dozens of eyes previously fixed on the fascinating scene now slewed toward Francis. "Sorry, cousin," he said to Lucas, sounding anything but contrite, "but I've heard it, too."

"And I." George Burnham waved his quizzing glass in the air to emphasize his agreement.

"I, too," came from somewhere to Lucas's right, followed by a veritable chorus of affirmatives.

"So speaks the jury of my peers," he muttered dryly.

Deirdre spun and gaped at him. Several gold curls had come loose from the tight knot, and Lucas was once again reminded of the fiery creature who had faced him down all those years before. He half expected her to give him a well-remembered blast of temper.

She did.

"How can you be so *blithe* about this?" she shouted, actually shaking a fist in his face. "Stand up for yourself!"

"Mrs. Macvail, perhaps you ought to listen . . ." His cousin stepped forward and barely avoided being coshed on the chin when Deirdre rounded on him, fist still in the air.

"Oh, cork it, Francis!" she snapped. Then, spinning again, she pleaded, "I cannot do this alone. For God's sake, Lucas, for once, show some emotion!"

Awed, he stared down into the deliciously flushed face, and noticed suddenly that there was something a bit unfocused about her fierce gaze. Ignoring the muttering masses, he leaned forward to take a closer look. When Deirdre pulled her hand back to muffle

135

a hiccup, his vague suspicions were confirmed. His glorious, fiery, avenging angel was foxed. And ready to start a ballroom brawl for his honor.

Well, had there been even a smidgen of doubt, this would have blasted it. Never before had two blithering, bumbling fools been so well suited for each other.

Show some emotion, she'd said. Given a choice, his exhibition of emotion would involve hauling her into his arms and kissing her until they both expired from lack of air. No, he decided, far more effective to toss her over his shoulder and carry her out the door and all the way to Northumberland.

What a shame his own cup-shot state would probably have him dropping her on her delectable posterior before they reached the foyer.

She was still glaring at him, blissfully unaware of the thoughts rolling through his head. He rather suspected that, should he pucker up just then, she would pop him smartly in the mouth.

"Mrs. Macvail," he said softly, fighting a smile, "you are a wonder."

"No," she shot back, "I am a hazard. Evan said so."

"Did he indeed?"

Her brow furrowed. "Well, no. To be precise, he said my dress was a hazard. Do you think so?"

"I think we ought to leave my opinion of your dress until another time. For now, I suppose, we must deal with our audience."

She plunked her hands onto her hips again. "I trust you are going to put a stop to all these ludicrous slurs against you."

"What? And deprive Polite Society of its finest moment of righteous indignation? I think not."

"Oh, Lucas!"

He shrugged. "Just look at it this way, my dear: In a matter of days I have been accused of deceit, dastardly scheming against a lady, and murder. There is nothing left to be thrown at me."

Deirdre cast up her hands in disgust, but held her tongue. No one else seemed to have much to say, either. The following silence might have dragged on indefinitely had not someone seen fit to break it with a rather impressive bellow from the doorway.

"Curse you, Conovar! You have made a contract of honor, and I will not allow you to break it!"

Lucas turned slowly to face the new arrival. "Well, I'll be damned," he murmured. "It appears I was wrong."

12

L ORD VAER HAD arrived. And he did not appear to be in the party spirit. In fact, Deirdre mused as she surveyed his brilliantly red face and bulging eyes, someone had really best find him a cool drink and a chair before he launched his spirit into the hereafter.

"I won't have it, Conovar," he announced, shaking his fist as he stalked into the room. "You wanted my daughter, and you're damn well going to have her!"

There was a faint, distressed squeak from the crowd. Miss Vaer, Deirdre assumed. The squeak was followed by a muffled thump. Miss Vaer again, probably. The poor girl must have fainted and not been caught. Neither would be much of a surprise. Such a scene must have been quite horrifying to the girl. And anyone who might have been counted upon to halt her fall was otherwise occupied in watching Lord Vaer and Lucas.

Lucas's brows were elevated, and there was a dull flush around his collar. Otherwise, he looked perfectly calm. "Perhaps this is a discussion we ought to have in private, Vaer."

"I think not. Seems you have a nasty habit of saying one thing in private and doing another in public. I want to be certain you can't weasel out of this."

This time there was a hushed murmuring from the audience. Apparently, Deirdre decided, people felt confident that they could speak out against Lucas en masse with impunity. A solitary attack on his honor, however, caused collective nervousness.

She could see a muscle twitching in his jaw. "I suggest you restrain yourself from assaulting my honor, sir," he ground out. "I will only tolerate so much."

"*You* tolerate?" Vaer's face was now an alarming shade of purple. "God's teeth, man! You offered for my daughter, then pay court to another woman, and you dare to mention what *you* will tolerate?"

With an abruptness that startled her, he rounded on Deirdre. "Heed my words, madam. He will not marry you. Might set you up prettily as his bit o' muslin, but he won't hand over the ring. Not that he would have in any case, mind you, but he has a prior attachment. To my daughter!"

Deirdre glanced down to find Lucas's hand gripping her elbow. It took a moment for her to realize he was, in fact, holding her up. She hadn't even noticed that her knees had gone to jelly. She'd been too busy absorbing the farce in front of her.

"Is it true?" she demanded, grateful that her voice was stronger than her legs. "Are you engaged?"

"Deirdre—"

"Not that it matters to me, Your Grace, but it might matter a great deal to Miss Vaer."

"Damn you, Vaer," Lucas muttered, then turned his back on the fuming viscount and grasped Dierdre's other arm, forcing her to face him. "No. It is not true. There is no engagement. There has been no—"

"No engagement?" Vaer sputtered. "Did we not sit in White's less than a fortnight ago discussing settlements? I say we did, sir!"

"And I say it was nothing more than the most casual of explorations. For heaven's sake, man, you bloody well know that!"

"I know nothing of the sort. What I know is that I mentioned her twenty thousand, and you countered with the land in Hampshire and the hunting box in Scotland."

As Deirdre watched, Lucas's mouth thinned further and the red flush crept upward toward his jaw. "There is no hunting box, Vaer. Now, Deirdre, please—"

"No hunting box, hmm? I specifically recall mention of it, Conovar. In Argyll, I believe. And damn me if I wouldn't remember mention of a place in such prime deer territory."

Lucas ignored him. "Deirdre, listen to me. Yes, yes, I know it doesn't matter to you, but I still want you to know I made no offer for anyone. Anyone since you seven years ago. I thought about it, spoke to Vaer . . ."

She believed him, felt relief slide through her body like a warm breeze, replacing the sadly vanished glow from the champagne. She knew he would have to marry at some point, but, oh, she was happy to know it would not be to Elspeth Vaer with her upthrust nose and smug smile.

She was even more gladdened to know that Lucas had not lied to her.

"Red Branch something!" Vaer crowed. "That was the name of the place. See, Conovar? I remember it all. Refute me if you can!"

"Red Branch . . . Oh, God," Deirdre whispered, too much becoming clear too quickly. "Not you. Tell me it isn't you who owns my home." He said nothing, merely tightened his grip on her arms. *"Tell me it isn't you!"*

"Deirdre, I'm sorry. I meant to . . . I was going to . . ."

"When, Lucas? When did you buy the lien?"

"Listen to me, I—"

"When?"

He flinched at the sharp exclamation. "A long time ago," he admitted. "Perhaps six months after you and Jonas moved in. I intended to—"

Numb now, oblivious to the fury she knew was bubbling deep within her, Deirdre closed her eyes and said, "I can imagine exactly what you intended. Why didn't you cast us out? You've had years to do it."

Her eyes snapped open when he gave her a quick shake. "Tell me what I *ever* did to injure you. You tell me what ghastly revenge I ever enacted against you and Jonas, and maybe you'll think again before asking me something like that."

True. Perhaps it was true, she conceded. But she could not excuse the fact that he had owned her *home*, the one place she had ever felt completely at peace, for nearly seven years. He had taken her money, raised the rent—or allowed it to be raised—had a tight hold over her almost from the first moment they had met.

Seven years of her life had gone, in one way or another, to Lucas Gower. And she'd felt so horribly guilty for thinking ill of him.

"You lied to me, Lucas."

"I did no such thing. I simply did not tell you that I owned a piece of property in Scotland."

"Fine. Play semantics if you wish. I imagine the rules are rather the same as chess: maneuver your opponent into check. Just tell me now that you did not buy the cottage . . . that you didn't keep your ownership of it in order to have your revenge."

"Oh, for pity's sake, Deirdre—" He broke off suddenly, eyes bleak.

"You cannot deny it. Oh, Lucas." Composing her features, willing her shaky legs to support her, she glanced coldly down at his hands, where they wrapped warmly and completely around her upper arms. "Release me, please."

"Deirdre."

"Let go of me, Your Grace."

He did. Of course he did—at least as far as letting his hands drop. He had been working on letting go of Deirdre Macvail for a very long time and, he thought grimly, had developed a certain proficiency at the motions.

"What do we do now?" he asked hoarsely.

She rubbed absently at her arms and gave him a level stare. "*We* do nothing. I am going to go compose a letter to my solicitor, instructing him to find me another house. I suggest you take Lord Vaer back to your club and come to an agreement as to whether or not you are going to marry his daughter. Who"—she peered into the crowd—"will quite probably have something to say on the matter when she regains consciousness. Listen to what she has to say, Your Grace."

Deirdre stepped around him without sparing him another glance. "As for you, Lord Vaer, you ought to be ashamed of yourself."

The man flushed and blustered, "Sorry about that bit o' muslin bit, Mrs. Macvail. Didn't mean anything by it."

"Yes, you did. But I imagine you were simply putting into words what the rest of Society is thinking, so I will not take offense. When I said you ought to be ashamed, however, I was referring to your participation in this appalling drama. I assume you were aiming for more in the match than a little house in

141

Scotland. A coronet for your daughter, perhaps? A Hampshire estate for you? A ducal grandson. That must be it." She shuddered visibly. "Dear God, you all disgust me."

She squared her shoulders, lifted her chin, and made her way through the parting crowd. Lucas shoved Vaer out of the way and went after her. "Deirdre, wait." He did not think she would have stopped had he not snared her wrist and planted himself solidly in front of her. "I want you to know, I was going to give you the house."

She refused to look at him. "I beg your pardon?"

"Red Branch Cottage. I'd made up my mind to sign it over to you. It should be yours."

Her smile would have frozen molten lead. "Would you care to say that again, a bit louder, perhaps? I daresay there are a few people in the back who did not hear you the first time."

"What the hell . . ." Glancing back at the several dozen rapt faces, he cursed harshly. "You bloody well know I didn't mean . . . I never intended to make you my . . . er . . ."

"Bit o' muslin?" she supplied blandly. "Well, that is most handy for you, Your Grace, as you possess nothing which would have tempted me anyway."

She tried to pull her arm from his grasp. He held on. "Damn it, Deirdre," he muttered, voice low and urgent, "don't do this. Don't you dare shut me out. Get angry, for God's sake. Shout at me . . . like you did once, all those years ago."

"Haven't we been through this before? I am not the same girl I was then. And I have no need to shout at you. It would only irritate my throat, and you already know precisely what you've done wrong. Now, take your hands off me. Please."

Her blasted cool was beginning to tear at his. "Come now, Mrs. Macvail. Here is your opportunity to have at me—in front of half the ton, no less. Don't be shy," he taunted, driven to desperation by her unflappable indifference. "Take your best shot. Can't you? God knows what happened to you in Scotland, but you most certainly are not the same girl who arrived here seven years ago. You are a pale shadow of her at best. What? *Nothing* to say?"

Something—ah, yes, something—flashed in the depths of her

eyes. "Very well, Your Grace. Tell me why Jonas had to leave the regiment."

"What?"

"You wouldn't tell me before. I want to know now. Why did he lose his commission?"

"Bloody hell, Deirdre. This is hardly the time or place to be discussing your husband."

"No?" She gestured to the still-enthralled crowd. "I would say it is the best of times and places. We all want to know." She leaned past him and stared fiercely at George Burnham. "Don't we all want to know, Mr. Burnham?"

"I . . . er . . . Yes, certainly, madam," the fellow stammered.

"There. You see?" Deirdre turned back to Lucas in triumph. "So tell us."

"For the last time, this is not about Jonas. This is about—"

"You? No, Your Grace. It is not. Trust me, not everything is about you."

Now she sounded smug, and Lucas saw red. "Fine. You want to know why Jonas was stripped of his commission. Fine." He could almost hear Jonas Macvail's raucous laugh. The blighted sod was taunting him even now, from well beyond the grave.

"I'll tell you, Deirdre. He was drummed out because he had a rather unfortunate predilection for going on leave whenever he wanted. And he seemed to have those urges frequently. Whenever a pretty face smiled invitingly at him, as a matter of fact." He drew a harsh breath. "There. Are you satisfied now? Does it help you in any way to know that your beloved Jonas liked the ladies? Will you be able to keep him alive even longer by lying in bed at night, wondering if he stopped loving them when he started loving you? *Well?*"

His head snapped back when her hand cracked against his cheek.

"You told me to take my best shot, Your Grace. I would venture to say I will be more satisfied with it than you will with yours. Now, do me the immeasurable favor of getting out of my way and out of my life!" With that she jerked her captive arm from his grasp and stalked toward the door.

Lucas mutely lifted his hand to his cheek, pressed it where hers

143

had struck. He saw her nearly plow over Althorpe, who had the misfortune to be in her path.

"Did you know, Evan?" she demanded.

"I . . . ah, about Jonas?"

"No. About my home. Did you know he owned my home?"

"I . . ." Althorpe shuffled his feet for a moment. "Yes. I knew."

Deirdre stared hard into his averted face and then, with a brisk nod, walked around him and out the door.

She left a deafening silence in her wake. For what seemed an eternity, no one moved. No one spoke. Then several people slipped quickly past Lucas and away. A faint buzzing started among the guests. A few more left. Off, no doubt, to spread the delicious tale now that it was clear the show was over.

Francis stopped as he reached Lucas. "Masterfully done, cousin," he announced with an unpleasant smile. "It takes a goodly amount of skill to treat a woman like both a whore and a naive little fool in the space of one evening. Truly masterful."

Burnham took his place an instant later. "Always knew you were a boor, Conovar. Surpassed yourself with this one, though."

The next ten minutes or so took on the properties of a reverse receiving line in hell. It occurred to Lucas that he could simply move away from the path to the door, but he did not possess the requisite energy.

The party clearly was over, and one by one the guests filed out. Some moved slowly, others with gleeful speed. Vaer thundered by, hauling his son and daughter with him. There was nothing animated or calculating about his expression, Lucas was forced to admit, but his pace was impressive.

"My children certainly won't be marrying you or anyone connected with you, Conovar," he snapped as he stalked past. "Hunting box be damned!"

Olivia did not bother speaking to him. She merely stared at him for a long moment. Then she stomped one slippered foot down atop his and huffed out of the room.

Had he been wearing boots, it would have been a futile act. As it was, however, his evening shoes did little to protect his instep. Lucas gritted his teeth, cursed silently, and resisted the urge to hop up and down on his uninjured limb.

"I expect that stung." He lifted his gaze from the little heel print on his shoe to find Lady Leverham studying him intently from beneath her drooping turban. "You dropped your lance, dear boy," she announced sadly. "Poor show for any knight." Then she patted his still-flaming cheek and trundled after her charges.

By this time the room was nearly empty. Lucas cringed as he saw Lady Hythe gather her shawl about her rigid shoulders and make her way toward him. He contemplated making a dive for the nearest window. After being blasted, singed, walloped, and stomped on, he did not think he would survive a tongue-lashing as well.

The countess stopped in front of him, shaking her head wearily. "You know, Conovar, I really am at a loss for words."

"Please, my lady. I would greatly appreciate it if you would not—"

"You are genuinely in love with her, aren't you?"

He felt his jaw dropping. "What was that?"

"I would not have believed it had it not been so terribly obvious. Well." Her pixie face creased into a bemused frown. "I suppose I should pity you, but I cannot. You deserve no such sentiment. The poor girl *does*. Come along, Hythe. I am ready to go home."

Like Livvy, the earl said nothing. He shrugged, face expressionless as always, and followed his mother out.

Lucas closed his jaw with an audible click. "I'll be damned," he muttered.

"You just might at that, old trout." Althorpe was leaning against the near wall, arms crossed over his chest. "Gripping performance all around. Dare I ask if there is an encore planned?"

Lucas glared at him. "With friends like you, I need chain mail."

"Oh, I'm not your friend, Conovar. I am merely an entertaining diversion at times. And, I must say, it was rather nice to have the roles reversed for once."

"Delighted to oblige," Lucas muttered.

"Of course you are. You've always been such a gracious fellow when it comes to public displays of emotions you don't possess." Althorpe levered himself away from the wall. "So was Lady Flighty correct? Are you in love with Deirdre?"

"Don't be absurd!" Lucas snapped. His pride had already taken enough of a beating. He did not think he could stand telling the truth and having Althorpe laugh in his face. "I simply thought to offer her—Oh, the hell with it."

"How infernal are our thoughts this eve. 'So farewell hope, and with hope farewell fear. Farewell remorse: all good to me is lost—' "

"Oh, for God's sake, don't blather Shakespeare at me now! I'm not in the mood, and you'll only get it wrong anyway."

Althorpe's fair brows rose until they nearly met his Byronic shock of fair hair. "Well, well. The king has spoken. For the record, Your Grace, that was not Shakespeare; it was Milton. *Paradise Lost*." He gave an insolent salute and spun on his heel.

"Where are you going?"

"I am going to see if Mrs. Macvail will accept my abject apologies for not telling her the truth. Then I am going home."

Lucas ran a weary hand over his eyes. "I need a drink. Come with me to Watier's?"

Althorpe gave a short laugh. "An invitation? Good heavens, a first! And no, thank you. I have better things to do."

Left alone, feeling somewhere in the vicinity of three inches tall, Lucas stood in the middle of the cleared room and waited for his legs to obey the command to move. When they did, he limped off in search of his hat and coat. They were not hard to find in the end. In fact, he nearly stepped on them as he scanned the vacant foyer for Peters. The butler had made his own eloquent statement by leaving the coat neatly folded in the middle of the floor, hat centered on top.

So the news had already spread throughout the large house. No doubt it would be all over Town by the time he reached the street.

Lucas glanced around the hall, debated finding a bellpull and tugging on it until someone arrived. He could try to find Deirdre himself, but imagined she would knock him over the head with a chamber pot should he burst into her bedroom.

In the end he opted for his own bedchamber. If he were to be battered again that night, he decided he should be the one doing the beating. He thought there was a formidable copy of *Paradise Lost* in his library. He could pound his head against that for a

146

few hours. Then he would decide what on earth he was going to do next.

"I think leaving Town for a few days would be a very good idea." Deirdre looked up hopefully from her facedown position on the bed, expecting her hostess to protest. "Only till Monday or Tuesday. I know you think me a terrible coward, but—"

"Dear girl." Lady Leverham rose from her chair and crossed the room to plop down on the mattress. She stroked Deirdre's tumbled curls. "I think you the most astonishingly brave creature in the Realm."

"Oh, please . . ."

"Well, I do!" The lady fumbled about her person for a handkerchief and came up with a pungent vinaigrette. "Do you need . . . ? No, no. Hold on a moment." She ended up collecting a handkerchief from Deirdre's dressing table. "Here you go, my dear."

"Thank you." Deirdre mopped at her damp cheeks, then noisily blew her nose. "You do not mind, then? Going away for a bit?"

"Not in the least. I think that would be a very good idea. My sister lives but two hours' drive from here. She will be delighted to have company."

Deirdre's shoulders sagged in relief. "You are too kind, madam."

"Oh, piffle. Some country air will do me a world of good. It will do us all good."

Deirdre wasn't certain that a few rural breezes would cure what ailed her, but they would at least blow away the weakest of the thoughts. "Could we go tomorrow?"

"As early as you like."

Her own mother had never encouraged confidences, had brushed off any tentative attempts she had made to share her adolescent woes. Now, as an adult, Deirdre did not know how to begin sharing with this warm, doting woman whose kindness had come to mean so much that it tugged at her heart.

"I cannot go home," she said quietly.

"Perhaps not." Lady Leverham gently stroked several new tears from her cheek. "But you have a home with us as long as you

147

need it. There is the house near Tarbet as well as the ones here and in Edinburgh. Take your pick, love. You know you are more than welcome."

Deirdre did not think she could stand to live in Tarbet, not when she would see her rosy little cottage every time she went to town. Perhaps Edinburgh . . .

"I thank you, with all my heart." She reached up to squeeze the woman's plump hand. "I . . . I don't have to decide just yet."

"No, you don't. We'll have a few days in the sun, then come back and see Livvy settled with her future earl. There will be plenty of time to make plans after that."

Deirdre recalled her words to Lord Vaer and winced. "I'm not certain Livvy's future earl will come up to snuff after tonight." Perhaps, she thought, that wasn't such a tragedy. "Lord Vaer might prove resistant to having his son marry into this family."

Lady Leverham smiled. "Oh, he might, but Teddy will make up his own mind. They always do."

"I wouldn't be so certain," Deirdre said doubtfully. "Young Mr. Vaer has never impressed me as having much of a backbone."

"Ah, but he possesses other things. Honestly, my dear, you mustn't look at me as if I've spoken in Chinese. I know all about men's brains. They use them so rarely, but tend to do the right thing when they do."

Deirdre chuckled. She couldn't help it. "I do adore you, madam."

"And I you, dear girl. Now, what are you going to do about Conovar?"

"I am not going to do anything about Conovar," she replied tightly, all amusement gone. "I am going to do my very best to avoid him during whatever time I must spend here. Then I am going to vacate *his* house and never think of him again."

"Mmm. Well, if you are determined to do so, I won't try to dissuade you. I must say, however, that the pair of you seem to have done rather nicely together of late."

"I was being polite!" Deirdre snapped, then added quietly, "Forgive me, my lady. I am not myself tonight."

"No? I rather think you have been precisely yourself, and it has been splendid to see." Lady Leverham raised a conciliatory hand

148

at Deirdre's sharp look. "I won't say any more on the subject. We have more important matters to consider just now. For instance, which of us is going to tell dearest Olivia that she is going to miss the Winslow fete?"

"Oh. Oh, dear. I hadn't even thought . . ."

Deirdre groaned and dropped her forehead onto the counterpane. It was a brief moment of weakness. She was on her feet moments later, and preparing for battle with some enthusiasm. She knew that if there were one thing that would keep her from wallowing in her own heartbreak, it was a good tantrum from someone else.

13

FOUR DAYS. FOUR days of staying completely out of Deirdre's life, and all Lucas could find out from his determined inquiries was that she had left Town.

Oh, he'd wanted to obey her decree that he leave her alone, if only because it was the sole thing she had ever asked of him. But he couldn't. Not finding her home the first day had been no great surprise. Calls, shopping, strolls in the park . . . He had created a number of explanations, any preferable to the probability that she *was* home and refusing his call.

The entire Leverham-Macvail coterie had been conspicuous in its absence from the opera that night. Everyone knew Lady Leverham did not miss a performance of Handel's *Rinaldo*. Lady Leverham did not miss anything with a connection to the Crusades.

By late afternoon of the second day, when he had been again informed by the redoubtable Peters that Mrs. Macvail was not in, Lucas had become suspicious. When she failed to appear at Lady Winslow's costume ball, he was certain something was amiss. On the third day he'd started asking questions of everyone he could get to speak to him.

He knew there was more to the story than he was receiving, but no one seemed willing to enlighten him. In fact, whenever he had tried, as tactfully as possible, to glean some information, even the loosest tongues in the ton had ceased flapping. Teddy Vaer, the garrulous fool himself, had shut up like a netted clam when Lucas got within ten feet.

Thoroughly annoyed and verging on frantic, he had tried to locate Althorpe. That uncooperative bounder was nowhere to be found. A desperate man by the third day, Lucas had finally turned to desperate means. He'd cornered Lady Hythe.

He had gotten straight to the point. "Where is Mrs. Macvail?"

Despite the fact that the woman clearly would have preferred to speak to the devil, she'd put on an impressive show. He had managed to maneuver her into a corner of the Tarrant ballroom and, when it became evident that the cut direct was not going to work, the countess had stiffened her spine, stuck her chin into the air, and glared at his waistcoat buttons.

"If you were a gentleman, Conovar," she'd announced tartly, "you would not ask me to betray a friend's confidence. I will tell you nothing."

"If I were *not* a gentleman, my lady, and you not the mother of an old acquaintance, I would be conducting this interview with a good deal more force."

It was undoubtedly the least respectful address the countess had ever received, though clearly no more than she would have expected from him. But it seemed to work. She snapped her ridiculous little fan open and tried to step back, but Lucas had her trapped by a wall and a formidable potted plant.

It had taken him a good half hour to stalk her all the way around the cavernous room, and now it looked like the only reward he was going to get for his effort was to have her swat him on the chin.

He'd been ready to abandon the whole thing in disgust when she announced, "I will not tell you where Deirdre is, young man. I will, however, tell you this: For some unfathomable reason, the girl seems determined to continually forgive you for your appalling treatment of her. I do not think you have any idea of what a gift that is, but if you have an ounce of brains in your head, you will figure it out!"

Then, with formidable strength for such a tiny creature, she had pushed past him, leaving him to glare at the wall.

Of course he knew what a gift he had been given. And he fully intended to express his gratitude every day for the rest of his life. Once he'd gotten Deirdre back, of course. He had recently come to the distressing conclusion that as inconceivably successful as he'd been in bringing her into his life—twice—he was a complete and utter failure at keeping her there.

He wondered if there were a book somewhere on the subject. *A Bumbling Gentleman's Guide for the Prevention of Alienating the Woman He Adores.* No doubt sales of that one would be immense, if only it existed—and if only men weren't so bloody resistant to lay even the lowest of heart cards on the table.

Lucas was more than ready to lay out the whole damned suit.

Now, low on options and at a total loss as to where the Leverham household might have gone, he was slouched in his favorite chair at his club, hoping that a brandy would produce a helpful vision. One benefit to being something of a persona non grata, he decided, was that no one bothered him. No nasty new tales had surfaced in the past several days, but neither had the old ones disappeared. No one save the occasional footman came anywhere near him. He was approaching the half-empty point in his snifter, when a familiar figure sauntered through the door.

"Althorpe!" he bellowed, making his target, several footmen, and those club members present jump. "Bring your sorry self over here!"

Althorpe obeyed but not, Lucas noticed, without some reluctance. "Well, this is a new style for you," he commented blandly, gesturing to Lucas's unshaven jaw and wrinkled coat. "Did Lowry quit again, or are you looking to take up where Brummell left off?"

"Shut up. Sit down." Lucas jerked his chin toward the facing chair. "Damn it, man, sit!" Then before his order had been obeyed, "Where in the hell have you been?"

Althorpe took his seat with aggravating slowness. "Bath. Auntie Wilhelmina was taking the waters, and the noxious stuff tends to relax her purse strings along with her gout. I was only gone for three days." He jumped when Lucas's glass hit the table. "Why?"

"Because I've been looking for you all week. No one will tell me where Deirdre is."

"And you think I know?"

"Yes. I think you know. I think *everyone* knows but me."

"Hmm." Althorpe flagged down a footman and requested a

brandy. "Did it ever occur to you that perhaps Mrs. Macvail does not want you to know where she is?"

Lucas's fingers curled around the arms of his chair. "Yes, Althorpe, it occurred to me. And I don't give a damn if she wants to be found. I intend to find her."

"Why?"

"*Why?* I should think that would be perfectly obvious."

"Humor me." Althorpe's brandy arrived. "What is so important that it cannot wait for her return?"

Lucas came halfway out of his seat. "She is returning?"

"Sit down, Conovar. Before I tell you anything, I want an answer. How do you plan to hurt her this time?"

Stunned, Lucas dropped back into his seat. "That isn't fair, man."

"No? It seems to me that you've rolled right over Deirdre at every opportunity. What do you plan to do this time? Hand over a detailed log of her husband's transgressions?"

"Damn you, Althorpe . . ."

"Damn *you*, Conovar! You've gone through life having everything you wanted dropped at your feet. And you've taken it all without so much as a by-your-leave or a thought for what anyone else wants. Well, Deirdre didn't want you seven years ago, and it bloody well looks like she doesn't want you now!"

"I need her."

"And furthermore, if you think I . . ." Althorpe squinted at him. "What was that?"

"I need her," Lucas repeated. "This has nothing to do with wanting . . . though there is that, too. I *need* her in my life."

"And what of her needs?"

Lucas shook his head. "I'm not so arrogant as to think I can answer all of them. But I'd like to try."

"You'd like to try." Althorpe snorted in disgust. "Well, I'm certain she would be just overjoyed with the prospect of having you blundering through her life like a half-blind bull searching for the red cape."

"Perhaps not, but that's her choice, isn't it?"

"Ah, a choice. You intend to give her one, then."

"Althorpe."

153

"Quite right, it is her choice. So I suppose I might as well tell you. Deirdre and Olivia have been at Lady Leverham's sister's home at Windsor. I escorted them there myself. They should have returned by now."

This time, Lucas all but shot from his seat. "Thank you. I . . . thank you."

Althorpe shrugged. "You would have found out sooner or later. Before you go haring off, however, there are several more things you really should hear."

Gratitude won out over eagerness. "And those are?"

"Your cousin was to join them the second day and escort them back this morning."

Lucas cursed under his breath. The last scene he wanted to imagine was of Deirdre and Francis lounging in the sunlight on some idyllic Surrey estate. "Fine. Francis was there. What else?"

"She was justifiably upset by this latest chapter in your gothic novel of betrayal and revenge."

"Hell. I've owned up to that one, and she knows the rest is untrue."

"Does she?" Althorpe demanded. "Does anyone but you know what is untrue and what isn't? All evidence points against you, my friend."

"Deirdre knows," Lucas said flatly. "Now, was there more?"

"Only this. You don't deserve her."

"Of course I don't deserve her." He ran a hand wearily across the back of his neck. "What man possibly could?"

Althorpe stared at him for a long moment, then waved him away. "Go on, then. I haven't anything else to say."

Lucas was out the door and on the street seconds later, leaving his hat and stick behind. He wouldn't need them. Unless, of course, he had to fend off the collective rage of the Leverham household. In that case, his boots ought to serve well enough for a desperate escape. He started jogging through the light London fog toward Berkeley Square. With divine providence, Deirdre would speak to him.

He was winded by the time he reached the Leverhams' front door. He paused for a minute to lean against the jamb and regain his breath before pounding at the brass knocker. It took the butler a damnably long time to appear. When he did, his greeting was something less than gracious.

"Yes, Your Grace?"

Lucas drew a shaky breath and demanded, "I wish to see Mrs. Macvail."

He half expected to receive a faceful of painted wood, but Peters pulled the door inward and stepped aside. "If you will follow me, Your Grace, I will inquire as to whether Mrs. Macvail is in."

Lucas followed the man's rigid back up the stairs and allowed himself to be shut in the parlor. He paced the confines of the room as he waited, berating himself for not going home first. A shave, a bath, and a change of clothes would have been a good idea. Any of the three alone would have been an improvement over his current state. Not that how he looked mattered much. Words mattered, and he had a great many planned.

When the door opened, he nearly leapt toward it. But it was not Deirdre's slender form that entered. Peters gave him a bland look and announced, "I regret to inform you that Mrs. Macvail is not in."

If the man possessed any regret whatsoever, Lucas decided, it was that he could not accompany the announcement with a swift kick to the departing ducal posterior.

"Check again," he suggested grimly. "You might be surprised by what you find. I will wait as long as necessary."

Peters did not budge. "I do not know when Mrs. Macvail will be available, Your Grace. Perhaps not for a long time." The man's ramrod-straight back managed to stiffen even further. "An extremely long time."

Lucas had a strong urge to plop down in the nearest chair, cross his arms, thrust out his jaw, and inform the insolent sod that he wasn't going anywhere until he'd seen Mrs. Macvail. An extremely strong urge.

He resisted it. "Very well," he muttered, the words sticking in his throat. "Very well."

Wishing he had his stick, just so he could jauntily swing it as he left, he plodded from the room.

"Have you a message for Mrs. Macvail, Your Grace?" Peters's step, as he followed into the hall, was audibly light.

"Yes." Lucas came to halt on the landing. "You may tell her that I will—No." He started down the stairs, eyes fixed squarely on the door below. "I have no message."

Deirdre stood by an upstairs window and watched him go. He paused at the bottom of the stairs, and she was ready to step hurriedly back should he turn and look up. He did not, but continued on his way.

She knew she ought to have faced him, perhaps even listened to what he had to say. She simply didn't feel strong enough. There had been so much ill sentiment between them. And a few brief days of accord. It was very hard on the spirit, she decided, to have one's emotions bounced around so.

Better, she knew, to just stay away from the Duke of Conovar. She didn't think she could handle any more disappointment.

As she watched, he turned the corner and disappeared down Hill Street. "Oh, Lucas." She sighed, her breath condensing on the cool glass. She stroked a finger down the patch but wavered at the bottom. Then, instead of making the familiar upward curve to the left, forming a J, she drew a straight line the other way. "Why couldn't we have met now, for the first time?"

Silly, she chided herself, clearing the window with a single swipe of her palm. Had they not met all those years before, she would probably not be here now. She would not have met Jonas, not have fallen in love with him and his family.

People blamed the Duke of Conovar for her sorrows, conveniently ignoring the fact that he had been responsible for the joy as well.

Shaking her head to dispel the heavy thoughts, she prepared for bed. Tomorrow she would decide how best to get through the rest of the Season. For now she needed a good night's sleep and a pleasant dream or two.

After donning her nightgown, she sat at the dressing table and removed the last pins from her hair. It fell heavily over her shoulders and halfway down her back in thick curls. Ignoring the silver-backed brush for the moment, Deirdre propped her chin on her palm and regarded her reflection in the mirror. It was something she did as seldom and briefly as possible. Her opinion, gleaned from many years of experience, was that she never saw in her face what others did.

To her eyes she always looked pale, gaunt, and slightly muted, as if she'd missed some vital illumination. The image that looked back at her now was unfamiliar somehow. In the candlelight her skin had a rosy tint. And with her hair uncustomarily free to frame her face, the sharp angles were softened. Most surprising was the soft glint in her eyes. They gazed boldly back, speaking of some knowledge gained and strength bolstered.

Perhaps the days at Windsor had helped after all. She certainly hadn't felt rested while there. Beyond the sunshine and fresh air, there had been little to inspire feelings of peace. Lady Leverham had fretted and fussed, urging plates full of sugary pastries and nattering vague monologues about Crusades. Deirdre did not know much about King Richard the Lionhearted beyond the typical schoolroom text. She was reasonably certain, however, that the man had not found his solace in lemon cakes.

Livvy, furious at having been dragged away from her social demesne, had pouted, squabbled with Francis, and written long letters to Teddy Vaer which had gone promptly into the fire. Deirdre was somewhat heartened by the destruction. If Olivia did not post her missives, it was likely there was no engagement. Deirdre hoped Livvy would tell her of any such development, but considering the girl's present frame of mind, she quite probably wouldn't share anything more intimate than her laundry list.

No, it had not been a particularly peaceful interlude. The only quiet moments had been when Olivia and Francis had been apart, or taken their bickering out of doors. Apparently Francis was in full agreement with Deirdre as to Teddy Vaer's character. Not that he ever said anything which wasn't absolutely true, but no young lady wanted to hear that her favored suitor was a soft-headed, indolent fop.

Sighing, Deirdre decided she really should check on Olivia. The girl had been uncustomarily subdued during the drive back and, after reading the large number of messages left by disappointed playmates, had retired to her bed. All signs pointed to an epic sulk.

If Olivia truly wanted Mr. Vaer, and if he had the gumption to defy what would certainly be severe disapproval from his parents, there was little Deirdre could do about it. But she could not banish the conviction that it was a very poor match indeed.

She twisted her hair into a loose braid, donned her dressing gown, and padded into the hall. She had no idea what she was going to say should she find Olivia awake. Simple logic and dubiously sage advice would not work. Not with Livvy. Perhaps, she thought wryly, she ought to go into wide-eyed raptures over the indolent Teddy's vast appeal. Throughout history there had never been anything so capable of cooling young ardor than the unconditional blessing of an authority figure.

No light showed from beneath Livvy's door. Not that it indicated much of anything. Olivia had been known to do some of her very best moaning in the dark. Deirdre tapped gently at the panels. Receiving no answer, she turned the handle and crept inside.

In the faint light of her candle, she could see the familiar tumble of clothing. The girl always packed and unpacked as if she were standing in the midst of a wind squall. Smiling slightly, Deirdre moved farther into the room. The lump in the middle of the bed did not move.

The lack of motion did not disturb Deirdre. Livvy, once asleep, slept like the dead. The precise, centered location of the mass was a different matter. Livvy slept like the dead—in the wake of a battle, limbs sprawled in every direction.

Alarmed now, Deirdre rushed forward and threw back the neatly arranged quilt. The pile of rolled clothing wavered for a moment, then separated and spilled over the sheets.

"Oh, dear God."

Her first impulse was to run shouting back into the hall and rouse the entire household. She bit her knuckle to stifle the cry. Waking the Leverhams would serve no purpose, at least not yet. Drawing a deep breath, she forced her racing heart to calm. A cursory glance around the chamber offered no clues as to where Livvy had gone. Then a draft lifted the gauzy curtains of the corner window.

Deirdre did not know what she expected to see when she got there and leaned out. A rope of sheets, perhaps? But there was only brick and ivy stretching to the garden below.

Biting hard at her lip, she scanned the room again. Oh, she had a very good, though perfectly horrifying idea where Livvy had gone. She just needed to be sure. No, she amended, what she truly needed was to learn that this was all an elaborate prank, that Livvy was giggling in another chamber, anticipating the shock her cold-hearted guardian would have on finding her missing from her bed.

The Macvail siblings were known practical jokers. This, how-ever, was not even remotely equivalent to putting frogs in Deirdre's stocking drawer. She liked frogs. Cold chills and immi-nent demise from a failed heart were not nearly so innocuous.

Perhaps she would have noticed the sheet of paper on the writing desk sooner had she not been accustomed to seeing the surface covered with anything *but* paper. Now the collection of gloves and ribbons had been shoved to the side. Legs shaky, fin-gers more so, she crossed the room and lifted the sheet.

Dearest DeeDee,
I hope you will not be too upset with me. Yes, you will, but I trust it will not last long. I am only doing what you did, eloping with the man I love. Do not fret, please. We are going to Grettna Green . . .

How very like Olivia, Deirdre thought vaguely, to misspell Gretna. Her next thought was that she really needed to sit down. Letting the note drift to the floor, she sank weakly onto the padded stool.

"Dear Lord," she whispered, half lament and half prayer. Then she muttered, "Oh, hell."

Lucas was sound asleep, when a hand roughly jostled his shoulder. "Back away, Lancelot," he mumbled, fumbling for his sword, "I spied the fair maiden first."

"I will not contest that, Your Grace. Wake up, if you please."

He was shaken again. "Damn it . . . er, forsooth . . ." He dragged his eyes open. "Christ, man, you look like hell."

"I apologize if my appearance offends you, Your Grace, but I am very much afraid I lose a great deal of my beauty when dragged from a sound sleep."

Lucas came fully awake and found he was brandishing an empty bottle under his valet's nose. "What time is it?"

"Nearly one, Your Grace."

"One? I never sleep till one."

"No, you are most reliable at being awake at either one o'clock." Lowry stifled a yawn and blinked red-rimmed eyes. "You have a visitor."

Lucas noticed the man's candle and belatedly realized it was still night. "At this hour? For God's sake, what on earth possessed you to wake me—"

"It is Mrs. Macvail, Your Grace. She is most anxious to speak with you."

"Deirdre?" Lucas bolted from the bed. Deirdre was in his house.

"I . . . ah, beg your pardon, Your Grace."

He paused impatiently in the doorway. "What is it?"

"May I suggest a dressing gown? As you retired early, the fires were allowed to go out, and it is rather chilly tonight."

"Oh, hang the . . ." He felt the faint draft first, looked down after. He was stark naked. "Lowry, find my . . ." The valet handed over the heavy silk robe. "Remind me to increase your salary."

"Certainly, Your Grace. It will be my pleasure."

Knotting the belt as he went, Lucas hurried down the hall. He came very close to going tip over tail when he saw Deirdre.

She was pacing the floor at the base of the stairs, midnight cloak swirling with her steps. Gold curls had escaped the loose braid to curl wildly around her pale face. She resembled every distressed damsel in every legendary tale, and for a moment, Lucas decided Lady Leverham was not so dotty after all. There was something to be said for living in the time of chivalry.

"Deirdre?"

Her head came up abruptly, her eyes meeting his. In the candle-light he could see faint, silvery tear marks beneath them. "It's Livvy, Lucas. She's run off with Teddy Vaer . . . to Gretna Green. I . . . I know it's horribly late . . . and I wouldn't have come to you

160

if I thought I could rely on anyone else to be of any use. I just . . . didn't know what else to do."

The knight-errant felt his pride and elation deflate a bit. Of course she hadn't wanted to turn to him. But she had. "Deirdre . . ."

"Please, Lucas. Don't think about it. If you do, you might refuse, and I *need* you!" Crying openly now, she sagged against the banister. "He will make her miserable. I know it. I cannot . . . I cannot allow her to be like me and make such a huge decision with no thought. Please . . ."

Lucas did not need to think out his decision. "Hastings!" he bellowed at the hovering, heavy-eyed butler. "Send a groom over to the Falcon for a running team. I want the barouche readied immediately." To Deirdre he said, "Go wait for me in the library. And for God's sake, pour yourself some brandy. You are going to need it."

Then, taking the stairs three at a time, he ran back to his chamber to dress.

14

Less than an hour later, they were speeding north out of London in Lucas's carriage. The interior was small, but it was light and quick, and that was all Deirdre cared about now.

"I don't suppose it would go over very well if I were to tell you to calm down," Lucas said as they rolled through the last of the city streets. "There is nothing you can do, Deirdre, and you're so tightly coiled that I fear you will launch yourself right out the window."

She would have snapped at him had he not been absolutely right. The pleats she had twisted into her skirts were no doubt permanent, and the muscles in her back were so tight she could feel them. Even with the light carriage and sturdy team, they had more than twenty hours ahead of them. Working herself into a state during the first leg of the journey would serve no purpose whatsoever.

She forced her fingers to release the crumpled muslin. "You're right, of course. I just—dear heaven, I don't even know what to say to you. I cannot even think clearly."

"What do you feel you must say? It seems to me we've covered all the vital points already. Livvy has eloped with a wholly unsuitable man; you think me lower than an earthworm. What is there left to be said?"

The words were spoken lightly enough, but Deirdre would have had to be far less perceptive than she was to miss the edge to Lucas's voice. He sounded weary, slightly petulant—and hurt.

"I know I could apologize, Lucas. I suppose you have a right to expect an apology. I should never have struck you. And I should

never have aired our private affairs in the middle of a ball. But . . .
I don't want to apologize. I don't feel I should have to."

"Then don't," he replied curtly. "We don't have to discuss the
matter at all."

She stared at him in surprise. This was not what she had
expected from him—her persistent companion on the path of
most resistance. "I know you came to the house several times
while I was gone," she said gently. "And again earlier tonight.
You must have wanted to talk to me. I'm ready, Lucas, and
willing."

The swaying carriage lantern threw a rhythmic pattern of light
across his face. He looked thinner, she realized, than he had that
first night in Edinburgh. His cheekbones seemed more prominent,
his whisker-shadowed jaw sharper. He also looked decidedly
annoyed.

He regarded her for a long moment before speaking. "Yes, you
are very gracious. You know, Deirdre, for four days I planned and
replanned what I would say when you decided to see me. Forgive
me, but I find suddenly that I don't want to have one of our epic
conversations."

"And why not? Can you at least tell me that?"

"To be perfectly honest, my dear, this is overly well-trodden
ground. I will merely go on protesting my good intentions—"
He raised a hand when she opened her mouth to argue. "My
good intentions of late. I take full responsibility for my less-than-
charitable feelings of seven years ago. I will go on protesting; you
will continue to think the very worst of me and say so with
impressive reserve and eloquence. I cannot fight that, Deirdre. I
simply have no weapons against that beautiful, impregnable wall
you've built around yourself."

"Lucas . . ."

"Try to see all this from my point of view. I am the undisputed
villain in your Celtic tale: the greedy king who wanted a beautiful
woman so much that he was ruthless in his pursuit. Who killed the
man she chose and drove her to noble suicide. Oh, don't look so
surprised. I know the story. Everyone knows the story.

"I'm not a villain, Deirdre. I didn't kill Jonas, and I'm not
responsible for any of your sorrows now. I am merely a man—just

163

a man with ordinary pride and desires and resentments—trying to get through life as I think I ought. I've committed my share of sins, but they're old sins, and suddenly I'm weary of flagellating myself for them."

He slumped back against the squabs and rubbed a hand roughly over his neck. Stunned, Deirdre met his shadowed gaze. "You think I've behaved like a martyr."

"No. I think you've simply done what I have: tried to get on with your life as best you can. But tonight I came to the conclusion that while you have forgiveness down to an art, you do not forget. I was clumsy and bitter seven years ago, Deirdre, but I was never malicious. Now I'm tired."

"Why did you agree to help me tonight if you feel that way?"

"Because you asked," he said simply. "And because, though you might have a hard time believing me, I care for Olivia. I always have. Ah, Deirdre, I am sorry about the house. Can you just believe me and leave it at that?"

"I . . ."

"No hurry. You have a good twenty hours to decide." He reached up and turned the oil knob on the lamp, dimming the light to a faint glow. "Try to sleep. We have a long ride ahead of us."

He stretched his legs out as much as he could, crossed his arms over his chest, and closed his eyes. Shutting her out. Deirdre watched him for countless minutes, waiting for him to look at her once more, to say anything to make her comfortable with him again.

But that, she knew in her heart, wasn't his job. He was right. She had forgiven him, and fairly easily. She hadn't forgotten. Instead she had carried a list of his slights against her in some little mental pocket. She had taken her own comfort in knowing it was there—should his undeniable, irresistible appeal chip away another piece of her shell.

"Oh, Lucas," she mouthed silently. You're right. You're so very right.

She would tell him when he awoke. She would apologize sincerely, and tell him that she did not think him malicious, nor lower than an earthworm. She didn't think she could tell him precisely what she thought he *was*. That one would take some serious consideration on her part.

Following his lead, she leaned back and closed her eyes, for all the good it would do. Her nerves were jittering and sleep was never so elusive as when it was most desired. Convinced she could feel each long mile roll by, she gave in to her scattered thoughts. She thought about Olivia, somewhere on the road ahead, perhaps already regretting her decision.

She remembered her own giddy flight to Gretna Green: the feel of Jonas's coat sleeve beneath her hand, the sound of his boot heels ringing over the blacksmith's stone floor, his catlike smile when she signed the smudged wedding certificate . . .

"We had a good run, didn't we, love?" he asked, lifting her hand to his lips.

She glanced at her arm, was startled to see a black sleeve. "Jonas." She tugged her hand from his, placed it against his pale cheek. "I have to say good-bye now."

"Of course you do. Damn well past time, too. I didn't deserve half so many years."

Deirdre reached out to trace the full lips, the familiar dark brows above the startling blue eyes. He moved just out of reach. "Oh, Jonas, I did love you."

"I know, sweetheart. I know. But you'll love him, too."

"I don't think so, Jonas."

"Liar." He grinned at her, that grin he always used when *he* was not quite telling the truth. "You'll love old Lucas. Hell, you already do . . ."

Deirdre came awake with a start, heart pounding. It took her a minute to orient herself, to see that her sleeve was pale gray in the lamplight and to adjust to the quick rocking of the carriage.

She pressed a hand over her breast and took a steadying breath. She had no idea how long she had been asleep. It could have been minutes or hours. Long enough to have a dream so vivid that she could almost hear Jonas's voice echoing in her ear.

You'll love old Lucas. . . .

She darted a quick look across the carriage. Lucas was still sleeping, his face relaxed and chest rising with his slow breaths. Of course she didn't love him. She had no intention of ever handing her heart over to another man. But it wouldn't be so difficult to love this one.

His boots were wedged beside her smaller ones, and she could not resist scooting over and moving one foot so it was propped next to his. The difference in size made her smile. In that moment, grinning foolishly at a very large, very male foot, she felt warmer and safer than she had in a great many years.

You'll love old Lucas. . . .

Deirdre pressed a hand over her annoyingly trembly midsection. "Oh, dear God," she whispered, and clapped her free hand to her forehead.

"Deirdre, are you ill?"

The light suddenly flared again. She looked up to see Lucas releasing the lamp. Her gaze skittered past the unshaven jaw to very intense, very open gray eyes. "I . . . no, I . . ."

"We can stop if you like."

Lucas didn't especially like the color in her cheeks. Oh, the flush was lovely against the ivory skin, but there was something feverish about it. With her hands pressed against her belly and brow, Deirdre did not look at all well. "We can stop," he repeated, more firmly this time.

"No. No, I am fine." When he moved to rap against the roof, she nearly leapt to stop him. "Truly. I am fine, merely worrying about Olivia. I . . . I did not mean to wake you with my fidgeting."

He had not been asleep. He knew better than to try with Deirdre seated not three feet away. He had alternately watched her and closed his eyes, contenting himself with listening to her breathe.

"You have something you need to say, don't you?"

She nodded, withdrawing into her seat, then almost immediately shook her head and bit her lower lip. "I'm not sure what there is to say, other than that I'm so terribly sorry . . . for all of this. For . . . I . . . I should never have dragged you into my concerns."

He wanted to tell her how very much it meant that she had come to him. How only some vestige of wisdom had kept him from hauling her right back out the door of his house—in his dressing gown—and into the first hack he could find. At the time

166

he would have done anything to keep her from changing her mind and leaving him behind.

He cleared his throat instead and insisted, "You would have been mad to do this alone. I don't mind that you came to me. Not at all. Olivia is as close to a sister as I've ever had."

Deirdre smiled sadly. "I can only imagine how that went over the years. She has always been so headstrong, so impulsive. I should have known, should have seen this coming—"

"Rubbish. Olivia's nature aside, not even the worst of fools could have predicted that Teddy Vaer would go along with such a scheme, let alone orchestrate it." Lucas thumped his fist against the wood paneling, bitterly cursing himself for spending so many years in a snit that he had allowed the closest person he had ever had to a sister to grow into womanhood without the brother he could have been in the absence of the real thing. "What in God's name possessed them?"

There was a heavy pause. Then, "Love," Deirdre said wearily. "At least I can only hope it was overpowering love. And I imagine the collective disapproval only fueled it further. There is nothing like the knowledge of an enraged parent to quicken a flight. Poor Teddy. I rather expect his mother is just the sort to have always expressed her displeasure with the back of a hairbrush."

Without thinking, Lucas offered, "My father preferred birch switches. They grew to epic proportions over the years."

Deirdre's head snapped up. "Your father beat you with a stick?"

"Of course. Frequently. Sometimes just to prove he could."

"Oh, Lucas, how awful!"

He shrugged. "You would be surprised how one can start accepting such things."

"I would be surprised indeed! My father, brute though he was, only lifted his hand to me once, when I tried to refuse—" She broke off, and he watched as the flush returned to her cheeks. He knew without a doubt what she had been about to say, and his jaw clenched.

"When you tried to refuse my suit. My God, he *struck* you for it. And still forced you to accept me."

"I ..." Deirdre's gaze dropped, and Lucas could tell she

167

wanted to lie, to comfort him. His heart twisted. "Yes. He had already agreed to the settlement and ... well, the title was so important to him."

Oh, Lucas had known that from the beginning. Richard Fallam had very nearly slavered over the thought that he would share a grandson with a duke. What Lucas had not known, or rather had not allowed himself to contemplate, was the length to which the man would go to see his daughter wedded to a lord.

"I did not see you for some days after that scene. Dear God ... he did not ..."

She reached out, clasped her hand tightly over his. "It doesn't matter, Lucas. It was so long ago."

The bruises had faded quickly, she recalled. And she had almost been able to believe her father really only wanted the best for her. Almost. What had hurt more was her mother's utter refusal to intervene. Jonas Macvail had. How could she not have loved the one person who had ever offered her a choice in anything?

"Lucas, really—"

"I would have killed him. Had I known, I would have killed him."

She believed him, and was stunned to realize he had felt so strongly. "Thank you," she said softly. "God help me for being grateful for something so wrong, but I am." She withdrew her hand and numbly curled up on the seat. "Am I doing wrong here, Lucas? Should I have let Olivia make this decision without interfering?"

"I don't know," he replied bluntly. "Perhaps. But even if true love sent the pair to flight, it's deep love that had you taking off after her. I would venture to say that makes all the difference."

"I would venture to say Olivia won't agree."

"Maybe not now. Later, who knows?" He paused and brushed some invisible debris off his leg. "What would you have done if someone had come after you? Would you have changed your mind or would you have married Jonas then and there anyway?"

Deirdre remembered constantly looking back over her shoulder, remembered expecting to hear Lucas's voice booming through every posting house where she and Jonas had stopped. "I suppose if someone had come after me out of love, I might have paused. But anyone interfering would have done so out of anger and wounded pride. Nothing that could possibly have made me look beyond what I felt for Jonas."

Lucas did not respond, and Deirdre really had nothing more to say. Or rather, nothing she was willing to express. Once spoken, words could never be taken back, after all. So they sat silently for a time. Outside the carriage dark fields rolled by with the occasional stone cottage. She imagined the people inside—sleeping, or just rising to stoke the fire and prepare for the day of hard work. Or making love . . .

"Deirdre."

"Hmm?" She jumped in surprise and flushed anew.

"I . . . Did you ever . . . ?" Lucas shook his head and grimaced. "Never mind. I . . . ah . . . I really ought to have asked you this before, but what on earth do you intend to do when we find them?"

"Thank you for your confidence that we will."

"A good recruit never questions the strategy of his intrepid leader." He gestured out the window at the wide, well-traveled road. "Besides, there's only one way to get to Scotland if you're in a hurry. We'll find them. So what are you going to do, Madam General, at the end of this campaign?"

Deirdre realized she had absolutely no idea. She simply had not thought the matter out clearly. Unable to resist the impulse, she laughed—a bit hysterically, but it felt marvelous nonetheless. "I don't suppose you have any rope lying about in this contraption?"

"Not to my knowledge. Why? Are you contemplating tying one young fool to the roof and another to the back on the return to Town?"

"Well, there's a thought. I'll have to ponder which goes where."

Lucas chuckled. "You could always alternate."

"What a wonderful suggestion. But no, I once had a thought about dragging Livvy back to Tarbet and keeping her restrained there until she turned thirty. I'm sorely tempted to do that now."

"You would be gray-haired and wizened within a month."

"No doubt." Deirdre reached up with a rueful smile and touched her hair. "It has already begun."

Without thinking, Lucas reached across and snared one loose curl. It was the first time he had seen Deirdre's hair loose since their brief, ill-fated betrothal. He wound the curl around his finger and gently stroked the feathery ends. It was, he realized, something he had wanted to do for more than six years.

"It all looks gold to me," he said softly.

He nearly stopped breathing when she reached up to trace a fingertip over his temple. "The silver suits you. It speaks of . . . experience. A full life."

"Deirdre . . ." Lucas let the gold curl slide through his fingers as he cupped her face with his trembling hand. Her eyes widened, her lips parted slightly in what might have been a surprised, quiet gasp. "Are we all right again, the two of us?"

Perhaps it was nothing more than his hopeful imagination, but she seemed to press her cheek ever so lightly into his palm. "Do you mean have I forgiven you for being rightfully angry? Or are you telling me that I am forgiven for being such a paragon of self-righteous indignation?"

"Yes," he said, then leaned forward slowly, so slowly that he was barely moving, certain she would jerk away before his lips met hers . . .

They nearly bumped noses when the carriage rocked to a halt.

Deirdre's eyes, soft and opaque a moment earlier, sharpened. She dropped her hand from where it had rested against his temple and pulled back into the corner of the seat. Lucas was left holding nothing but air.

The carriage rocked again, and the coachman's ruddy face appeared in the window. Lucas jerked it down with unnecessary force. "What is it?" he snapped.

The man's eyes slewed from Lucas to Deirdre, where she sat studiously examining her lap. "Beggin' your pardon, Your Grace, but the team's slowin' a bit. We can run 'em for a few more hours, but only if we stop for wind an' water at the next postin' house."

"And if we keep on?"

"We'll need to swap by dawn."

Lucas thought for a moment. "Stop, then."

"Aye, Your Grace. Shouldn't be more 'n a mile."

A mile. Not nearly enough time to properly complete what he had begun. Lucas cursed silently. And ached acutely. He wanted to kiss Deirdre. He wanted it so much that he hurt. But he had a very good idea that he would require several hours to do it right. Several hours of learning her cheeks, her eyelids, the hollow of her throat, of learning the contour of her lips with his own.

"Deirdre, sweetheart," he began, ready to explain exactly what it was that he planned to do once they'd completed their stop.

"A mile. I wonder where we are." She was briskly smoothing hopelessly wrinkled skirts. "We must be in Buckinghamshire by now. Did you know that Lord Althorpe's estate is in Buckinghamshire? Near Marsh Gibbon, I believe. But of course you would already know that. You've known Evan rather longer than I—"

"Deirdre."

"Hmm? What?"

"You are prattling."

"Am I? I was merely commenting—"

"Deirdre, love—"

"Don't!" she said so sharply that he flinched. "Please." Her voice softened. "I cannot . . . Lucas, I cannot take it when you use that tone, those words with me."

"What words?"

"Love. Sweetheart." Her hands fluttered above her lap. "I cannot take it."

Baffled, he reached to grasp her hands and still them. She jerked away. "Sweet—Deirdre, what is there to take? You feel it, too. Whatever it is, you feel it."

"What I feel is stifled and exhausted, Your Grace. I will be glad of some air. Most glad."

She all but pressed her face to the window, away from him. Lucas, having absolutely no idea what to say, slowly slid to the opposite corner. Confused, hurt, his fingertips still tingling from the warmth of her skin, he stared at her in agonizing silence until they pulled into the inn yard.

It got worse from there. They stayed only long enough to rest

171

the team and make use of the place's facilities. Then they were off again. The next stretch passed in near silence, broken only by polite words as they shared the repast Lucas's cook had packed. Deirdre was pale and solemn; Lucas nearly sullen.

In thirty years he had known a great many women, a good many of them intimately. And never once had he come close to comprehending the innermost workings of the female mind. Come to think of it, he mused grimly, he hadn't had much luck at understanding the outermost workings, either.

Hadn't he and Deirdre just shared a . . . Well, he couldn't find a precise word for what they had shared. A moment? Too bland. A moment of mind-searing passion? Too melodramatic and, he thought, probably just a matter of wishful thinking on his part.

In the end he took the cowardly option of burying his nose in a day-old newspaper taken from the inn. As if he could possibly read with the insufficient light and the carriage jolting along. Finally, after not reading the same page a half-dozen times, he peered over the top. Deirdre was staring out the window into the darkness, seeing God only knew what.

At that moment Lucas would have given nearly every pence he possessed to be reading her thoughts, insufficient light and all.

For her own part Deirdre would have given a good half of her meager savings to be anywhere other than where she was.

She had loved only one man, had kissed only one man. The sweet, almost sharp desire to meet Lucas's lips with her own had frightened her. More than that, it had nearly overwhelmed her. She had spent so many years resenting him, hating him insofar as she could hate anyone.

Now she wasn't certain what she felt, but it was far from hate.

She had dragged him out of his home and on a fast, fierce journey that would cover most of England. It had seemed to make so much sense at the time. Who better to involve in the chase than the man who had unwillingly—but graciously—been dragged into her and Livvy's affairs since the night in Edinburgh. And his noble strength was so appealing.

Lucas Gower had never seemed overly affected by anything. Not her sniping at him in the wake of their betrothal, not her flight, and most recently, not by the vicious rumors that had circulated through the ton. In the moment when she had felt an utter failure, he had been the natural choice to take charge. And he had.

Lucas Gower had been confident and cavalier. The Duke of Conovar had been—was—everything accommodating and . . . kind. Beyond that, he had awakened sensations she'd thought gone forever.

"Lucas." She needed to talk to him before she turned cowardly. He glanced up from the paper he was studiously reading in the lamplight. Deirdre noted the *Brackley Observer* on the front page and nearly smiled. For a man who no doubt read the *Times* each morning, a brush with the *Observer* must be a step down in the world indeed. "Lucas, I . . . want you to understand what happened."

He lowered the paper several inches but did not set it aside. "Yes?"

She took a deep breath. "I did feel something. Of course I did." The paper dropped another inch.

"Would you care to elaborate on that?" he asked, his voice expressionless.

"No, I wouldn't actually, but you deserve an explanation."

"I'm listening."

"I think I have an idea what life was like for you in your family. Hard, yes. I could cry for the little boy who learned to ride impossible beasts in order to please a father who couldn't be pleased. I hate the idea that you got so much anger from your father when you should have had only approval. I wish he could have talked to you once in a while rather than yelling . . ."

Lucas smiled thinly. "This is fascinating, Deirdre, but hardly news. I've had the same thoughts for thirty years."

"I know." She knotted her fingers in her lap. "I'm saying this as a way of explaining who I am. What my family made me. I never had *anything* from my parents, you see. No approval, no anger. Nothing. Until I suddenly became valuable as a commodity. Then they paid attention. They yelled and bullied and made it abundantly clear that I *meant* nothing. Except as a means to socially elevate them."

She blinked away hot tears. "Jonas was the first person who ever really talked to me. He wanted me, knowing I couldn't bring anything to him but myself. It astonished me. I fell in love with him. How could I not? I was so *grateful*. And everything got tied into that gratitude—everything I felt for him."

"Deirdre, you don't need to—"

"Yes. Yes, I do. Because when you touched me and I felt so much, I felt that gratitude, too. Because you've been so kind to me, to Olivia, because I could tell you actually wanted me."

"Of course I want—"

"Lucas. I want you, too."

The paper slid to the floor.

He felt his jaw dropping—and other parts of him rising. "Deirdre . . ."

"But it won't work, Lucas. It cannot. Because I don't want to feel grateful. It doesn't last, gratitude, any more than passion does. And I don't ever want to feel that disappointment again." She met his gaze squarely. "Do you understand now?"

No, he thought, not entirely. He'd gotten lost somewhere around the wanting him part. But he'd be damned if he would admit as much. All he needed was a few minutes to catch up. And an hour or so of ravishing that lush mouth, of course.

"I understand," he said solemnly, and moved toward her.

"Good." The brilliant smile she gave him halted him in midscoot. "I am so glad. I think I'll be able to sleep now."

"What?"

"It's been gnawing at me. For days, really. Ever since I saw you sitting all alone at the theater. I haven't really slept well since then, and now I know why." She gave a soft laugh. "Thank you."

"For what?"

"For understanding me. You are a very good man."

With that she curled her legs beneath her, rested her head against her folded cloak, and closed her eyes. Lucas stayed precisely where he was, half off his own seat, wondering when he had lost his basic comprehension of the English language.

He knew the moment she fell asleep. A soft sigh escaped her lips, and her entire body relaxed. He watched her for a very long time, watched the soft rise and fall of her breasts. And he realized he would give everything he possessed, even his life, to have her sleeping in his arms for one night.

174

Slowly, so as not to wake her, he eased onto the seat by her side. She tensed for a moment and whispered something unintelligible as he gently wrapped one arm about her and leaned her head onto his shoulder. Then she curved her body against his as naturally as if she had been doing it for years, and went still.

As they rolled into the night, Lucas held the one woman he had ever wanted in his life. The only one he had ever loved. And he silently vowed never to let her go.

15

Deirdre's eyes opened to bright sunlight and fawn brocade. It took her a moment to figure out where she was. And where she was was curled up on Lucas's lap. Her cheek rested against his chest; her bottom was nestled quite comfortably atop his thighs.

She had no idea how she had come to be there. Nor how Lucas had come to occupy the seat that had been hers the night before. His back rested against the paneling, and his legs stretched along the seat. Judging from his steady breathing, he was very much asleep.

Deirdre's first impulse was to spring across the carriage. He had his arms wrapped firmly around her waist, however, and she knew he would wake if she tried to disengage herself. She did not want him awake. She wanted him to remain quite oblivious to the fact that she had somehow crawled into his lap during the night.

"Good morning, Mrs. Macvail."

She did spring into the opposite seat then, scrambling on rubbery legs. Lucas let out a muffled grunt. When she'd settled herself, flushed and speechless, and mustered just enough nerve to look at him, she saw that he had curled up slightly, his knees bent.

"I . . . ah, good morning. Is it still morning?"

Lucas grunted again, then let out a pained chuckle as he reached for his pocket watch. "Barely. It's nearly eleven. Are you always so spritely when you wake?"

"I rarely wake up on top . . . er . . ." Deirdre raised her hands helplessly, then let them drop into her lap. "Could we possibly not talk to each other until I've regained a modicum of composure?"

This time he laughed aloud. "I believe I like you in the morning. You release some of that perfect control."

She shot him a look, then quickly averted her eyes and pressed herself into the corner as he stretched. There simply was not enough room in the carriage for her, a very large man, and her great humiliation.

"Before you regain that composure, dare I ask why you're so flustered?"

Deirdre was still too rattled to decide if he were having a lovely laugh at her expense. She decided he was, but opted for polite coolness. "How kind of you to pretend ignorance," she muttered, "but I apparently made bold with your person."

"No, actually you didn't. But since you'd rather not speak of the matter . . ." He stretched again and peered out the window. "We should be stopping soon."

Thankfully they did. When they pulled into the coaching yard some ten minutes later, Deirdre sprang out the door before the carriage stopped rolling. And was forced to stand foolishly by while Lucas took his leisurely time in disembarking.

Inside, the innkeeper's wife gave him a long look before ushering them upstairs. For her own part, Deirdre preferred not to notice how very attractive he looked, even in his rumpled state. Or rather because of it. All he needed was a silver ear hoop to go with his sleepy eyes, whiskered jaw, and loose shirt to make him the perfect image of a lazy corsair.

A quick glance in the hall mirror as they passed told her she looked like the business end of a mop that had been used to swab the decks.

A hushed conversation between Lucas and the other woman produced a satisfied nod on his part, a husky chuckle on hers, and two private chambers upstairs.

Deirdre availed herself as well as she could of the basin of water and soap that the lady provided. "Cocky bounder," she muttered to herself as she scrubbed at her warm cheeks. She decided she did *not* like Lucas Gower in the morning. The smug, slumberous smiles alone would set a reasonable woman's teeth on edge.

It hardly mattered that they would set a dead woman's heart thumping, too.

She dried off with more force than was necessary and heaved

the towel across the room. Feeling somewhat fresher though no less exhausted, and certainly no less humiliated, she headed back downstairs. Lucas was not the important matter at hand. She would simply remind herself of that should he get too close again.

He was already waiting for her, his damp hair and shirt collar testifying to his attempts at a similarly impromptu bath. A large basket sat at his feet. "I didn't think you would sit still long enough to have a decent meal here."

Deirdre's stomach clenched at the thought of eating. Food was rather low on her list at the moment. She was grateful, however, for the thought and thanked him. Then, on the same breath, she demanded, "Have they been here?"

"Less than three hours ago. And they are in a large coach. We should be able to catch up before they reach the border."

"Oh, thank heaven." Deirdre was already halfway out the door. "Please, Lucas, do hurry."

He did. Stiff as he was from a night in the carriage, he was more than ready to get back in. He and Deirdre had some unfinished business, and when a man had life-important matters to deal with, he would just as soon begin immediately.

Of course, he lost some of his resolve once he was settled across from her again. *Mrs. Macvail, I believe we should get married as soon as we get to Scotland* was hardly normal breakfast conversation—even if the breakfast were taking place in a carriage rattling toward Gretna Green. So he opted instead for a slightly less dramatic option.

"Scone?" he asked politely, reaching into the basket.

"No, thank you," she replied, but distractedly accepted one anyway. "I am not hungry."

Lucas waited until she had taken a healthy bite before unstopping the carafe of tea. He would have preferred coffee, but the stuff was hot. It was also, if the smell were any indication, strong enough to clean the carriage's axles. For what it had cost him, it ought to taste like champagne and effectively protect him from all ills till eternity. The lost highwaymen of the past century, he decided, were alive and well and thriving in the hostelry trade.

He passed Deirdre a cup and a second scone. She had devoured the first. *Mrs. Macvail, I believe we should* . . . "We should reach Gretna around dawn tomorrow. If we have to go that far."

She nodded and sipped at her tea. He saw her wince and prepared himself. Considering the fact that his mouth already tasted as if something had crawled in and died, the tea was not so bad. It was the last time, he vowed, that he would rush off to Scotland without being properly prepared.

It was, he amended the ridiculous thought, the last time he would rush off to Scotland. He had every intention of breaking the return journey at his estate in Northumberland—and staying there with his wife for the rest of his natural life.

It was such an appealing concept. The problem, of course, was convincing Deirdre just how very appealing it was.

Perhaps he needed a new approach. There was the issue of honor. *Mrs. Macvail, you do realize this journey has put you in the most compromising position. I feel it is my duty as a man of honor to*—He abandoned that one quickly. Deirdre would probably throw her cup at him should the proposal even hint at anything approaching pity.

Mrs. Macvail, since we have driven all this way, I cannot help but think we should avail ourselves of Gretna's famous attractions when we arrive . . . He rolled his eyes in disgust. That would have her leaping from the carriage in horror.

Deirdre, I'm rather desperately in love with you. I think I always have been. And if you refuse me, I fear my heart might lose interest in beating.

There was nothing quite so terrifying as the bare truth.

"Deirdre—"

"It has all been a mistake, Lucas."

He blinked at her. "What was that?"

"Everything between us, from the very beginning, has been a series of dismal mistakes." She had set her cup aside and was twisting new pleats into her irreparably creased skirts. "I believe it is past time to put a stop to it."

"Well." Intrigued, delighted, he leaned forward until his knees bumped against hers. "I could not agree more."

"Oh, good. I was . . . worried. We seem to have become

friends somehow, despite all the troubles, and I do hate to give up friendships."

"Mmm. But life must progress."

She nodded, eyes fixed on where her skirts met his breeches. "Precisely. Which is why I feel we mustn't see each other again after this journey is through."

"What?" he snapped, making her jump and nearly rattling the teacups.

"I thought you understood me ... agreed with me," she stammered. "We are like a keg of gunpowder and a careless spark, Lucas. No matter how cautious we are, something terrible always happens when we are together. You said as much yourself: There is no way for us to have a comfortable meeting of the minds."

"To hell with our minds, then," he growled, and hauled her out of her seat and back into his lap, where she belonged.

Any chance to protest was lost immediately. Deirdre's hands were helpless between her chest and his. And the moment she opened her mouth, his descended to cover it with a searing power that took her breath away. Then she thought she might never breathe again.

Nothing could possibly have prepared her for the sensations that washed over her at such a rough meeting. Warmth unfurled and sparked inside her, sending a tingling heat to every inch of skin where it met his—and some where it did not. Her hands clenched convulsively, her lips parted under the relentless assault. There was nothing gentle in the kiss, nothing restrained. Lucas tasted of strong tea and stronger need, and it was, Deirdre decided hazily, impossibly sweet.

It was also *wrong*. Distance. She had just suggested—no, demanded—distance. Miles, in fact. Instead she was as close to him as flushed skin and some rumpled clothing would allow.

Tugging fiercely, she pulled her hands free. And promptly buried them in the thick hair at the nape of his neck. He breathed his approval and slid his own hands around her back to draw her closer, all the while devouring her mouth as if it were coated with honey.

On and on it went, this relentless kiss, as new to her experience

180

as it seemed completely natural. Deirdre felt Lucas's thighs rocking beneath hers, felt the rocking of the carriage beneath them both. She met the hungry thrust of his tongue, reveled in the velvet-rough feeling against hers. When she finally dragged her face away to draw a much-needed breath, Lucas buried his lips in the base of her throat, trailing a fiery path from there up to the sensitive spot just beneath her ear.

She dropped her hands to his shoulders, moaned softly, and tilted her head to give him better access. When his teeth closed gently over her lobe, she sighed and relinquished the last ghost of control. Feeling as if every bone in her body had melted away, she slumped against his chest.

She heard him chuckle, felt the gentle rumble along with his quickened heartbeat against her cheek.

"What was that about gunpowder and flame, Mrs. Macvail?"

She rested her forehead against his shirt and struggled to get air into her burning lungs. She had never thought a person could forget how to breathe. His hand, stroking lazy circles over her back, did not help much. Oh, it felt lovely, but did nothing to settle her frantic pulse.

"Stop that," she panted.

"Stop what?" His touch feathered upward to her nape, raising the fine hairs there and making her stomach do a giddy flip. "That?"

She shuddered deliciously, sighed, then demanded, "Keep your hands to yourself for a moment, please. I cannot think."

"And we can't have that now, can we?"

She nearly moaned when his hands dropped away—then gasped when they slid between their bodies, brushing firmly against her breasts. Her swift, deep breath had each of his knuckles sliding over the taut fabric of her bodice, "I said—"

"You said to keep my hands to myself. And I am doing so. This, my dear, is the only monklike pose I know."

Summoning what little strength she possessed, Deirdre braced her trembling hands against his shoulders and pushed herself away. Monklike, indeed, his hands were linked over his chest. A quick glance at his decidedly impious smile told her he knew exactly the result getting them there had caused.

"Very clever," she muttered, resisting the urge to press herself against those very clever fingers again. "Now, release me so I can go back to my seat."

His dark brows rose into devilish arcs. "I am not holding you, my dear. You are sitting on me."

He was absolutely right. She made a weak attempt to slide onto the seat beside him, but he promptly unlinked his hands and, with impressive speed, wrapped his arms firmly around her back. "No. I don't think I will release you after all."

"You'll have to, eventually."

As far as Lucas was concerned, eventually meant fifty years or so. Of course, considering the state of his body, it would be gentlemanly to remove her from his lap now. He was not feeling much like a gentleman, however. He was entertaining the very appealing possibility of switching their positions, dispensing with the barrier of miserable clothing between them, and showing Deirdre precisely what his definition of release was.

He wondered what she would say to another stop at an inn so soon after the last one.

No. He intended their first time to be far different from a hot tumble in a carriage or hired room. He envisioned the massive bed in the master suite of his Northumberland estate: acres of soft mattress and fine linen sheets. He imagined Deirdre's hair loose and glowing like molten gold in the firelight, her sublimely soft skin flushed and heated and displayed in all its glory for his slow exploration.

They could not be more than a few hours from Darlington. From there it would only be another three or four to Blyth. A late arrival would hardly matter. His staff would have his bed ready for him anyway, as it always was. A light supper, perhaps, beside the fire in his chamber. He had never explored the well-documented uses of Northumberland clotted cream. If he were very fortunate, he might be able to persuade Deirdre to join him on the sensual expedition.

Judging from her eager participation in the kiss, he thought he'd struck gold there. No, he amended, he had always known her immense value. What he had never guessed at was the fire banked deep beneath the surface. If he had, he would never have let her go. He would have ridden through hell to stop her before she reached Gretna Green. He would have flattened Jonas Macvail with one knightly blow, tossed Deirdre over his saddle, and thundered away, flag at full mast . . .

"Stop!"

Jostled back into some semblance of reality, Lucas shook his head to clear it, then surveyed his visibly affected but oddly empty lap with surprise. Deirdre, he discovered, was crouched on the seat beside him, her delectable bottom pressed against his side, her face pressed to the window.

"Stop!" she cried again. "For God's sake, Lucas, make the driver stop!"

Confused, still half in his erotic reverie, he obeyed. He banged his fist against the trap. Moments later the carriage shuddered to a slow roll.

"Deirdre, what . . ." he began, but for the second time that day, she was tumbling out the door without sparing him a backward look. "Well, hell," he muttered, and, taking some care for his spring-taut muscles, clambered after her.

Deirdre gathered up her skirts and hurried toward the glossy black coach resting by the side of the road. The vehicle had caught her attention as they passed it; a glimpse of black curls through the window had had her scrambling to get a better look. Now she broke into a run, fervent prayers filling her mind.

I'll never ask for anything for myself again, she vowed, if only you'll let this be Olivia, and let us talk.

She got a brief glimpse of a young boy at the head of the team. Too young, certainly, to have been driving. Images of highway robbery flashed into her head as she raced toward the coach. Not here, she thought resolutely. Not on the busiest road between England and Scotland.

"Deirdre, damn it . . . !"

She heard Lucas pounding behind her but did not stop until she'd reached the door. Skidding to a halt, she seized the handle.

She landed hard on her posterior when the door swung outward, shoving her with it. Coughing and clearing dust from her eyes and mouth, she peered up at the portal, and a familiar dark head poked out.

"For heaven's sake, DeeDee, what on earth are you doing here?" Olivia, looking far too lovely to have spent more than twelve hours on the run, stepped from the coach, crouched down beside Deirdre, and then nearly sent them both rolling in the dirt when she gave her an enthusiastic hug. "I am ever so glad to see you! You have no idea how glad. But, good Lord, what an awful mess you are! Did you run all the way from Town?"

Deirdre was spared the necessity of responding by Lucas's arrival. He glared at Livvy, then reached down and hauled Deirdre up by the arm. "One of these days, madam," he said fiercely, "we are going to have a talk about launching oneself out of a moving vehicle."

She ignored him. "Olivia, do you have *any* idea what you've done?"

The girl had the gall to roll her eyes and grumble, "I have done nothing yet, DeeDee, save take a very long drive in deadly dull country. Had you caught up with us tomorrow instead, I no doubt would be telling you I'd gotten married."

"Well, thank heaven for small blessings," Deirdre shot back. "What possessed you to run off like that? I've been heartsick, Livvy. Do you hear me? Heartsick!" She glanced down when she felt a tug at her skirt. Lucas had bent over and was staring intently beneath the coach. "Not now, Lucas."

"Ah, Deirdre, I believe you might want to—"

"Not *now*!" She turned her attention back to Olivia. "All right. Where is he?" This time Lucas grabbed a handful of fabric and all but hauled her to the ground. "For pity's sake, what is it?"

"I'm not entirely certain, my dear, but there appears to be a body lying on the other side."

"A *body*? My God." She crouched down for a better look. All she could see was a pair of dark breeches and dusty boots. "Olivia?" she quavered, groping behind her for her sister-in-law's hand.

"Oh, he isn't dead, merely unconscious. He took a bump on the head, though I daresay all the liquor he consumed contributed to the effect. Although, when one ponders the matter, it really must have been the other way about. He had most of a bottle of something at the last posting house. The knock on the head was subsequent."

"The knock . . ." Deirdre allowed Lucas to help her up, then watched hazily as he strode around to have a better look at the fallen man. "Whiskey. Livvy, you didn't . . . he didn't . . . try to force himself on you?"

"Force himself? Good Lord, no. He fell off the box."

"Fell . . . ?" Wondering whether she perhaps had unwittingly consumed some liquor with the appallingly strong tea, Deirdre rubbed her hand over her forehead. "What was he doing atop the box, dearest?" she asked as patiently as she could.

"What a silly question. It is where he sits, noddy. Or rather, where he sat. We decided he would do better on the ground until he regained consciousness and we could move on. But now you are here, and we can simply take your carriage." Olivia squeezed her hand tightly. "Did I tell you how glad I am that you are here? I am, DeeDee. Prodigiously glad."

Deciding she was going to have to get rational answers for herself, Deirdre stalked around the coach, Livvy's hand held fast in hers. Lucas was crouched beside the supine figure, obscuring the man from the chest up.

"Is he . . . ?" Deirdre tucked Olivia firmly behind her. "Is he . . . dead?"

"Drunk, I would say. We'll find out soon enough." Lucas braced his hands against his thighs and slowly rose to his feet. "All right, Brat. Where is he?"

Deirdre stared down at the unfamiliar, pockmarked face which could only belong to the coach's driver, and felt her heart give a relieved thump. It was short-lived. She had a few words to say to Mr. Vaer, among them a severe scolding for leaving Livvy alone in the road while he hied off God knew where.

"Yes, Livvy. Where is he?"

The girl flushed and stared down at the hem of her pristine, yellow dress. "He . . . er . . . went to answer nature," she mumbled. "He'll be back any moment now."

Even as she spoke, there was the crunch of boot heels on dried grass. "Well, I'll be damned. The cavalry has arrived! I must say, I'm delighted to see you, Mrs. Macvail. Dearest Olivia was

185

becoming quite distraught at the thought of being married without you in attendance. Weren't you, my love?"

Deirdre's jaw was completely slack as she watched Olivia run happily into the open arms of Francis Gower.

16

I T WAS A beautiful wedding.

At least Deirdre kept insisting that it was a beautiful wedding. As far as Lucas was concerned, its only recommendation was that it had been blessedly short. The heavy-eyed Archbishop of York, collar askew, had performed the ceremony himself at six in the morning.

Only for the Duke of Conovar, the man had muttered on being dragged from his bed, would he rise before the bloody sun.

Had he had his druthers, Lucas would have used his not-insignificant authority to have his cousin coshed over the head and shipped off to Botany Bay. But Olivia had been adamant, Deirdre had been adamant, and Francis had been uncustomarily silent. So the ducal influence had procured a special license and a sleepy archbishop, and now the former Miss Macvail was Mrs. Francis Gower.

In between ordering him about and fluttering around the glowing lovers, Deirdre had managed to explain the discrepancy between the bridegroom they had found and the one they had expected. Apparently Olivia had neglected to mention precisely with whom she was eloping. Lucas really wished she had. He might have traveled with a hefty cudgel, then, and such a weapon would have come in most handily right now. He was ready to cosh himself over the head, and hence gain even temporary reprieve from the dismal situation.

They must have been quite a sight, pulling into York. Of course, it had been somewhere around four in the morning, so only the innkeeper there had been witness to the procession. Lucas's coachman had taken over Francis's vehicle; Francis had been at the reins of Lucas's. Olivia and Deirdre had ridden in the former; Lucas and Francis's slowly recovering driver in the latter. The fellow had come to sufficiently to stick his head out the window and retch just as they pulled into the posting house yard.

By the time the wedding was over, Lucas had been well pounded into submission by the bizarre chain of events, and had not so much as peeped a protest when Deirdre suggested that they go north from York to his Northumberland estate immediately. So there they were: the happy couple, the delighted sister-in-law, and one grouchy, exhausted duke who wanted nothing more than to haul Deirdre upstairs into bed and absorb her thoroughly before sleeping for the next fortnight.

As it was, he was forced to entertain his blasted cousin and curse the fact that his housekeeper had put Deirdre in the bed-chamber farthest from his own.

After an hour at the supper table, with Francis and Olivia all but drooling over each other, he abruptly excused himself and took dubious solace in his library, propriety be damned. Francis could bloody well take his port in the presence of the ladies. Lucas had better things to do.

There was a mammoth pile of estate business demanding his attention, but he had a far more pleasant interlude in mind. He planned to empty the port decanter at hand and rattle his glowering father's portrait off the wall with his snores.

He'd done no more than pour the first glass when some-one rapped at the door. His responding snarl ought to have warned off even his fearless butler, but the door swung inward any-way. The nasty comment died on his lips when Deirdre slipped into the room.

A peach silk gown had replaced her creased muslin. It was several sizes too large, years out of fashion, and she looked like heaven incarnate. Lucas squinted at the dress. It was so familiar . . .

"That is what you were wearing when we met!" he declared, vastly pleased with himself for remembering. And women thought men took no interest in such things.

Smiling, Deirdre dropped gracefully into the facing wing chair and drew her slippered feet up beneath her skirts. "The day we met," she said cheerfully, "I was wearing a godawful, frothy white thing. You, on the other hand, were wearing black."

She was right. He had been rather fond of that black coat and had mourned its loss. He had dropped a spoonful of chocolate soufflé down the lapel when she'd walked by him and even Lowry's best efforts had not been able to remove the stain.

"The Jermyn fete, then. I distinctly remember that dress."

"At the Jermyn fete, I wore a godawful, frothy white thing. You wore black." Apparently taking pity on him, she reached out to pat his knee and announced, "I'm sure you do remember this dress. It belonged to your mother. I'm afraid I had to send a maid to riffle through her belongings. My dress is destined for the rag bin and I left my valise in your London foyer."

Lucas vaguely recalled tripping over some hard object as he'd hustled her out the door and into the carriage. "The dress suits you." And it did, especially when she wrapped her arms around her knees, leaned forward, and gave him a delightful view behind the sagging bodice. "My memory, unfortunately, suits a doddering old man."

"Oh, I don't know. It seems to me you made a very good point not long ago about the value of forgetting."

He did remember that. "I'm sorry. I was unduly harsh."

"No, you were forthright. There is a difference, and I appreciate what it is." She rocked slowly, and he forced himself to keep his eyes on her wistful face. "Some things really are best forgotten."

"I never meant to forget anything about you," he said gently. "I didn't think I had."

"You should, Lucas. You should forget a great deal about me."

"And what in God's name is that supposed to mean?"

Now she hugged her legs tightly against her chest and looked past him, toward the shaded windows. "It means I am so frequently wrong about so many things. And I'm not nearly as good as I thought at admitting it. I . . . oh, forget I said . . ." Her quick smile did not reach her eyes. "There, you see? Best forgotten."

No, he didn't see. In fact, he had no idea what she was saying. She stalled his protest, however, by announcing, "You really

189

ought to give your cousin a chance. He's a good man. A very good man."

He did protest now. "Francis is an overdressed, preening, sharp-tongued fop who delights in mocking me at every turn. I have never liked him, and he returns the sentiment tenfold."

"I'm sorry you think so. You're wrong, you know."

"Wrong? He is wearing an *aqua* coat! And a yellow—"

"Lucas. Don't." She regarded him solemnly. "As for his appearance, he would look very much like you if he dressed as you do."

"Are you telling me he wears all the colors of the rainbow to keep from resembling me? That rather proves my point."

"Actually, I believe it refutes it. I've come to know Francis quite well over the past weeks, and I truly believe he would very much welcome being like you . . . being liked *by* you."

"Oh, good Lord, Deirdre." Lucas snorted. "Francis has been thumbing his nose at me since he was in short pants and trailing after me wherever I went."

"Mmm. And you are how many years older? Five? I would venture to guess he wanted your attention rather badly and chose the only way he knew to get it. Did your fathers get along?"

He blinked at her in surprise. "They loathed each other. Actually, they loathed everyone."

"I see." She leaned back then, eyes soft. "What a marvelous legacy to pass on to their sons. The horses and gaming and hell-for-leather driving are part of it, aren't they?"

Oh, yes. Every crackbrained, dangerous act had been to please the old duke. Even the recent purchase of the beast from hell. "I enjoy the livelier pursuits," Lucas muttered. "It is expected of me."

"And of Francis. Have you ever seen him behind the reins? Of course you have. Well, I'll tell you, Lucas—his expression when he is there reminds me very strongly of you." She shrugged. "But that's neither here nor there. I came in to ask you to at least offer them your felicitations."

"Interesting request from a woman who shot out of London as if the devil were on her heels to halt an impetuous marriage."

"I was wrong," Deirdre retorted. "As I frequently am. And to my credit, I was trying to prevent Olivia from making a *bad* marriage, not merely an impetuous one. I think Francis is precisely the right man for her."

"Do you?"

"Yes. I wish they had let me into their secret . . . or rather I wish I hadn't been so blind that I missed the obvious signs of their falling in love. But it has all ended well, and I must say I am proud of both of them. They are perfectly suited and ought to be commended for knowing it."

Lucas studied her face intently for a sign—any indication—that she might be aware that *her* perfect mate was seated not three feet away. All he saw was staggering beauty and satisfaction at another man's job well-done.

"What about you, Deirdre?" he demanded gruffly. "Will you know when the right man comes along?"

She tilted her head, gave him a slightly pitying smile and faint laugh. "Some things only happen once in a lifetime. One grasps them or misses them entirely. I won't be marrying again."

With that pronouncement she dropped her feet to the floor and stood. "Please, Lucas. Think on what I've said. You have a great deal more influence over people than you believe."

"Deirdre . . ." He reached out to stop her but she was already at the door.

"There's someone who wants very much to speak to you. Listen to what he says, too. In your present frame of mind, I fear that might be difficult."

"What do you know of my present frame of mind?"

"Your neck is sporting the delightful rash you get whenever you are upset. Ah, don't scratch!" she scolded, then she was gone.

He muttered a curse and waited for the door to open again. So his cousin wanted to speak, did he? Well, let him. Lucas pondered Deirdre's words, dismissed them, and pondered again. He recalled Francis as a small boy, always lagging five steps behind. True, he'd been a sporting little fellow, manfully trudging through mud, gorse bushes, and streams to keep up. Then again, he'd also ended most of those jaunts by whacking at Lucas's knees with a stick.

He would very much welcome being like you . . . being liked by you . . . And the Duke of Cumberland was an altar boy, Lucas thought sardonically.

This time, when the knock came at the door, he managed a reasonably polite, "Enter."

Francis had exchanged his brilliantly blue coat for a far more sedate russet one. A very familiar russet coat.

"Damn it, is that my coat?" Lucas demanded.

His cousin paused with his rump halfway into the chair. "No, as a matter of fact, it is not. It is *my* coat."

Lucas waved him into his seat. "Looks just like one of mine."

"Meyer?"

"I . . . yes, actually. You have your coats made by Meyer?"

"For years now." Francis eyed the port decanter hopefully. Lucas automatically poured a glass and handed it over. "Thank you. Yes, I have Meyer do my coats, but no one makes breeches like Stultz."

"Best cut in Town."

"Quite. Gloves?"

"Plimpton in Maddox Street," Lucas replied decisively. "No one's thumbs compare."

"You won't hear me arguing." Francis leaned forward, tilted his glass in challenge. "But the capper . . . Waistcoats?"

Lucas folded his arms over his chest. "Doubled or single-breasted?"

"Single."

"Collar or lapel?"

"Collar."

Lucas narrowed his eyes, paused, then announced, "Schweitzer and Davidson!"

"Good man!" His cousin slapped his knee in delight. "Wouldn't go anywhere else." He proferred his glass; Lucas clinked his against it. Satisfied, Francis leaned back. "So Deirdre said you wanted to talk to me."

Lucas hurriedly swallowed a mouthful of port. "Not at all. She said you wanted to speak with me."

For a moment they eyed each other, smiles fading. Then Francis shook his head and gave a wry laugh. "Splendid woman, isn't she?"

192

"Extraordinary." Lucas sighed. "You did not have anything to say to me, did you?"

"Oh, I usually have a great deal to say, but decorum prevents . . . Well, damn. Sorry, man. Old habit."

"We have a slew of them, don't we? Old habits of blasting each other. Seems to me our respective papas encouraged it."

Francis glanced up at the portrait above the mantel. "Bitter old curs. The nasty things they used to say about each other behind their backs . . ." He turned an earnest gaze on his cousin. "Which reminds me. I have no idea if you'll believe me, but I'm not the one who has been dragging your name through the muck. Truly—"

"I know."

Francis blinked in surprise. "You do?"

"For several days now."

"Then who . . . ?"

Lucas waved the question away and plied the bottle again. "Doesn't matter. It will all end soon enough." He lifted his glass. "On to far loftier matters. Allow me to make a belated toast to you and your lovely wife. May you have years of happiness and peace . . . er . . ."

"Gives one pause, doesn't it?" Francis chuckled. "Peace with Olivia. We certainly had a rocky path to love. But I decided long ago to have her and settle for the happiness."

"That makes sense, I suppose. Do satisfy my curiosity on one matter, if you will. What happened to Teddy Vaer?"

"Ah, poor sod. It really didn't take much to convince Olivia how ill-suited they were. I merely dropped a few hints as to his character . . . and his mama's, of course. And . . ."

"Yes?"

"Well, I kissed her in between the finest hints. Worked wonders."

Lucas was very tempted to ask for details. Hadn't he tried kissing Deirdre into submission? It hadn't worked very well at all, so far as he could tell. Minutes later she had gone bolting out of the carriage.

Yes, he would have appreciated some advice in the matter, but he chafed at the concept of getting it from his cousin. So instead he offered, "Deirdre seems to think you've both chosen well."

"Deirdre is a very wise lady. Olivia and I shall do splendidly together. I have her reading Shakespeare at the moment."

Lucas nodded. "A noble endeavor."

"Yes, well, it was part of a bargain, actually."

"Oh? And your part?"

Francis squirmed in his seat and grumbled something unintelligible. When Lucas gave him a blank look, he sighed and muttered, "I'm to get spectacles."

"Good heavens. Do you need them?"

"I don't think so, but she says I make her nervous behind the reins, so . . ." Francis spread his hands and shrugged. "What's a fellow to do?"

"What indeed?" Lucas sipped thoughtfully at his drink. "How did you propose?"

"I didn't. I told her to be waiting in Leverham's garden Tuesday night with a valise."

"And it worked." Lucas gazed at his cousin in open admiration.

"Almost." Francis tossed back his port and smiled fondly. "She brought three valises."

Olivia removed her ear from the keyhole. "They are laughing!" she announced delightedly.

"Well, good." Deirdre assisted the girl to her feet. "I thought they would connect if given the chance." The breath went out of her lungs when Livvy enveloped her in a fierce hug.

"Oh, DeeDee, you are the very best sister in the whole world!"

"I am the *only* sister you've ever had, so that compliment loses some of its veracity, dearest."

"Bosh. I know precisely what I'm saying." Livvy glanced back toward the keyhole. "Perhaps I ought to stay and hear the rest."

"Perhaps you ought to leave the gentlemen to their conversation. I wish to speak with you anyway."

Livvy rolled her eyes. "Not a deceased don discourse, please!"

"Not even close." Deirdre guided the girl down the hall and into the elegant parlor. "Though you might find this more distasteful. I hope not." She sank onto a tufted brocade sofa and pulled Livvy with her. "I probably should have done this far sooner, but . . . Do you have any questions about . . . tonight?"

Livvy regarded her blankly for a moment, then flushed and laughed at the same time. "None at all, as it happens. Francis explained everything to me already."

Deirdre sat back, stunned. "He did?"

"Right down to the feather bit. He said he did not want there to be any surprises. We had rather a lot of time to talk, you know, on the way here."

Deirdre did not think she wanted to know what the feather bit was. "Livvy, sweetheart, I just want to make certain you understand what happens between a husband and wife in bed."

"Thank you, DeeDee, but I assure you I am quite clear on the matter. Dear Francis was very thorough about what part goes where and why—and why some parts go some places for no reason whatsoever." Olivia leaned forward, eyes bright. "I do hope you realize, widow or not, that a bed is not absolutely necessary. One can make do with a carpet or chair or even a grassy field."

Deirdre held up her hand to stall further explanations. "Yes, I am aware of that, dearest. I must say, Francis was very thorough indeed."

"Oh, I did not mean to say he was pushing about it. He merely wanted there to be—"

"To be no surprises. Don't fret. I think it was very well-done of him."

"You do?" Livvy beamed.

"Most certainly. I . . ." *I wish someone had done the same for me.* "I think you two have made a very good start—and it will only get better for you. Just know, if there is ever anything you wish to discuss, I will be here for you."

"I know." Livvy chewed thoughtfully at her lip for a moment, then said, "I do have a question for you."

"Yes?"

"Do you . . . Well, do you . . . *did* you like it? When Jonas . . . ? I mean, Francis has kissed me. Quite a few times, to be truthful, and I liked that very much. But the rest? He said I might not like it so very much the first time, but that he would make every effort.

195

And that after, it would be absolute heaven." She leaned forward, grasped Deirdre's hands. "Is it heaven?"

Deirdre closed her eyes and remembered sweet nights in heather-scented sheets, recalled the immense pleasure in being held, touched. Then she remembered a kiss that had completely turned her world upside down. And how she had wanted more, known somehow that making love with Lucas would be unlike anything she had ever known. Like heaven.

"Yes," she said gently, squeezing her sister's hands. "It is heaven."

"Oh. Oh, I am so glad." Livvy positively glowed. "I know Francis would not lie to me deliberately, but men do tend to exaggerate when it comes to matters of physical prowess."

"Olivia!"

"Well, they do! Nasey was forever catching trout this big"— she spread her arms—"which would somehow shrink to a quarter the size somewhere between the stream and supper table. And I know Lord Fremont hasn't bagged half so many foxes as he claims."

"Oh, Livvy." Deirdre shook her head in fond resignation. "I am going to miss you so terribly."

"Miss me? Good heavens, where am I going?"

"You will be in London, dearest, or at Francis's estate in Berkshire. I will be . . . in Scotland." Somewhere.

"Oh, pooh. We'll be up to visit you, and you will come to stay with us. We shall be together quite often." Olivia's confident smile grew sly. "Besides, I rather expect you will be in your own London residence before the end of the Season."

"What a perfectly ghastly thing to say to your sister, dear!" Deirdre teased. "You know how I feel about London. And a town house is hardly within my means."

"Oh, don't be dense! Lucky has a perfectly stunning house, and I have a very good idea how he feels about you."

"Olivia . . ."

"Yes, yes. I know. You were terribly peeved with him about Red Branch Cottage. I quite worried for a day after that, but then the two of you came charging after me like frantic parents. Tell me, DeeDee . . . look me in the eye and tell me you don't like him exceedingly well."

She couldn't. "I do like him. Of course I do. I don't want you imagining any attachment, though, Olivia. There isn't one . . . and will not be."

"Whyever not? Goodness, you ninny! The two of you are positively made for each other. And you cannot help falling in love, you know, when it is right. Just look at me and Francis . . ." Livvy cast up her hands and gave a familiar, melodramatic sigh. "Oh, I know that expression. Well, I also know something else. Something you did not intend for me to discover yet."

"And what is that, pray?"

"I found the locket, DeeDee. Yes, you hid it rather well in my valise, but I found it. You've let go of my brother at last and, much as I appreciate your giving the locket with his miniature to me, I am even more grateful that you've finally decided to move on."

Astonished, Deirdre gaped at her sister. "Oh, Livvy. When did you grow up?"

"It has been a slow process, I know, but it happens to everyone. Now, for your advance knowledge, I intend to be far better dressed at your wedding than you were at mine. Pale pink silk, I think, with a garland of white roses . . ."

The sound of boot heels ringing down the hallway stopped her in mid-rhapsody. A moment later Lucas and Francis appeared in the doorway. It was the first time Deirdre had seen them smile in each other's presence, and her heart swelled. They needed each other, these scions of a cold family. And with them the next generation of Gowers stood every chance of being extremely fine people indeed.

"May we join you?" Lucas asked politely.

Francis didn't bother waiting for an invitation. He strode into the room, grinning broadly, and, waiting only long enough for Deirdre to scoot out of the way, plopped down beside his wife. "Did you miss me?" he demanded, wrapping a proprietary arm around her shoulders.

"Terribly!" Olivia snuggled against him, nearly purring.

Deirdre stifled a smile. Lucas grunted—but it had far less force than his customary grunt. Then he entered and took a seat a good fifteen feet from the happy couple.

"We'll be off to Tarbet first thing in the morning," Francis announced cheerfully. "Then on to Edinburgh. Olivia wants to show me off to her cronies . . . even if I am not an earl."

"No, my love, you are not an earl," Livvy said tartly, "but you *are* very rich, so I need not be ashamed of you."

Both Lucas and Deirdre averted their eyes from the subsequent embrace. Yes, she thought, Francis and Olivia would be very happy together. And that meant her job as guardian was done. Not that she'd done such a good job. Livvy had seen to her future herself. And had been far better at it than Deirdre herself.

All that was left for her to do now was to return to London, pack up their belongings, clear up whatever mess their flight had left behind, and— She had no idea what she would do then. Return to Tarbet probably, pack up her belongings, and close up her life there.

"You'll see Mrs. Macvail back to Town, won't you, Conovar?" Francis asked. Apparently he and Olivia had come up briefly for air. "We'll be leaving before you get up tomorrow, and we're . . . er . . . ready to retire. I want to be certain everything is set now."

"If you would prefer to stay here, I can take the mail coach, Lucas." Deirdre almost hoped he would agree. She was not sure how she was going to manage another day with him in the confines of his carriage.

"Hmm?" He turned from his examination of the lily-painted wall. "Ah. No. There is no need for you to do that. I will escort you back to Town."

He did not sound especially happy about the prospect. "Really," she insisted, "I do not mind."

"And I said I would take you."

"Lucas—"

"We can discuss the matter in the morning," he said gruffly. "Until then . . ."

"We will bid you a good night, then." Olivia sprang to her feet, hauling a slightly slower but clearly willing Francis with her. "I am sure we will see you again before too long, Lucky, but I want to thank you for all you did today. I am glad you were at my wedding, since Jonas couldn't be." He looked rather taken aback when she bounded across the room to enthusiastically throw her arms around his neck, but he eventually returned the embrace.

"Cousin." Francis sketched a brief bow. "I'll see you in London, then."

Lucas nodded. "The first bottle at Watier's is mine."

"Mrs. Macvail." Francis turned to Deirdre. "You've done me several great services today. I am in your debt. If there is ever anything I can do for you . . ."

"Thank you, Francis." Deirdre rose to meet Olivia's embrace. "Be good to each other till next we meet."

"You, too," Olivia said firmly, tossing Lucas a quick smile. "Till next we meet."

Then, hand in hand, the newlyweds scuttled out of the room.

Lucas was staring at the opposite wall this time. Deirdre watched him for a few moments, taking in the stern, beautiful face and rigid bearing. He still was not happy about the turn of events, she could tell, but he would learn.

"Lucas."

He turned slowly, as if he had forgotten she was there. "Hmm?"

"I . . ." I think I would like it if you would kiss me again. "I suppose I should retire. It has been quite a day."

"Yes, it has." He tilted his head back and grimaced at the ceiling. "I remember a time when weddings were simple affairs. You set a date, invited those people most likely to give good gifts, and simply showed up at the church. No mess, no jaunts across the bloody country, no one inconvenienced."

Deirdre flinched. Perhaps he hadn't meant to slap at her, but he had. "Does it really matter? When two people are in love, little details become unimportant. If anything, all they require is the people nearest to their heart."

"Details, my dear, are *never* unimportant. Although I must say that dragging one's nearest and dearest hundreds of miles is an impressively effective way of determining one's value. Damned cocky, but effective." He ran a hand over his eyes. "God, I'm tired."

"Yes, I'm sure you are." Not knowing how to deal with this

mood of his, nor with the fact that he had not once looked at her since entering the room, Deirdre rose shakily to her feet. "I'll bid you good night, then."

He stopped her as she reached the door. "Deirdre."

"Yes?"

Now he was studying the toes of his boots. "I . . . Ah, hell. Good night. I will see you in the morning. We can make our plans then."

"Very well, Lucas."

She closed the door quietly behind her and headed for the stairs. Oh, it hurt, but she knew what she had to do. When she reached her chamber, she crossed directly to the desk. Withdrawing a sheet of crested paper, she composed the three lines that would either complete or ruin her life.

17

LUCAS ARRIVED HOME less than two days later, grim and bleary from the grueling drive. Without Deirdre's company, the journey had been pure hell. He had considered staying in Northumberland, but abandoned the idea as quickly as it had formed. It would simply have been too painful to remain on the estate. She had fled from him twice, both times from the home he had always loved. Now he was beginning to hate the place with all his heart.

Perhaps he should have gone after her when she left him that night in the parlor. No, he amended, he *knew* he should have gone after her. But he had been afraid that anything he said would frighten her off for good. More importantly, he had been afraid that even looking at her would have him bounding from his seat like a ravening animal and devouring her on the spot. He hadn't wanted that. Nor had he wanted to fumble about for words. He'd intended to propose properly the next morning—in the rose bower—and then to rush back to York for another encounter with the grumbling archbishop.

He'd had no way of knowing that he would wake up the following morning to find her gone.

The sun was nearing its peak as he made his weary way through his London house and to his bedchamber. He planned to crawl under the covers and stay there for the next twenty years or so. Perhaps by then he would be too riddled with some delightful affliction like gout to notice the persistent ache around his heart.

Lowry appeared in the dressing room doorway just as Lucas was shucking his boots. The valet had obviously been enjoying a leisurely morning, as his waistcoat was misbuttoned and one shirt-tail peeked from beneath it. "Your Grace. I did not expect you back so soon."

"Well, you will have plenty of time to refill the empty decanters," Lucas muttered as he struggled with the second boot. "I should be asleep for the next decade or so."

Lowry hurried to help with the boot. Once freed, Lucas dropped back onto the mattress, his legs hanging over the edge. He would have been content to stay just as he was, but he was still wearing his breeches and shirt and both were slightly ripe. Oblivion, he decided, would have to wait until he'd had a bath.

He propped himself on his elbows and mustered the strength to complete the ascent. "Hot water, Lowry," he commanded. "Lots of it."

The valet retrieved the coat from the floor and promptly held it away from his person. "I should say so." He gingerly lifted the boots with the fingertips of his other hand. "Just set that on the floor, Your Grace. I am confident it will walk to me on its own."

Lucas had managed to get himself onto his feet and out of his shirt. He dropped it on the floor. He couldn't be bothered to respond to Lowry's customary insolence. Getting out of his breeches would require all of his attention. They seemed to have been soldered to his legs sometime during the drive.

"Have some brandy sent up as well." So what if it was not yet noon? As far as his body was concerned, it was still night four days past. Or something like that. Brandy seemed like a very good idea.

"I would suggest having some coffee in it," Lowry announced, heading for the dressing room. He gave the crumpled shirt a wide berth. "Shall I order tea for Her Grace?"

"Who?" Lucas paused, one leg halfway out of the breeches.

"The duchess, Your Grace. I assume she arrived with you?"

Lucas squinted across the chamber. Lowry looked perfectly serious. "Perhaps you might tell me exactly who you assume arrived with me."

202

"Why, your new wife, of course. Pardon the informality, Your Grace, but the young lady formerly known as Olivia Macvail."

There was a resounding crash as Lucas, forgetting that sudden movements were not advisable when hobbled by partially removed clothing, hit the floor hard. He postponed the series of violent curses to demand, "Where in the hell did you get the impression that I had married Olivia Macvail?"

Lowry had hurried back and now stood surveying Lucas from above, a frown creasing his customarily pinched face into deeper lines. "I take it I am mistaken, then."

"Damned right you're mistaken." Lucas struggled to get himself into some semblance of an upright position. This time his unfettered elbows kept getting in the way. "Well?" he snapped. He shoved away the valet's ostensibly helping hand. "That isn't what I meant! About Miss Macvail . . ."

"All of London assumes you married the lady, Your Grace." Lowry stepped back to a wise distance as Lucas finally shoved himself to his feet. "It was in this morning's paper." He scuttled off, leaving Lucas to mutter vague invectives and to untangle the breeches from around his knees.

The valet was back moments later, newspaper gripped in his fists. *"Parties have reported,"* he read aloud, *"an elopement of a dramatic but not wholly unexpected nature. The Duke of C., whose character has recently been a topic of lively debate, has quitted Town in the company of a certain Miss M. The lady's guardian, Mrs. M., who, intimate acquaintances say, has been grievously wronged by the duke in the past, followed soon after. It is not known, even to the editor of this newspaper, where the parties have gone, but the assumption is Gretna Green. . . ."*

Seething, Lucas stalked naked across the room to seize the paper. It was just as Lowry had recited. "Bloody hell," he cursed. "What an infernal mess!"

"To be sure, Your Grace."

Lucas crumpled the paper and tossed it aside. "What else is being said?"

"It is hardly my place to gossip—"

"What else?"

203

Lowry scrambled backward again. "I will tell you, Your Grace, if you will promise to contain your rage."

"Lowry!" Lucas bellowed, hands extended toward the man's throat.

"People are saying you intend to install the duchess . . . er . . . Miss Macvail permanently in some remote household in the north while you establish Mrs. Macvail in a household here in Town, where she will be subject to the full censure of Society."

Lucas's jaw nearly came to rest on his chest. "What an appalling, absurd piece of tripe!"

"I am most relieved to hear so, Your Grace."

"Not that I owe you an explanation, but Miss Macvail ran off with my bloody cousin. Mrs. Macvail and I followed."

"Well, that ought to make for an interesting twist to the tale when it gets out," Evan Althorpe drawled from the doorway. "Sorry to barge in like this, but I heard you were back in Town and thought I'd better come ascertain just who was in residence."

Lucas rounded on him. "How did you get in?"

"Standard way: right past the butler. I simply followed the shouting up here." Althorpe saluted the stealthily departing Lowry. "Splendid rendition of the current *on-dits*. I couldn't have done it better myself."

Lucas waited until the door had closed behind the valet before announcing coldly, "High praise, indeed, from the man who created the awful tale."

Althorpe sauntered across the room and slid gracefully into a chair. "So you figured that out, did you? I rather wondered if you would." He propped one booted foot on the opposite knee and regarded Lucas blandly. "For the sake of clarity, I did not feed this most recent nonsense to the newspaper. It really is amazing what rot the ton will take up with the merest suggestion."

"I ought to kill you."

"That, old trout, is your opinion. I might disagree. And I have rather definite opinions of my own regarding being murdered by a naked madman."

Cursing fluently, Lucas stalked across the room and dragged his dressing gown from its hook. "While I decide just how violently deranged I am, you may tell my why you did it."

"Not clever enough to figure that one out, hmm? It's quite simple, really, albeit thoroughly humbling to admit. Though now that I think on it, we've been through the issues before. You've gotten everything I've ever wanted, Conovar, and deserved none of it. Beyond that, you are consistently arrogant, condescending, and insulting. Beyond *that*"—Althorpe leaned forward in his chair, his customarily pleasant features twisted angrily—"your behavior to Mrs. Macvail has been villainous."

"You want her." Stunned by his realization, Lucas blinked and repeated, "You want her."

"Well, give the man a medal! I don't suppose you recall who first brought the lovely Deirdre Fallam to your attention."

"You did."

"Very good, sir! Now, tell me what I said to you at the time." When Lucas did not respond, Althorpe hissed, "Don't recall that part, I see. What a shock. Let me tell you what I said, Conovar: I said, 'I have just met the woman I am going to marry.' You laughed. Do you remember that? And demanded to see the unfortunate creature."

"Althorpe, I did not—"

"You did. Less than a sennight later, you made your hellish arrangement with her father."

Lucas did not want to admit how familiar the tale was sounding now. Shaken, he made his way to the bed and perched on the edge. "You waited rather patiently for your revenge against me."

Althorpe snorted. "Don't overestimate your importance in this scenario. I was perfectly satisfied when Deirdre jilted you at the altar. Until she returned, twice as beautiful as before and ten times more battered, and the whole thing began anew. I couldn't watch you tread all over her again."

"So you started spreading rumors."

"Don't think I'm proud of it, Conovar. I might be a jealous, bitter fellow, but I am not without a conscience. I even considered admitting all, consequences be damned, but then you went haring off in the middle of the night."

Lucas tried to rekindle some of his fury. Instead he found he was simply confused. "So why did you come here now?"

205

"I came to ascertain whether the rumors that grew from mine were true. And to flatten your face if by some chance they were."

"God." Lucas buried his face in his hands. "When did I become the sort of man people could suspect of such behavior?" He looked up bleakly. "Why didn't you press your suit with Deirdre when you could?"

"Who says I didn't?" Althorpe gave a harsh chuckle. "Oh, I tried. I made rather a nuisance of myself, dropped any number of subtle hints as to my feelings."

"And—?"

"And it didn't work. Mrs. Macvail has this terribly pervasive ailment that makes her immune even to my considerable charm."

"And what is that?"

"She is completely in love with you."

This time, it was Lucas's turn to laugh, a sharp, pained sound. "She left me. Again, in Northumberland. That, Althorpe, is how completely she loves me. I all but handed her my heart, and she ran back to Scotland."

"I have absolutely no idea why I should even care—guilt, perhaps—but what did she say before she left?"

"Say?" Lucas staggered to his feet and retrieved Deirdre's note from the bedside table, where he had placed it. It had not left his fist during the entire drive back, and was now creased and soiled. He unfolded it carefully. *"Lucas,"* he read aloud, *"I am leaving with Francis and Olivia. Try to understand. I know my own value. Deirdre."* He turned stinging eyes to the man least likely to help. "What in God's name am I supposed to do with that?"

Althorpe draped one arm over the back of his chair and drawled, " 'When mighty kings lose their jewels, they gird their loins and storm the mine.' "

"I suppose I should have expected that. Go ahead, spout more butchered Shakespeare at me."

"God spare me from the witless." Althorpe rolled his eyes. "That is not Shakespeare, you idiot. It is from McNally's version of 'Deirdre of the Sorrows.' I don't suppose you ever bothered to read it."

206

Lucas shook his head. "I only vaguely remember the tale from my days in the schoolroom."

"Well, I am not about to educate the illiterate heathen." Althorpe rose to his feet. "Since it appears you are not going to murder me just now, I believe I will take my leave."

"Go." Lucas waved him away. "For what it's worth, I am sorry for my behavior over the years. I won't expose your part in this."

"Thank you. Before I depart, I do have one question for you. How did you deduce it was me behind the rumors?"

"It was the night of the Leverham ball. You were the only one I ever told the name of the property I'd purchased in Scotland. I certainly didn't give Vaer the specifics, so . . ."

"Ah, yes, Red Branch Cottage. Your mine, King Conovar."

Lucas looked up blearily. "I'm *what*?"

"You are a disgrace to the hallowed ranks of Etonians. The *mine*, you ass! It's a hell of a trek, but the worth of the jewel should get you past that minor inconvenience." Althorpe headed toward the door. "Do me a favor, old trout. Don't invite me to this wedding. I might be compelled to object when given the opportunity, and I have a feeling you would not forgive me again."

Lucas wasn't listening. He was too busy scrambling for the bellpull and trying to ascertain whether he could make it another day without expiring due to his own potent aroma.

Deirdre buried her face in a white Alba rose and breathed deeply. The garden had burst into bloom in her absence, welcoming her home with a blaze of color. In the five days since she had returned, she had spent as much time as she could there, unable to face the inside. Even now, Donald, the grizzled manservant, was building packing crates behind the kitchen to add to those already spread over the dining room floor.

A day of his rhythmic tapping away with his hammer had set Olivia and Francis to grumbling. His rough baritone on "Jamie Telfer in the Fair Dodhead" had sent them fleeing from the house an hour past, destination unknown. Deirdre couldn't blame them, really. It was a terribly melodramatic ballad, and Donald sang all forty-odd verses with raspy relish. Then he sang them again. It was his favorite song. Had Deirdre had anywhere to go, she might have fled, too.

Waiting, she had decided on the second morning, was a non-activity designed by God to test a woman's spirits and faith to their limits. Both of hers were at a low ebb. By the end of the third day, she had cleaned the cottage top to bottom—twice. Within twenty-four hours after that, she had removed a legion of weeds, and some struggling shoots, which she later suspected had not been weeds at all, from all sides of the house. Last night she had cried herself to sleep.

Now, determined to find contentment if it killed her and the effort just might—she wandered slowly among the familiar paths, stopping occasionally to touch a velvet petal or breathe in the comforting scent of summer roses. Moving from the Alba, she reached for a tiny *rosa moyesii*. Already past its seasonal prime, the crimson-tipped plant would drop its petals soon and not bring forth more. It was a hardy creature, though, and Deirdre knew it would survive the winter with ease to bloom the following June.

She did not want to consider the growing likelihood that she wouldn't be there to see it.

She ran her fingertips over the delicate, lacy green, cupped the vivid blossom in her palm, and bent to gently caress her cheek with its lightly fragrant petals.

"O my love is like a red, red rose, that's newly sprung in June."

She raised her head slowly, trying to keep her smile from blooming as brilliantly as the flowers. Heart lodged in her throat, she said huskily, "Well, if it isn't a bonny English laddie quoting our Rabbie. You'll have good Scots rolling in their graves."

He looked awful, she thought, as she faced him across the flower bed. A veritable scarecrow, with a good week's worth of whiskers covering his jaw and his shirt hem hanging out from beneath his coat. Grim-faced, slightly gaunt, his clothing looking as if it had been through a wringer, Lucas Gower was still the most beautiful man she knew.

She stood and waited for him to respond to her weak sally. He took a step forward, eyes fixed boldly on hers. "Fare thee well, my only love."

"Are you leaving so soon, then?"

"Fare thee well a while." The next step had him standing in the middle of her best perennials.

She planted her hands on her hips and did her best to glare at him. "That is Scotland's finest lupine you're wading through. Oh, and there go my lilies!"

"And I will come again, my love."

"Oh, Lucas."

"Though it were ten thousand miles."

He was standing directly in front of her now, and she thought she might cry. "Oh, my darling," she sighed, and stepped into his arms. They closed around her with breathtaking force, holding her so close that she could feel the beat of his heart against her cheek. "I thought you weren't going to come. What took you so long?"

His lips brushed over her brow. "I had to figure out that you wanted me to."

"That took you four days?"

"Two. I went back to London. A third to rush north again . . ."

"And the rest? A day to learn Burns for me?"

He chuckled and rubbed his cheek against her hair. "That was courtesy of the very nice farmer who pulled my carriage out of his field. It seems I took a wrong turn at Dumbarton. He set me right and gave me something to read on the way."

"God bless the Scots and Robert Burns."

"Mmm. How did I do?"

She lifted her face, fought against the tears prickling at the back of her eyes. "Too English," she said, voice catching, "but it was music to me."

Lucas loosened his grip and raised his hands to gently cradle her jaw in his palms. "I'll learn to recite the whole bloody volume with a brogue for you, sweetheart. I'll walk to the Highlands. I'll—" His head jerked up, and he glanced around sharply. "What is that infernal noise?"

"Music," she replied, crying and laughing at once. "Donald is singing while he works."

"Donald?"

"Oh, aye, my strapping Strathclyde laddie." When his eyes went bleak, she stroked his cheek and added, "Sixty, if he's a day, and he *never* quotes Burns for me."

Lucas's tense jaw relaxed. "What is he doing, beyond the debatable singing? Tearing the cottage down?"

"No, he's building packing crates. I knew I couldn't stay here forever."

His hands tightened in her loose hair. "Oh, Deirdre," he muttered harshly.

"I said I couldn't stay. But I would have waited for you forever, Lucas, somewhere. Even if you never came for me. But you did come."

"Though it were ten thousand miles," he said. "Though it were a hundred thousand. You mean that much to me, Deirdre. Do you understand that now? Do you ... Well, damn. I cannot do this properly with Donald pounding and howling away. Come along."

He grasped her hand and stalked from the garden. She lifted her skirts and matched his brisk pace. "Where are we going?"

"Somewhere where we can be alone. I loathe crowds."

Recalling the fact that nearly every time they'd met had been in the center of London, she grinned to herself but did not complain. When Lucas veered toward the village road, she gently tugged him toward the lake path. Moments later they broke through the pines and reached the shores of blindingly beautiful Loch Lomond.

Lucas came to an abrupt halt at the rocky edge and gave a reverent sigh. "It is," he announced huskily, "exactly the color of your eyes." Then he turned his back on the sight and gathered Deirdre back into his arms. "Forgive me if I would rather look into them than the imitator."

He kept his eyes locked on hers as he lowered his face. The last thing she saw, before their lips met and she saw stars, was earth-shattering love cast in his silver eyes.

"Do you know now?" he demanded long minutes later. "Do you know how much you mean to me?"

Breathless, tingling from head to foot, she nodded. "Do you

understand why I needed to leave? I had to see if you would come after me this time."

He spread his hands over her back, drew her so close that she could no longer tell where his body stopped and hers began. "For the record, my love, I intend to hold you just like this for the next millennium or so. Should you happen to break away, however, rest assured that I would come after you. No matter where you went, no matter how far, I would find you."

The tears had started again. She would have dashed them away had she not been determined to keep her hands just where they were, wrapped around Lucas's waist, for the next millennium or so.

"Don't, sweetheart, please," he begged. "I cannot bear to see you cry. God, when I saw that blasted painting, I thought it would tear me apart. I'm almost glad someone bought it before I could. I don't know that I would have survived having it on my wall. And I would have put it somewhere where I would see it every day, you know."

She sniffled, then shook her head with a faint smile. "Will you mind very much if *Deirdre of the Sorrows* is relegated to the attics for a while?"

He frowned down at her. "Do you mean to tell me . . . ?"

"I own the painting. Mr. Raeburn sold it to me even before he painted it, long before it went to London and everyone saw it." She managed an amused sigh. "Had I known what he was doing, I would have taken the blasted thing as he wanted, and not handed over the shilling."

"You gave Henry Raeburn a *shilling* for a portrait?"

"Well, I insisted on paying something. But we did bargain. I suggested a pound. What *are* you laughing at, Lucas?"

"Oh, Deirdre. Not that I could ever put your value to me in monetary terms, but I offered a thousand pounds for the thing."

"You did?" Inordinately pleased, she beamed at him. "That was appallingly extravagant of you, but very gratifying."

"I am very glad you find it so, my dear, because I intend to take it from you."

"Oh, you do, do you?"

He nodded. "I think it would make a splendid wedding gift.

211

What do you say? Then we'll have Raeburn paint *Her Grace, the Joyous Duchess of Conovar* with a thoroughly satisfied smile on her face."

Heart bursting, she smiled up at him. "Like this?"

"Joyous, certainly." He glanced speculatively over her shoulder at the pine copse. "What do you say we work on the satisfied?"

Weak-kneed now, she whispered, "I like that idea very m—" She squeaked as he swept her into his arms and strode briskly away from the loch.

They nearly made it.

"Well, damn!" he cursed, halting abruptly at the edge of the copse.

"What?" Thrilled, impatient, she shoved at his shoulder. "What are you stopping for, you daft man?"

"Oh, Deirdre." The emotion in his eyes nearly undid her. "I have been head over heels for you for seven years. I can bloody well wait until I have you properly tied to me."

She didn't think she could, but he looked so very noble and adamant that she muffled her disappointed moan. She'd very nearly resigned herself to the longest hours of her life when inspiration struck. "Remember where we are, laddie." At his blank yet definitely strained look, she grinned and explained, "This is Scotland. We can have a handfast marriage till tomorrow."

"And then?"

"Well, if I decide I don't love you truly, madly, deeply after all, I'll leave . . ." She laughed when his arms tightened dangerously. "Tomorrow we'll go see old Reverend MacRae and let him make it official."

Lucas scowled. "So this handfasting isn't official, then?"

She rolled her eyes. "As if it matters. It is in the eyes of God. What more do you want right now?"

He hesitated for less than a second before demanding, "What do we do?"

"Well, I'm not completely certain." She thought witnesses might be required, but decided not to mention it. "I believe all we do is take each other with love and honor."

His eyes slewed to the pines again. "I thought we were about to do that anyway."

"Oh, Lucas. Be serious. And put me down."

"No."

"Very well, then." She wrapped her arms firmly around his neck and placed a quick kiss at the base of his throat. "I'll begin. I take you, Lucas Gower, to husband—with all my love, all my honor, and my very warm, very eager body."

His grip faltered for an instant, but he recovered admirably, cleared his throat, and declared, "I take you, Deirdre Fallam Macvail, to wife—with all my love, all my honor, and my . . . er . . . ah . . ."

"Good enough," Deirdre said, and dragged his mouth down to hers for a searing kiss.

His eyes, when he opened them long minutes later, were vague and slightly crossed. "Are we married now?"

"Absolutely."

"Thank God," he groaned, and plunged into the trees at a dead run.

Want to know a secret?
It's sexy, informative, fun, and FREE!!!

❧ PILLOW TALK ❧

Join Pillow Talk and get advance information and sneak peeks at the best in romance coming from Ballantine. All you have to do is fill out the information below!

♥ My top five favorite authors are: _____

_____

_____

_____

_____

♥ Number of books I buy per month: ❏ 0-2 ❏ 3-5 ❏ 6 or more

♥ Preference: ❏ Regency Romance ❏ Historical Romance
　　　　　　❏ Contemporary Romance ❏ Other

♥ I read books by new authors: ❏ frequently ❏ sometimes ❏ rarely

Please print clearly:
Name _____

Address_____

City/State/Zip_____

Don't forget to visit us at
www.randomhouse.com/BB/loveletters

jensen